Trial by Song

The Faery Trials, Volume 1

Alicia Gaile

Published by Snowy Wings Publishing, 2017.

For Mom, Dad, and Aunt Mikie, who took me to the forest where I first saw the faeries dance.

Chapter 1

Dangling from his second-story window, Jack stared up at the carved yellow eyes of the sentinel balanced on the sill. From this angle, the pumpkin's crooked grin appeared sinister. Rather than repel spirits from the Otherworld, it leered as if to say they were already there.

Under its flaming gaze, Jack was man enough to admit that he'd made a mistake. He wasn't strong enough to climb back inside to safety—his arms shook just trying to keep his chin above the ledge. With every second his guitar strap rode up his chest. Already it had a stranglehold across the base of his windpipe.

He eyed the distance to the ground. Naked spears of withered forsythia jutted up, brittle sentries in closed ranks to keep him from sneaking away.

His sneakers scraped the wood siding trying to find footholds. He held his breath, hoping his family inside couldn't hear. His left hand slipped.

One moment he dangled fifteen feet in the air, and the next his heels slammed into his mother's flower bed so hard white-hot darts stabbed up through his ankles and his breath whooshed out in a shrill hiss.

"You know," said a mild, mocking voice from behind him as two hands slid under his arms to hoist him to his feet. "When people say 'break a leg' you're not actually supposed to do it." His brother, Logan, patted the dirt off him. Jack shook him off quickly to check that his guitar was alright. Logan swung his green gaze from Jack to the window and back again.

"I get that this is your first time sneaking out and all, but don't you think out the window is a bit melodramatic?"

Jack shrugged.

"Didn't have much choice. Mom's still awake, and her door's wide open. Douglas got called out on patrol. She's been in there pacing for over an hour. She'd be blowing up your phone too if she didn't think it was buried beneath a pile of clothes in some cheap motel around here." It helped that Logan was

1

twenty and free to do as he pleased. Logan buffed his fingernails against his tan sweater with a flash of teeth.

"It's still early."

Jack limped past him to the driveway where Logan's faded, white Mustang idled. The trunk yawned open, but Jack laid his acoustic guitar across the cracked leather back seat and fastened the seat belt over it for good measure.

"Really?" Logan's reflection shook its head in the rearview mirror as he slid behind the wheel. Jack tightened the belt until the guitar rested flush against the cushion. He ran his thumb over the faint signature below the bridge. "I know how you drive. I could buy ten cars for what that guitar's worth." But Logan wasn't listening. His face had gone very stiff. His eyes fixed on Jack's bedroom window. Jack whirled around to see their mother's flannel-clad figure leaning out at them.

Despite being close to sixty their mother, Edna Sorley, seemed to defy middle age. Its only signs were the ever-widening streaks of gray hair she was too busy to color, and the trench-like frown lines earned over decades of wrangling her seven sons.

She jabbed her finger down at them.

"Get back in the house right now, do you hear me? I expect this from him, but you, Jack?"

Jack clenched his fist and looked at the ground. If he raised his head he'd have to face the betrayed expression that held him back every other time he'd tried to chase his dream. Logan watched from the driver's seat, waiting to see what he would do.

Jack gritted his teeth.

Far away as she was, his mother saw the exact moment she lost him.

"Don't even think about getting in that car! Do you hear me? Jack? Jack!"

Jack didn't hesitate again. He dove into the passenger seat. Logan grinned and threw the car in reverse. They barely cleared the driveway before Jack's pocket buzzed. 'Keith,' the name of their oldest brother, flashed across the outer screen. Jack stuffed his hand-me-down phone into his pocket and pinched the bridge of his nose. As soon as one call went to voicemail, a new one came in.

Logan wrinkled his nose with sympathy.

"I feel for you, man—I really do. Just remember, come March she can't legally ground you anymore."

They bounced over deep ruts where chunks of well-worn asphalt had broken loose. Taking his eyes from the road, Logan leaned over to inspect his teeth in his side mirror. They hit a bump that sent their stomachs somersaulting. Logan grinned, but Jack pressed his fist against his forehead, trying to convince himself that if Logan hadn't killed himself in the four years since he got his license he could keep the record going for at least one more night. He was in enough trouble without Logan wrecking the car.

"She can't help herself." Jack defended their mother out of habit. "The fae have been more active than usual lately. Haven't you noticed?"

"Nope," Logan said, popping the 'p'. He leaned forward to drape a brown wave of hair over his eyes using the rear-view mirror. Just when he seemed satisfied, another rut made his head bounce and his hair tumbled back to the way it looked before. Jack resisted the urge to check on his guitar.

"Every time I'm uptown I see goblins lurking in the shadows. The park is crawling with hags, and a band of spriggans set up camp in the woods behind the school. Vinny had to throw out his entire harvest this year because the fae put a curse on his land. Even Keith couldn't save it. Keith!"

Logan shrugged.

"You know how he is. Maybe he didn't want to risk interfering. A lot of farmers had bad yields this season. Someone would notice if Vinny's crop wasn't affected." Jack studied his faded sneakers.

"Winterthorn is back."

Logan mashed the breaks.

The shriek of skidding tires raised the hair along Jack's arms. He tasted burnt rubber, and the smell stung his eyes.

They whipped toward the edge of the road, and Jack flung both hands at the dashboard as if that would save them from careening into the ditch. They skidded to a stop, spraying gravel into the two-foot drop-off.

Breathing unevenly, Jack pressed his nose to the glass to see how narrowly they'd avoided disaster. Logan yanked him around by his plaid, cotton sleeve. All laughter was gone from his face now.

"You saw Winterthorn—with your eyes? He's back and you didn't say anything?"

Jack squirmed.

"He may have seen me too." When Logan's face spasmed, Jack rushed to explain. The words tumbled over themselves. "It was about a month ago. I was on my way to talk Stevie into convincing her brother to let me compete tonight. There was a funeral heading up Main Street. He was following them—the Wild Hunt was with him. I-I've never seen anything like them. They were massive! They had red, glowing eyes, and their teeth were like—" Logan released his sleeve to pinch the back of his neck. Jack cringed to a stop.

"I don't care what they looked like. Focus. Did he recognize you?" Jack grimaced.

"I don't know," he admitted. "It happened too fast. As soon as I looked up we locked eyes and I froze up—just like in the stories. It was like he'd turned me to stone. If he hadn't turned his head I think I would've just…. But he kept walking, and as soon as he broke the connection I could move again." Jack rubbed away the goosebumps that prickled the backs of his arms.

Outside a breeze kicked up bits of leaf and twig to pepper against the windshield. Logan sat back and ran his hand through his hair—completely undoing his earlier work.

"Look," he said after a moment, "he can't still be mad that Dad freed his girlfriend from that spell. That was decades ago for us and probably centuries for him. Now that Dad's gone he doesn't exactly have a reason to hold a grudge against any of us. I mean, we didn't do it. You said he was with a funeral. It was probably just a coincidence you were walking by." With each word his tone grew more confident.

Jack's doubt must have shown on his face because Logan thumped the steering wheel with the heel of his hand and barked with laughter.

"You're telling me that you'd risk running into him for fifteen minutes of spotlight and a chance at a little studio time?"

Jack nodded without hesitation.

"It's not just the studio time. There's bound to be talent scouts there tonight. When I win they'll—" Logan's nose wrinkled.

"It never occurred to you to just send in an audition tape like everyone else?"

Jack clenched his jaw, but the knot in his chest unraveled.

"This'll be my big break. Everyone will be there! News crews, possibly agents, even—"

Logan put a reassuring hand on his shoulder.

"You don't have to twist my arm. I already promised I'd take you. Besides, it's not like Winterthorn would attack in front of all those people—even if they can't see him. He probably won't even be there." He returned his attention to the wheel, projecting a confidence Jack wasn't sure that he shared. With a jerk, the Mustang rolled back onto the road.

Raindrops sprinkled the windshield, gathering into a steady drizzle as they passed from forest to farmland. Jack drummed his fingers against his knee. Immediately a soft, silver glow engulfed his hand. Static crackled over the speakers, drowning out the local rock station. He noticed Logan's uneasy glance and forced his hand still. The light winked out and the eighties rock ballad returned, but a heavy silence stretched between them.

"Thanks for doing this," Jack murmured twenty minutes later as the orange and purple lights of a Ferris wheel appeared in the distance.

"I was going to be out here anyway. Daisy called...." Logan waggled his eyebrows. Jack's stomach turned over.

"You mean you're not going to stay and watch?"

Logan shifted in his seat.

"I'll try, but Daisy usually has other plans." He rubbed a finger across his upper lip trying to hide a smirk at what he expected those plans to be. The anxiety Jack had been fighting since they left the house returned in full force.

"You're just going to leave me here?"

"Calm down." Logan swatted the air between them. "I'll be back by ten to get you. You'll be home and under house arrest long before the monsters come out to play."

The Mustang followed the line of yellow tape roping off a lane through the open field and pulled into a parking space behind an oversized red truck.

The two guys hopping down from the raised bed were football players Jack recognized from school—Carl McGuire and Kevin Shrouds. Aiden Doyle, long-faced with deep-set brown eyes, slid out of the driver's seat and scanned the field. When he spotted Jack, his burly features hardened in an arrogant dismissal before he turned back to his friends.

Jack exhaled gustily and tried to ignore them, but when the linebacker, Carl, crossed his eyes and mimed playing a flute Logan's eyebrow shot up. Jack wanted to bury his head under the seat.

While most of his classmates doodled during class, he filled the margins of his notebooks writing music. Three weeks ago, his homeroom teacher, whose wife taught Music Theory at the Oberlin Conservatory of Music, caught him writing out Stravinsky's 'Rite of Spring' from memory. Mr. Gryne spent all of homeroom that day and the next marveling at its accuracy, which only alienated Jack further from the other students who already thought he was odd.

"Logan, don't say anything. It's not a big deal." He sensed the storm gathering behind his brother's meticulously groomed façade.

"What? I'm just going to talk to them." Logan, the picture of innocence, opened his door. "Hey fellas!"

His voice—pure compulsion—formed a soft silver mist. It floated toward the group with unerring precision. Their heads swiveled just in time to inhale the cloud. In unison the arrogant expressions relaxed into vague, welcoming smiles even though none of them had met him before. Only the dark-skinned boy, Kevin, looked mildly confused as he scratched his head trying to place where he knew Logan from.

Still in the car, Jack suffered a stab of jealousy. Logan had been born with the gift of persuasion. All he had to do was open his mouth and he could convince anyone to do anything—well, not anything. According to Logan he couldn't force someone to do anything truly against their will, but so far as Jack had seen no one's will had ever gone against Logan's.

"This is a nice truck." Logan inspected the orange running lights on the scarlet pick-up.

"I know, right? Aiden's dad gave it to him for breaking the school passing record." The blonde wide-receiver, Carl, supplied the information with pride, as if friendship entitled him to a claim on Aiden's skill.

"You must have quite an arm." Logan held out his hand, palm up. "Prove it." The silver mist was thicker this time. To Jack's eye it was as if a smoke ring hit Aiden full in the face, but he knew Aiden didn't see a thing. He blinked several times as the suggestion took root then grinned at his buddies and dug in his pocket for his keys.

"It's about fifty yards to the trees," Logan said. "Think you can make it?" This time the suggestion was so thick that Aiden coughed, but after he recovered, he hefted his keys in his hand, eyed the distance across the field, and lobbed them as hard as he could over the rows of cars. Logan watched them sail into the shadows with a satisfied smirk. It was impossible to see where they landed in the dark. Carl whooped, Aiden preened, but Kevin cocked his head with a frown.

"Well, you sure showed me." Logan dusted off his hands. "Look, I've taken up enough of your time. Go enjoy the fair, fellas." This time he gave them only a small push, enough to make them forget the keys and the issues that came with not having them later when they were ready to go.

Aiden high-fived his friends, and they turned and walked off for the ticket booth without a backward glance. A father wrangling his three kids nearby twisted his head in the direction the keys had flown.

"Did he just...?"

"Yes. Yes, he did." Logan interlocked his fingers to stretch his arms full out in front of him.

"Isn't he going to need those later?" The dad asked wryly. Logan grinned. "Probably."

By that point Jack had dragged his guitar out of the back seat. He scowled when he drew level with Logan.

"What?" Logan's eyebrows lifted in response to Jack's scowl. "He did it, not me."

"You told him to."

"It's not like I told him to jump off a bridge. He's a show off. He wouldn't have done it if he didn't want the attention." Before Jack could follow that trail of logic to its disturbing implications, Logan's pocket jingled. He pulled out his cell phone, winced when he answered at the crackle of static from standing too close to Jack, and moved several steps away.

"Daisy! Of course, gorgeous. You're where?" He flashed Jack a not-so-apologetic smile and covered the mouthpiece. "She's waiting for me at the Ferris wheel. I gotta' go. Good luck with your show. Go knock 'em dead." He flashed a thumbs up and hurried off. Jack slipped his guitar strap over his head, taking comfort from the familiar weight resting against his back. The air hummed with magic, and the hairs on the back of his arms rose.

A pair of girls dressed in fishnet stockings, tulle skirts, and store-bought wings giggled as they passed. One glanced back and whispered something to her friend. Jack set his jaw. In hindsight maybe he should have put together a costume. A quick look around confirmed that even the laziest fair-goers had themed t-shirts or face paint. Jack wore only a pair of dark jeans and a thin cotton shirt with the sleeves rolled up to his elbows. He'd been going for unassuming, but tonight his lack of disguise made him more conspicuous.

He headed toward the ticket booth. It was easy to spot with the word 'Ticket' written in glowing bulbs. To make it feel spookier, someone had switched out the regular yellow lights with bulbous, green ones. By the emerald glow Jack made out a stooped figure standing to one side of the ticket window. His senses went on high alert, zeroing in on the bent form that was decidedly not-human. The next man in line didn't so much as glance at the fat, hairy fingers that reached out and snatched the bills from his hand. He blinked, looked down, and then bent to search the ground for his money. When he looked back up the goblin had settled a stack of brittle leaves on the counter disguised by glamour to look like the missing cash.

It was a trick as old as the relationship between humans and fae. No doubt by morning the 'money' would resume its true shape. The fair would believe they'd been robbed. No doubt the goblin would plant another stack of 'evidence' on an unsuspecting victim just to sit back and watch gleefully as the poor dupe's life upended around him.

The goblin's over-wide mouth pulled into a sinister grin as the next customer stepped up to the window. Suddenly, he lifted his gorilla-like snout and sniffed. Slanted red eyes swiveled to where Jack stood, and Jack quickly pretended to scan the crowd. His heart pounded and sweat dampened the thin material under his arms.

Had the goblin sensed him? It was hard to say. There were plenty of other sounds and smells that could have gotten its attention.

Just then, the opening chords of a guitar riff blasted above the noise of carnival games. Jack forgot about the goblin. He checked his watch, shook his wrist and held it up to his ear for good measure. The Battle of the Bands wasn't supposed to start for another fifteen minutes! He stared in dismay at the ticket line.

"Jack, over here!"

He looked around to see Stevie from the gas station waving to get his attention. Orange and purple lights glinted off her horn-rimmed glasses as she cut in front of a woman pushing a stroller. A glow-in-the-dark skull decorated the black t-shirt she wore beneath her gray blazer.

"Hey, glad you're here. They started early because Chemical Fire's fans were starting to go crazy. You don't have to buy a ticket. Come on, I'll take you in." She put an arm around Jack's shoulder, steering him past the ticket collectors. When one of the girls gave them a suspicious look, Stevie waved a laminated 'Stage Crew' tag hanging by a lanyard around her neck.

Chemical Fire was a local garage band that had gained a small following after playing a few bars in Cleveland. In person, Jack wasn't impressed. Only the lead guitarist had any real talent. The drummer looked like he had to concentrate to hold a steady beat, the backup singer kept trying to overshadow the lead, and the bass guitarist stood as far from the audience as the stage would allow, hiding behind her shoulder-length black hair. Still, Jack caught himself nodding along to their medley of horror movie themes.

An ear-splitting scream rose above the guitar's whine. It snapped at Jack's nerves like a rolled up wet towel, but judging from the bobbing, grinning heads around him, no one else heard.

Careful not to draw attention, he looked around until he spotted a forest troll at the back of the crowd. Eight-foot-tall and as wide as two grown men, it was hard to believe no one else noticed it even if they couldn't see it without Faery Sight.

The troll clutched a pink-haired pixie in its fist, squeezing until the insect-like body bulged with displaced organs. Baring mossy teeth in a mean smile, it shoved the pixie into its wide mouth. Seconds later a deep-bellied belch sprayed flecks of iridescent wing over the couple standing oblivious beside it.

Suddenly the thump of the music was too loud, the press of bodies too close. Jack wiped his palms against his jeans. His hands were shaking.

A roar of applause made him jump.

"Talk about a tough act to follow," crowed Stevie's brother, Corey, into the microphone. "But if anyone can do it, it's our next act, Straifield's very own Jack Sorley!" He preened for the audience in his black and gold Elvis costume while he waved Jack onstage.

For one moment Jack considered backing out. The fae were everywhere. There were even more of them than he expected. As soon as he started to play they would see the power glowing on his hands. If they caught him he would be lucky to meet an end as swift as the pixie's had been. They might stab out his eyes, or chop off his ears, or....

Stevie slapped him between the shoulder blades and shoved him toward the stage. Hundreds of eyes watched him. He couldn't turn back. With stiff movements Jack climbed the aluminum steps and pulled his guitar over his head.

Although he'd rehearsed all week, he didn't have a plan for what he was going to play. He trusted the right songs to come to him in the moment. It was the way his gift worked. But in that moment, with panic mounting to his brain, a void existed where the right notes should have been. Cold sweat filmed across his forehead.

This had never happened. He'd always been able to trust the music to be there when he needed it.

Stalling, he waved to the crowd. His hand shook visibly so he grasped the neck of his guitar in a too-tight grip. The silence grew uncomfortable.

Someone made a quacking sound and several people laughed.

Taking a deep breath, Jack lowered his head, settled his fingers over the strings and closed his eyes. Relax. One...two...three....

Rather than the up-tempo music the audience was expecting, the melody for a love song poured out. The light that blazed from Jack's fingertips was so intense it left the spotlights in shadow.

The troll jerked around, still grinding the pixie between its teeth. Its mean, black eyes narrowed on Jack.

At the edge of the stage a faery appeared in a puff of smoke. Her lime-green gaze fixed upon Jack with unwavering focus even as she shielded her face from the light of his song. By slow degrees she lowered her hand and began to move. She wound her body in a sinewy dance that defied the sweeping rhythm he set. She reached out, beckoning with long, pale hands.

Jack's fingers slipped. She recoiled from the sour note with a hiss that revealed two rows of yellow teeth. Jack recovered quickly and moved to the other side of the stage even though instinct screamed for him to keep her in sight. He faltered again when he glanced back to see her dragging her skeletal body onstage. Her head undulated in time to his song. Their eyes locked for a fraction of a second. Triumph blazed on her face as his legs locked in place. His breath caught in his throat. There was only one way to save himself.

Jack snapped his strings.

One moment the air was filled with music wrung from the Otherworld, and the next there was disoriented silence. The spellbound crowd blinked and shook their heads, trying to figure out where the ethereal music had gone.

"Guess I got a little carried away." Jack stammered into the microphone. "Thanks. You've been a great audience." In the precious seconds it took to make his small excuse, the faery hauled herself to the center of the platform. Throwing caution to the winds, Jack hopped to the ground and ran before she could lock gazes with him again. Stevie called after him, but Jack broke into a sprint. Boos and jeers chased him.

Chapter 2

"All I needed was five more minutes. Five minutes! They couldn't let me have that?" Jack strode up and down the empty livestock tent. Anger and humiliation burned hot inside him. Logan wouldn't answer his phone. Assuming he and Daisy were 'busy,' Jack sought refuge with the animals in the hope that his middle brother, Ross, would take him home if he came to pick up his prize cow, Bess. Since judging ended at four, Jack counted on the tent to be empty.

When he found Bess, Jack kicked the iron railing surrounding her pen. She swung her head over the top bar so that her wet nose soaked the yellow ribbon hanging next to her name. No one knew whether being the middle brother made him crabby or if a short fuse was the byproduct of his enhanced gift with animals, but Ross had never taken defeat gracefully. He would wait until all the other farmers collected their cattle before he showed his face in the tent.

Sighing, Jack stroked the space between Bess' eyes.

"I guess we're both losers tonight."

Bess raised her head sharply. The lights flickered and went out. With them went the heat, like someone sucked it out through a straw. Jack kept his hand on Bess' head to reassure her, but his eyes flicked around. They weren't the only ones in the tent anymore. The shadows drew closer, watching.

A sound like an exploding two-liter bottle went off followed by a thud that vibrated up through the ground. The force of the earth's shudder was enough to stagger him. Magic filled the air. Jack could taste the fine grit of it on his tongue. He coughed and covered his nose with the neck of his shirt.

Shifting his guitar so that it lay across his back and left his arms free, he hurried to the door of the tent and peered out.

The livestock tent backed against the edge of the parking lot. Lines of reflective, orange tape roped off the edge of the field to prevent drivers from barreling into the drainage ditch. Despite the precaution, a green four-door car stood nose-deep in sewage. Its windshield wipers screeched back and forth across the dry glass. Jack didn't know which was thicker, the fog blanketing the windows, or the residue of magic crackling in the air. As he emerged, several black shadows skittered into the night. Fearing the worst, he leapt the gulch, ran to the car, and tore open the door.

The driver sat slumped over the steering wheel. Black hair tumbled in all directions. Jack fumbled in his pocket for his phone, praying he would be able to find enough signal to go through.

The cellphone slipped between his fingers, clattering somewhere behind the brake pedal. Abandoning it for the moment, he leaned in to check if the girl was conscious.

"Are you okay?"

She groaned, and his head nearly hit the roof.

She peeled one shaking hand from the wheel to drag her hair back from her face. He only had time to register white, luminous skin before her eyes met his. His legs locked. All thoughts of concern wiped clear from his brain.

Fae. She was fae!

His eyes watered waiting for the hologram of high, rounded cheekbones and slim arching brows to dissolve into something grotesque. The facets of her eyes would lose their blue fire brilliance. The curved bow of her mouth was going to collapse any minute into a gaping maw with serrated teeth. In spite of himself, he drank the illusion in.

Seconds passed. The image never wavered.

Mud seeped into his sneakers thick and slimy as he sank deeper and deeper, but so long as her eyes held his there wasn't a thing he could do.

Her cranberry-colored lips parted, and Jack braced for the spell that would obliterate his free will.

"How bad is it?" Her lush curtain of lashes swept down in a wince.

His foot slipped, and he nearly went down. He was so stunned he barely registered that she had been the one to break the connection. Now was his chance to escape before her blue eyes snared him again. He put one hand on the door, preparing to shove clear and run when it occurred to him that the car was made of metal. She was surrounded by iron—the only substance lethal to the fae.

When he didn't respond, she reached for the latch on her seatbelt. She gave no reaction as the metal pieces slid between her hands. Jack shifted his weight, confused. He had no idea what concentration of iron it would take to burn her skin, but he'd always assumed even a trace would have some effect.

"What's your name?" he blurted out before his body recoiled in a wince. He wanted to kick himself. The fae never gave up their names willingly.

Her head came up slowly. By the time her eyes moved from his dirty sneakers to the top of his head Jack was certain she'd catalogued the color of his belt, the exact green of his eyes, and picked out every blond strand in his brown hair.

"Eira," she said, climbing stiffly out of the car. She wore snug, faded jeans and a black hoodie that only emphasized her striking complexion. While Jack gaped, she walked around the car. When she saw the shredded rubber that was all that remained of her tires, she gave the back wheel a kick.

"What kind of jackass would do something like this? Like I can afford new tires." She pressed the heel of her palms to her eyes. Pity cut through the fog in Jack's mind, though he knew better than to feel anything toward her.

"Do you want me to call you a tow truck?" He scooped his phone out from behind the pedals, but she shook her head.

"There's no point. I can't afford to have it towed. Ha! I can't even afford to catch a cab." There was a throaty edge to her voice as if she was fighting hard not to get hysterical. He offered his phone anyway, thinking she'd want to call her parents or ask a friend for a ride, but she shook her head again.

"It's alright. I'll think of something."

"My brother's a cop. He could give you a ride home."

Unsure of what else to do, Jack dialed Douglas. Static exploded across the line and a small spark zapped his eardrum. The shock nearly made him drop the phone. Eira raised an eyebrow.

"Bad signal." The tips of his ears heated in embarrassment.

Douglas answered on the first ring.

"So, are you a superstar now? Hope so. You're going to need that fame and fortune to buy your way back into Mom's good graces. She's left me seven messages to go down there and drag you back home in handcuffs."

"Not exactly...." Jack explained the situation while Eira stared forlornly at her car. He cupped his hand over his mouth and added in a rush, "Something weird is going on. You need to get over here fast."

"Weird how?" In the background, a siren wailed. Jack glanced over his shoulder. Eira had her back to him. His eyes surfed the black waves of her hair down to the small of her back before he caught himself and turned away.

"Just get over here!"

Before Douglas could ask any more questions, Jack hung up. He slipped his phone in his back pocket and tucked his hands beneath his arms, unsure what to do with himself while they waited.

"Thanks for your help," Eira said so softly he barely heard her. She sent him a shy smile. Adrenaline shot through him, setting off a tingling sensation deep in his chest. He cleared his throat and adjusted the guitar strap that was digging into the side of his neck.

An ominous crunch of metal sounded behind them, followed by peals of eldritch laughter. Eira whipped around with a small gasp. Jack watched her closely. She was silent for a long time, searching the gathering darkness.

"What's your name?" she asked unexpectedly. In the dim glare of the headlamps her eyes took on an eerie glow. Jack's smile faltered, and he gulped back a swarm of butterflies fluttering to escape his stomach. Did he dare answer? Names held power in the Otherworld. But then, she had given hers without a fight, and the fae couldn't lie.

"Jack." He held out his hand to see what she would do.

Without warning, the temperature plunged. Their breaths, which had been barely visible before, rose in opaque, white clouds. The searing cold sliced into his hands, and Jack crammed his fists under his armpits for warmth. Eira's teeth chattered. While she had the comfort of her hoodie, he wore only a thin, cotton shirt.

"C—c—come on. The heater st-still works," she said through chattering teeth.

Moments later they huddled side by side in the back seat of her car. His guitar rested across his lap. There was no room in the tight space, and the long neck stretched past her chest, nearly touching the window behind her.

"Why do you keep staring at me like that?" she asked, not looking at him. Jack flinched.

"Sorry. It's just that..." he hesitated before taking the plunge, "You look like one of the fae."

She eased as far from him as the cramped space would allow. The bridge of her nose wrinkled.

"Fae as in 'faery?' Like Puck from 'A Midsummer Night's Dream?'"

He snorted. If only they were that harmless. Scarlet seeped from the tips of his ears into his cheeks.

"That didn't come out right. Forget I said anything." He shielded his face with one hand, pretending to rub his forehead. If she wasn't fae then she probably thought he was a colossal moron. She shifted so that her back rested against the window and her bent knee brushed against his thigh. His heart somersaulted.

"No one's ever accused me of being an imaginary creature before. I can't decide whether to take that as a compliment or not. Why Jack, are you one of the Fair Folk?"

The idea repulsed him down to his marrow. His head came up to deliver a fierce denial, but the low current of laughter in her voice slid its warmth inside him, melting his disgust. Pulling a face, he turned toward her, and for the second time that night found himself snared in her gaze. He didn't know eyes came in that shade of blue. He considered telling her that, but a pressure in his chest made it difficult to speak. He wanted...he wasn't sure, but the look in her eye told him she knew and understood. Before he knew what he was doing, he leaned in to close the space between them.

A hard knock on the window jolted them apart. A beam of light glared through the foggy glass.

"Alright kids, step out of the car." The hard voice carried the edge of authority.

The door behind Eira swung open and a gloved hand hauled her into the night by the hood of her sweatshirt. Jack fumbled for his door, got hung up by his guitar, and struggled out into the blistering cold.

Eira lost her footing and fell against the car. The police officer caught her elbow and jerked her upright. Jack, annoyed by the cop's unnecessary roughness, opened his mouth to complain when he caught sight of the sterling silver star pinned to the brown leather jacket. Sheriff Doyle.

"Have you kids been drinking?" he asked, shining his flashlight into Jack's eyes as he rounded the trunk. Eira brushed his arm aside with a huff of impatience. The Sheriff bristled and raised the beam to her face.

The flashlight wobbled and nearly slipped from his hand. Eira shielded her eyes, and he took several rapid steps back. His free hand crept toward the holster at his hip before he balled it into a fist.

Jack wasn't sure he could handle any more surprises. The Sheriff thought Eira was fae too?

"Eirawen? Is that you? What happened to your car?"

The three of them looked around to see Aiden swing out of the passenger seat of Doyle's cruiser. Lingering resentment lined his face like someone who'd caught an earful for throwing away his car keys in an open field where any idiot could find them and drive off with his new truck. Every step he took closer to Eira thawed his expression to reveal one of unguarded delight.

"You know this girl?" His father didn't sound happy. Aiden walked over and pulled her into a one-armed hug. Doyle's hand spasmed as if he wanted to pull his son away but thought better of it.

"Yeah Dad, this is Eirawen Rothchild. We met at Youth Group last summer. How've you been?" Aiden beamed at her, oblivious to the tension in the air. If anything, his lack of awareness only seemed to make his father more suspicious. Jack frowned, trying to figure out what was going on.

"As you can see, I've been better," Eira replied with a rueful glance at the car. "I'm waiting on his brother to give me a ride home." She gestured toward Jack. Only then did Aiden notice he was there. His eyes narrowed.

"So, you were with her when this happened?"

"I didn't drive the car into the ditch, if that's what you're asking." Jack crossed his arms over his chest, but Aiden didn't care about his answer. Eira commanded his full attention.

"If you need a ride home Dad and I can—"

"I don't think that's a good idea," said his father just as Jack said, "My brother's already on his way." They looked at one another and Jack bit his tongue. Sheriff Doyle was the only person he'd ever met outside of his family who saw the fae too, and he wasn't sure how to feel about it. If Doyle knew about the fae, why didn't his son? It seemed like a dangerous secret to keep, particularly since the fae wouldn't hesitate to hurt Aiden to punish Doyle for seeing through their glamour. Maybe he thought he was protecting Aiden by keeping him in the dark. If so, it was a pretty high-stakes gamble.

Doyle regarded him with equal suspicion, and Jack realized that the only way to throw him off would be to appear just as susceptible to Eira as Aiden was. Channeling a move he'd seen Logan use a thousand times, he slid his arm around her waist and prayed she wouldn't slap him. Eira went stiff and glanced down at his hand. The heat that rose to his face was almost enough to combat the cold night, but a sudden, sharp bite of wind gave him all the excuse he needed to huddle closer to her body for warmth.

"You guys don't have to stick around. My brother will be here any minute." Ugh, he couldn't have sounded creepier if he tried. He was lucky she didn't plant an elbow in his ribs and spray him with some of Doyle's pepper spray. As it was, she took his sudden smarminess in stride and allowed him to wind her against his side.

Aiden wasn't about to bow out gracefully though. He bared his teeth in an aggressive attempt at charm.

"It's freezing, and we're already here. Seriously, I just saw a snowflake." He squinted up at the sky. "Come on, Eirawen." He held out his hand, but she wasn't listening. Her eyes were on the Sheriff, whose carefully neutral expression was betrayed by the barely bridled warning in his gaze. She leaned into Jack.

"I should probably stay. I'd hate for his brother to drive all the way out here for nothing."

"Not for nothing. He's got to pick him up. Jack doesn't even have his license." Aiden's tone made it clear that not having a driver's license qualified him to be put back in diapers. Jack gritted his teeth.

"At least I've got enough common sense not to throw my keys into the woods on a dare."

"Shut up!" For a guy who stood over six feet tall Aiden moved surprisingly fast. He shoved him—hard. Jack slammed back against the trunk of Eira's car. There was a loud crunch mixed with the twang of guitar strings. He bounced off the metal and went sprawling into six inches of mud.

Silence spiraled around them. Eira covered her mouth with her hand, and Doyle grabbed his son by the crook of the elbow. Jack couldn't move. The neck of his guitar hung limp against his side—at a complete right angle to the rest of its body.

"Jesus, Aiden," muttered his father, inserting himself between them. "Get in the car. You, girl. Go with him if you want a ride home." From his tone, Eira couldn't have been more to blame for the incident if she had picked up Jack's guitar and snapped it over her knee. Aiden wiped a fist under his nose and turned for the cruiser looking disoriented.

"I guess I should," Eira said in a tight voice. Jack closed his eyes, beyond frustrated. Was she really going to climb into the man's car when he clearly wanted her as far from him as possible?

"It's just that they're already here, and I'd hate for your brother to go so far out of his way." The words tumbled out in a rush, and a sudden gust of wind swirled up around her so that she had to use a hand to keep her long hair from flying in her face. Doyle turned up his collar against the breeze and glanced around with a wary eye. When Jack didn't respond, Eira ducked her head and hurried after Aiden.

"You should pick your fights more carefully," said Sheriff Doyle, watching her go. "This one wasn't worth it." Jack lifted his head to glare at him.

"Funny, from where I'm standing that looked a lot like an assault to me, Sheriff." Doyle rubbed at the stubble on his chin and stared vaguely in the opposite direction, telling Jack everything he needed to know about how the charge would be handled.

"It's getting late. You ought to head home. It's nearly midnight. Tonight's not a good night to be out." Doyle held out his hand to pull him to his feet, but Jack shrugged off the help. With a loud sucking sound, he stepped free of the mud and stomped off. His guitar's broken neck bounced against his shoulder with each step.

He made it to the corner of the livestock tent before he mustered enough courage to look. Slowly, he lifted the guitar over his head. His stomach dropped. Only a few stubborn strips of wood held the snapped neck together. A long crack cut straight down the back panel. It would take a woodworking master the likes of Tadgh Sorley to knit it back together, but Tadgh Sorley was gone.

A screen of tears blurred the image, and he lifted his face to keep them from falling. What would his brothers say when they saw it? What would his mother say? She hoarded what remained of his father's work, as if stockpiling enough of the pieces he'd poured his soul into she could put them together and bring him back again. The guitar was his father's last finished piece before a drunk driver ran him off the road ten years ago.

Jack's hand shook as he pulled back the white, vinyl, tent flap.

When he stepped inside, he was startled to find the shadows had drawn together to choke out the glow from the overhead lamps. Without the steady hum of electricity, the emptiness echoed the hollow chamber opened in his chest by the broken guitar. Head hung low, he waited for his eyes to adjust to the gloom. The dark haze didn't clear.

By slow degrees he registered a haunting perfume of spiced fruit. It overwhelmed the trampled straw, wet patties, and large animal smells. His mouth watered for the exotic flavor even as fear flooded his belly with a sobering wave of nausea.

The tent was deserted. Twenty minutes ago, there had been close to fifteen cows waiting to be picked up, but now every stall stood empty.

His sneakers squished as he cut a path to Bess' pen. She was gone. Her third-place ribbon still fluttered over the door. A withered vine looped around the latch, blackened where it touched the metal railing.

The air sweetened until it was as putrid as an orchard fermenting in the late autumn sun.

Hands shaking, Jack felt along the railing. The first pass turned up nothing, but the second time he found a small, leather pouch tied in place by a thin length of twisted vines. Jack's mouth went dry as he set down his broken guitar. He emptied the pouch into the palm of his hand and pale, round seeds spilled out. The memory of high-pitched laughter came back to him.

He clenched his fist around the bag. Seeds! The fae thought they could take Bess in exchange for seeds!

It was one loss too many.

Jack tore the vine off the stall latch and ground it beneath his foot. He knew better—dammit he did. Once the fae made an exchange it was safer to cut your losses and let them have their way. But tonight, he just didn't care.

Gateways between this world and the other sprang up where the elements of land, sea, and sky met. Knowing what to look for and actually finding a portal were two different things, but with so many fae at the fair he knew a portal must be nearby.

The drainage ditch that housed the front end of Eira's car fed a pond at the far end of the field. Mist hovered innocently over the black surface. Even from a distance Jack saw a clear line of hoof prints stamped into the bank.

Ten feet from the edge Jack had to pause and cover his nose.

Headlights ghosted over him, and he whirled around. A forest-green pickup was backing a trailer toward the livestock tent. It was his brother, Ross. Ross was disagreeable at the best of times. If he found out the fae had swiped Bess from practically right under Jack's nose he was liable to summon the nearest rabid animal to come along and bite Jack in the ass.

Panicking, Jack flung the seeds into the middle of the pond. They hit the surface with a loud smack before sinking.

"Bess is ours and I say you can't have her!"

First there was silence. It stretched long enough he thought nothing was going to happen. Then, the water stirred.

Jack knew enough about what lurked in the in-between places to back away, but no sooner had he moved one foot than a massive vine shot out of the sewage and wound around his leg. He tried to yell for Ross, but the plant undulated, lifting him up to slam him against the ground. His breath exploded out of him, and he saw stars. Digging his fingers into the mud, he scrambled and clawed to get free, but the vine dragged him steadily back into the water.

Smaller vines slithered beneath the surface and latched onto his wrists and torso. He lifted his head, praying his brother would get out of the truck and see him before he disappeared. There was time for one last gulp of air before the vines claimed their victim and dark, fetid water closed over his head.

Chapter 3

The vines grew a seed pod around him, pinning Jack's arms and legs to his sides. Struggling only burned through his oxygen, so he forced his body to go limp by counting a beat in his head. With each passing second the throbbing blood vessels in his eyes expanded until he thought they would burst. Black sludge barreled up his nose, forced his jaws apart, and slid down the back of his throat. He choked, but there was no room for air with mud oozing into his lungs.

The seed pod burst open, flinging him down through open air. Jack landed hard. His knees buckled, and he fell face-first onto uneven stone. Up from his belly erupted a hot wave of black waste.

The heaving went on and on, wringing the muscles of his throat raw. Tears and snot washed slime down his cheeks when he finally eased back onto his heels a short time later. He shivered, covered from head to toe in thick, heavy muck. Gagging, he slung his arms so that mud splattered the rocks with hard, loud slaps. The sound reverberated throughout the hollow hill. Uneasy, he looked around.

He was deep underground. The ceiling arched high above him, lost amid a forest of calcium formations. Small white orbs were bracketed here and there along the walls, casting huge shadows that made him feel disconcertingly small. There was no sign of the pond or the tunnel he had fallen through.

Despite the awful smell wafting from his clothes, a stronger one rose to mask it. Sweet. Coppery. Looking down, he saw a crimson-black trail winding through the puddle at his feet. Tracing the rivulet back to its source, he started dry heaving all over again.

Bess' head lay on its side. Her tongue protruded between her pale, rubbery lips. Black flies skated through its coating of sticky, white mucus. One blank, glassy eye stared up at him, and the severed muscles in her neck glistened in the yellow light.

Movement behind a large crystal jutting up from the ground sent him surging to his feet. Not knowing whether to stay or hide, Jack crept closer to see a dark, slender back and a braided pendulum of maple gold swayed in time with the faery's every move. She held a knife as long as his forearm in her small, brown fist. Blood coated her arms and splattered her face and neck. It drenched the filmy yellow material of her dress so that it hung crusted and stiff. Strung up on the wall in front of her was the rest of Bess' body. The white casing of her intestines ballooned from the jagged line down her belly.

Jack gulped for air, as if that would wash down his rising bile.

Steadily the faery's knife scraped through gristle and bone. *Skrip, skrip, skrip....* His stomach rebelled again, and he covered his mouth.

"You're a fool." She spoke without turning. "You came here with no way to bargain your way home." He wasn't surprised that she knew he was there. Slowly, he stepped out where she could see him. His tongue flicked out to wet his lips before recoiling from the taste it met there.

"I gave back the seeds. You were supposed to give her back."

Her laughter rang out high-pitched and eerie.

"You expect to return used goods for a full exchange? One who knows our secrets as you do knows what happens when mistletoe is planted at a gateway."

His mouth opened and closed in silent protest. He did know. In his haste and in the dark Jack hadn't recognized the seeds for what they were.

Mistletoe was a plant of great power in the Otherworld. It could be used in protection spells and love potions. It brought good luck and peaceful dreams. In some of the old stories it could make the bearer invisible or grant immortality. Jack swayed, stunned by the value the fae had bestowed upon Bess.

"It was unwise of you to travel here." The faery continued to hack at the carcass. "You more than most are vulnerable to what lurks in the Ash Queen's court."

"You had no right to take her," Jack insisted, refusing to acknowledge that the faery knew who he was. Her teeth clicked together with impatience.

"You left her unprotected, and it is the Eve of Samhain." She cleaned her knife against her thigh, and Jack tried not to notice the long bare leg exposed by a strategically high slit in the skirt. So far, she had not given him a clear glimpse of her face, but judging from the delicately sculpted muscles that glided beneath skin like aged bronze, when she turned she would be stunning. He clung to his anger, praying it would be enough to use as a shield.

"What am I supposed to tell my brothers?"

"I doubt you will have much opportunity to tell them anything. The Ash Queen will keep you." She bent to lift the bucket of organs she had harvested and moved away.

"Keep me?" He couldn't help the squeak in his voice. He knew what happened to people 'kept' by the Fair Folk. The fae were ageless and unchanging. Human limitations amused them, and any human under their thrall became a bystander in his own mind while his body gorged on whatever temptation the fae set before it.

The faery twisted to look at him. Her strange coloring and almost catlike features formed a vacuum that sucked the air from his lungs. Heat radiated from her like a hearth fire, though her expression was as cool as the first autumn frost. The tight coils of her hair were a vibrant rose-gold that she'd twisted back from her face, adorning it with ornaments carved from nuts and twig. But it was her honey-colored eyes that mesmerized him.

Immediately his brain threw up barriers against that thought. Finding her attractive was the first step toward self-destruction. He forced his eyes away and tried to think of something—anything—else. Another face rose in his mind—one with eyes like blue diamonds set against skin that shimmered like mother of pearl. His jaw clenched. Right, like that was much better.

"There has to be a way out," he said stubbornly. Before he could blink, the faery's blood-soaked hand seized his collar. Her fae eyes drilled into his. Magic gathered like static before a lightning bolt. Her power built until it became a single concentrated beam. He cried out as she attempted to brand her will against his mind.

Abruptly she let him go. She stared at him with a look he couldn't begin to understand. There were equal parts shock, confusion, and... was that hope? Jack gulped. The last thing he needed was to make himself interesting in Faerie.

She jerked her chin to indicate the space over his shoulder. "Follow the tunnel. It will take you past the Great Chamber of Muirias—take care not to be seen. Make your way to the corridor where the Urisk waits. If you can get past him you will come to the Treasury. Get that far, and I trust you to find your own way out." She lifted one bloodstained finger to her cheek as she considered him. Avid fascination sparkled in her gaze. Jack shivered. Careful to avoid her eyes, he searched her face. What trick was she playing?

Nodding his thanks—because saying it out loud put him in her debt—he set off down the tunnel she indicated. She produced a larger bowl from midair, drew out her knife, and went back to hack at poor Bess. The splatter of falling entrails echoed after him.

Shallow puddles announced his every step with tiny splashes that rang loud as cymbals to his ears. Dangling roots tickled his neck like spider legs. When one slithered against his cheek with a life of its own, Jack flailed and sank his teeth into his lip to keep from crying out.

Dirt showered down on his head. His arms shot out to brace on either side of the tunnel. As soon as his skin touched the wall, small bodies crawled up his sleeves. He sucked down a scream, smacking at his chest to kill the prickly creatures. They scuttled over him, burrowing beneath his clothes. In seconds, he had his shirt over his head, slapping it violently against the wall as white scorpion-looking things scurried to safety. One drove its stinger deep into the back of his arm. Within seconds, the insect's white body darkened as the stinger siphoned up his blood.

Horrified, Jack tore it out and smashed it beneath his foot where it burst like a grape. Jack swiped his hands over his shoulders, chest, and back again and again, frantic to remove every last one.

If the tunnel weren't so cold he'd have gone naked rather than risk one of them hiding in his clothes. Only after he turned his shirt inside and out several times and stomped on it for good measure was he willing to put it back on. Even after he was sure they were gone his skin prickled beneath the phantom swarm of invisible legs.

The wide tunnel narrowed the farther he went, and soon he had to crawl on his hands and knees. He prayed that the crawling things wouldn't come back for another attack. If they swarmed him now he had no room to fight them off. That thought alone almost convinced him to turn back.

His shoulders wedged between two sharp rocks.

Breathe, he willed himself. He clawed at the dirt, carving deep furrows that did nothing to break him free. Panic drew a tingling knot inside his chest. His heart slammed against his rib cage, each frantic beat more painful than the last.

Distant drumming traveled through the limestone. His breath wavered from his chest as he paused to listen. *Music? Here?*

He wriggled, desperate to get through the tunnel and find the source of the sound. Clawing and scrambling, Jack dug a path through the rocks. He crawled until a faint glow told him he had reached the Great Chamber of Muirias.

The music swelled. An arrangement of notes unlike anything he'd ever conceived played on an instrument he couldn't put a name to.

Every muscle in his body seized. Despite the tight space, his legs lashed out with a will of their own. His shin connected with stone hard enough to wring tears from his eyes. The music wrapped itself around his mind, probing, prodding, searching for a way in.

His right leg jerked violently, driving his kneecap into the wall. Momentum flipped him onto his side. The music turned his gift against him, burning the enchanted notes into his brain. Not only could he hear the spell, but his mind replayed and intensified its hold. The harder he fought, the more his body battered itself against the stones in its violent need to dance.

Desperate, he picked the tune apart, dissecting it into melody, meter, and notes until he broke it down into beat alone. One, two, three, four... one, two, three, four.... The tidal wave became a gentle, lapping stream. It washed over and around him, but so long as he concentrated on it note by note he could let it float through him without washing away his soul. He wasn't completely free of it though. He caught himself breathing in time to the beat, moving his arms in swoops like he was conducting.

He rolled back over and crawled in time to the simple count. On the first beat of each measure he inched forward, dragging himself along for the remaining three counts. It was slow going, but he congratulated himself on escaping the spell.

A clod of dirt near his elbow shifted, revealing a hole that looked down into the large cavern. The faery had called it the Great Chamber of Muirias so he expected to see a lavish ballroom or ornately carved chamber. Instead he saw an enormous cave. Bonfires sporadically lit the hall, throwing monstrous shadows around the room. Some of the rocks had been carved into pillars, but it was crude compared to the stories of Faerie elegance he'd heard as a boy.

The source of the music came from just below on a rounded platform of calcified rock. He hadn't recognized the instrument because it was a human rib cage with notches stabbed into the bones like a pipe organ. The musician fastened his mouth over the breastbone and his twelve fingers strained to play the morbid thing. Horrified, Jack wished he could scratch the sound from his ears.

Two humans writhed on the floor before the musician. One was a middle-aged man who wore slacks and a button-up shirt. Sweat darkened the fabric beneath his arms, across his chest and down his spine. Blood splattered the cave floor where his blistered feet danced holes through his shoes. The young woman beside him had no shoes at all. Her feet were so raw they glowed against the paleness of her ankles. Occasionally, flashes of pain cut through her blank expression, but just as quickly they vanished as she closed her eyes and succumbed to the music's spell.

The horror of it severed the last tethers binding Jack to the song's power.

But more musicians lent their music to the hall. A short distance away were a trio of the ugliest women Jack had ever seen half-submerged in a black pool. Their torsos were completely bare, and their shriveled breasts dragged on the ground. Webbed hands anchored them to the rocks where they flung back their heads and hissed to the darkened ceiling. They had an audience too—all men—a mixture of old and young. They sat cross-legged, swaying back and forth with their eyes closed in rapture.

There was a flurry of excitement as bright streaks of yellow light arced down from the ceiling. Hot on their heels came a galloping kelpie, snapping and snarling to drive them where it wanted the wailing willowisps to go. Jack flattened himself to the ground even though he knew he was safely hidden. One of the orbs broke away and passed close to where Jack huddled. It was bright as a shooting star, but deep in its center he thought he could make out a woman's face.

"He needs me! Give me back my baby—!" She came so close that Jack's spirit flared like a beacon in answer to her cry. The kelpie charged after it, sinking its pointed teeth into the fleeing soul and dragging it back to join the others. Jack felt a strange tearing sensation, as if a piece of his spirit broke off. If it did, she took it with her as the kelpie dragged her away.

Somewhere a child had lost his mother, would probably never know what happened to her. The watching fae jeered at her futile efforts to return to the family she'd lost.

Hot tears burned in the back of Jack's eyes. He'd never felt so helpless in his life. There were too many of them and already the kelpie had driven the souls away again with more yelps and barks of triumph.

Around the hall, hideous creatures cast their charms on all-too-willing prey. They lured them close to scabbed, scaly skin, tempted them to kiss and fondle parts he didn't want to think up names for. Jack saw what the humans saw—creatures of impossible beauty offering themselves eagerly—while his Faery Sight revealed the open sores, puss-filled sacs, and blubbery slime-covered flesh of what greeted those who gave in.

Despite the terror of it, the chamber called to the magic that flowed inside him. Music reigned here. Here they would appreciate the gift he had to offer. This was where he belonged. After all, had he not just proven he could break their spells...?

He saw how the humans worshiped the musicians and caught himself envying the fae. He longed to create music that hung in the air after the final notes faded, that haunted memories and lived inside those who heard it for the rest of their lives. Fae music held power, and Jack wanted it.

"I gotta get out of here," he said under his breath. In spite of his words, he glanced down again and nearly tumbled through the hole.

Lounging on a throne of sculpted limestone was a woman. A river of black hair rippled from the crown of her head over milk-white shoulders and down her back. Blood-red lips curved in a smile as glacial eyes surveyed the scene before her. She wore a red leather gown decorated with throwing knives. Jack missed several heartbeats before he realized she wasn't Eira.

The faery exuded such a strong magnetic pull that even thirty feet above her head Jack's senses tuned to her. This had to be the Ash Queen.

She beckoned with a curt, sweep of her hand.

The need to go to her crashed over Jack so hard that darts of pain rocketed up his thighs. In answer, a male faery of equal elegance approached her. He was as golden as she was fair, his hair carefully combed into waves back from his high brow. At her small gesture, the entire hall fell silent, as if they had merely been filling time until this moment arrived.

"Your scouts returned from the Wildwood empty-handed, Odhran." The lash of her voice made the golden faery flinch.

"Not empty-handed. They brought you tribute in the form of an exquisite white cow. Even now it is being prepared for your table."

"Tribute? Ha! They think gifts will spare them for failing to complete their mission. The child was alone and away from the protection spells the old witch wove on their house. Who knows when such an opportunity will rise again."

"They sprang their ill-conceived trap in the presence of iron. Griff claims a barrier prevented them from getting too close."

The Ash Queen tossed her head.

"What barrier? The old woman has been dead for over a fortnight. Even a true witch's spells would have lost their power by now."

"My apologies, Scatha. I thought they understood the importance of their task. They will not fail next time. For now, it is the feast of Samhain. The High King is dead and his court is scattered. For the first time in recorded memory the Solitary Fae have united under one banner—yours. Allow yourself to celebrate your victory." He made a circular motion with his hands and a small golden harp appeared out of thin air. Scatha's eyes flashed and she surged to her feet with a speed that made Jack gasp.

"Do not think you can pull my strings as easily as the ones in your hand, Harper. Finvarra's court will seek to save itself. Those prancing courtiers will never regard us as anything but vermin until each and every one of them has a taste of his own blood on our steel." A heavy broadsword appeared in her hand, aimed straight at Odhran's throat. "Once Winterthorn's allegiance is secured, Faerie will fall at our feet. We will chain them in our arenas and torment them for our sport!" A cry rose from the surrounding fae at her impassioned speech. Odhran scuttled back a safe distance from the Queen's blade.

"Your cunning is outdone only by your beauty, My Queen," said Odhran, bowing at the waist. With his nose mere inches from the ground, he strummed the golden harp.

As soon as his fingers touched the strings a lightning bolt zapped Jack straight through the heart. Crying out in shock and pain, he fell back. His head struck stone and lights whirled before his eyes. Jack touched his chest, half-expecting to find a hole burned through his shirt.

Below him the fae shrieked and squawked, falling on each other with teeth and claws. They were in a frenzy, and he didn't want to stick around to find out why. He scrambled down the tunnel as fast as he could on his hands and knees.

The light from the Great Chamber faded behind him. No helpful lamps illuminated his passage anymore, but fortunately the tunnel expanded. Soon he had enough room to stand. He picked his way carefully. His next obstacle was the Urisk, and according to the campfire stories his brothers used to tell, that was not the sort of monster he wanted to stumble across unexpectedly. They embodied loneliness, so ugly that one look at them could scare a man to death. Even the fae shunned them.

A dim red glow shone around a bend in the tunnel. Holding his breath, Jack inched forward to see a giant shape filling the entire tunnel. At least two-stories tall, the monster stood on one bent and twisted leg that had all the bunched power of a bull ready to charge. One muscular arm protruded from the center of its chest. Its long crocodile snout snapped at the air, and rough scales covered its misshapen body. The dim light came from the Urisk's pupil-less red eye.

It threw back its head and bayed. Jack flung his arms over his head as clods of dirt rained from the ceiling. It lurched forward until a thick, rattling chain pulled it up short. Around the Urisk's throat clamped a collar so tight the skin puckered above and below.

Jack's hope vanished. He'd have more luck flapping his arms and trying to fly home than slipping past that thing, and the den of temptation and torture behind him didn't offer a much better alternative. He sagged against the wall.

The Urisk snorted, and its spine curved forward so that its body resembled a question mark. The red glow all but went out as its eyelid lowered, and it bent to press the side of its head against—was that a door? The sight sent Jack's heart leaping, but it might as well have been on the other side of the moon, because there was no way he could get through with the Urisk sleeping on top of it.

A rush of frustration washed over Jack. His brother, Douglas, whose gift to go unnoticed could make him practically invisible, would be perfect for this. Jack didn't see how he could get past the Urisk without being seen, but ultimately, he didn't have a choice. Getting to his feet again he edged closer.

His first step sent a stone skittering across the ground.

Instantly, the Urisk bellowed and stomped and beat the wall with its massive fist. Jack covered his head and dove behind a stalagmite for cover. After a long time of bashing its body against the rocks the creature quieted again. Only then did Jack hear the music.

Simple, angelic, it floated through the air as gentle as a lullaby. The simple melody repeated again and again becoming an instrumental chant urging the monster to be still.

Eying the length of the Urisk's chain, Jack took a calculated risk, puckered his lips, and whistled.

At the first unexpected note the Urisk thrashed violently and fear cut Jack off mid-whistle. Wetting his lips hastily, he tried again, hugging the wall for all he was worth. When the Urisk realized the music was in the room with it instead of beyond the door, it lifted its snout and sniffed. Jack suddenly appreciated the cesspit that had dumped him into the Otherworld.

Ropes of drool hung from the monster's mouth. The nearer Jack got to those snapping jaws the harder it became to whistle on key. When the song wound down for the eighth time, he switched to humming before it started back up again. The lower register resonated with the song of the harp—for that was surely the instrument making that ethereal sound.

The Urisk closed its eye and doused Jack in darkness. Instinct kept him humming even though his heart threatened to leap out of his chest. He was close now. If he moved fast enough he just might make it to the door before the Urisk could catch him. But where was the monster? It would be a shame to get this far and run smack into its hand.

Sniff, sniff, sniff. Jack froze. Had it moved? Desperate, he groped for the door and brushed scales. Red light flared just before the ground at his feet imploded beneath an enormous fist. With a yell Jack dove for the door. He caught the handle and turned, but the latch had rusted tight. The Urisk's fist slammed down again. Jack twisted sideways and threw his weight on the handle. It turned, but not fast enough. The door swung in just as the Urisk's knuckles smashed into Jack's back. His feet left the earth, and he landed face-first several feet inside the door.

A pair of long, fat fingers prodded the crevice. Weakly, he tucked his legs out of reach.

The Urisk whined and snarled, straining to get to him. Safe, Jack collapsed.

The left side of his body throbbed from shoulder to hip. He moved his arm and felt a grinding sensation in his shoulder that didn't bode well. Carefully, he sat up. Muscles protested and joints popped.

A suit of armor lay in a heap on the ground not far from him. Despite looking as though it hadn't been used in a long time, the polished surface glowed with silver light.

"That would've come in handy five minutes ago," he muttered. His toe nudged the pile as he bent to pick up the shining breastplate. The helmet clattered from the top of the heap to land upside-down at his feet. Jack reeled back with a yell. The skull of its former owner was still lodged inside. Staggering, he tripped over a length of cloth lying on the ground. It tangled around his ankles, and when he looked down both of his feet had disappeared. He kicked frantically and sagged with relief when his feet reappeared the moment he got free.

The Treasury. When he'd heard that was his final destination he'd expected a room full of gold and jewels. Instead it appeared to be a room full of ... junk. A rusted sword here, a cracked cauldron there.... A tapestry hung on the wall depicting a woman with flowing black hair and pure-white skin wearing a crimson gown decorated with tiny stars. In her hands she held the same golden harp he had seen in the Great Chamber. She sat turned away to stare up at a full moon stitched in blinding silver threads. It looked so real he almost swore he saw her breathe. No. It must've been a draft rustling the fabric. With some effort, Jack wrenched his gaze away.

The Treasury was a large circular room arranged around a wide underground lake. Steam rose from the water and coated his skin in a sticky film. He gulped. It looked like he'd have to leave the same way he'd come in—hopefully there weren't any psychotic vines growing under the surface of this pool.

The thought made him jittery and he looked around again to make sure he didn't have another option. Below the tapestry on a simple stone dais stood the harp from the Great Chamber. Jack whirled around. Had the harper come in by another entrance to put it there? Silence echoed around him. Nothing moved.

Belatedly, it occurred to him that the music had stopped. He stared at the small instrument. It was unlike anything he had ever seen with intricate moldings of leaves and flowers transitioning through the four seasons as they followed the curve of the instrument's body. A bare winter branch formed the pillar that sprouted a crown of flower blossoms which faded into a pattern of leaves along the neck and withered away again around the ripe apple at its base. He glanced around again. No one was there. What sound would those golden strings make? Unable to resist the temptation, Jack plucked the longest string. It emitted a throaty hum.

Electricity sizzled up his arm. Pain and shock sent him crashing to his knees. His fingertips fused to the cold metal. Music bombarded his mind as every song the harp knew imprinted into his head in a brutal onslaught that would surely split his skull. With a mighty wrench, he yanked the harp off its pedestal.

Instantly the pain stopped.

Jack swayed. His temples throbbed with the memory of pain. He wanted to fling the harp across the room, but his hand refused to give up its prize. It had bonded to him, as much a part of him as his arm.

Drip, drip, drip. A drop of water landed on his shoulder. Jack was almost too afraid to look.

White fangs gaped wide in a mouth large enough to swallow him whole. Its skin matched the dark, murky, greenish-black of the water. Only the dragon's massive head hovered above the lake, but even that was enough to drown any hopes Jack had that he might make the swim to freedom.

The floor shook violently and Jack fell over. The harp clanged, sending up a single discordant note. A loud crack was the only warning before the Urisk barreled through the rock wall into the Treasury. His broken chain clanked off the stones as he moved. The water serpent swiveled its head in a fluid movement that suggested just how much of its bulk rested below the water. The Urisk didn't pause before tackling the great head. They slammed into the edge of the water, sending up a splash like a tidal wave.

Thrashing limbs and bellows of rage filled the cavern. Jack glanced at the murky water and back at the struggling giants. With both of them distracted it was his only chance to escape. But what if more serpents lurked below?

The Urisk's fist struck a vicious uppercut that sent the serpent careening toward Jack. Saber-long teeth snapped at his ankles. He dove into the water.

The dragon's horned tail sliced up to meet him. There wasn't time to move out of the way. The tip of one wicked spike gouged deep into the back of Jack's thigh.

Impaled, he hung helpless as the tail whipped ruthlessly back and forth. The scream that tore open his jaws signed his death sentence. Water flooded his lungs so quickly he was already half on the other side when the thrashing tail hurled him away. The blinding agony as his leg ripped free gave him one final push into oblivion.

Chapter 4

Jack floated in a haze of wry acceptance. Death-by-dragon-spike—that was unexpected. Warm light bathed his face, at odds with the cool liquid lapping at his back. Without warning his temple struck a rock. He flinched and the splash of water brought him back to his senses. Jack cracked his eyes open to see that he was drifting in the shallows along a riverbank. Black silt swirled back and forth with the movement of the current.

"My god, you're alive!"

A large hand probed the base of his jaw.

Fear leapt wild and feral against his rib cage. He tried to roll over. Instantly, pain ground him between its teeth. There was no part of him that didn't hurt. It felt as though someone had taken a grater to every inch of his skin. His muscles knotted, and his left leg dragged limply. That was nothing compared to the hunger raking at his belly.

Gasping, Jack fell back against an arm that supported his head out of the water. A wet leaf stuck to his cheek. Sunlight filtered through the web of branches overhead. The brilliance dazzled him.

"Where...?" The moment he opened his mouth the skin on his lips tore like tissue paper.

"Stay with me, Jack," his rescuer commanded. Frowning, Jack tried to place the vaguely familiar voice. He squinted at the face swimming above him until he recognized Sheriff Doyle. He was out of uniform, dressed in a plaid flannel shirt and jeans. He looked dressed for fishing, though Jack couldn't see any poles. By the light of day, he looked older than Jack remembered. Streaks of silver winged back from his temples and threaded through his dark brown hair.

"When is it?" Jack murmured. How much time had he lost in Faerie? Doyle grunted in frustration.

"Dammit, you need a hospital."

Jack's eyes snapped open. He tried to sit up. Whirling lights flashed in front of his eyes and nausea charged him like a ram. Doyle caught him under the arms and dragged him out of the water. Jack struggled, digging his hands into the riverbank for purchase. There was a muffled thrum from beneath the water. The harp! Ignoring the roiling in his belly, he slipped out of the Sheriff's grasp and flopped on top of the instrument to hide it.

"It's going to be alright, son." Doyle tried to be comforting but impatience put a bite in his voice. We need to get you out of here." He stepped back and patted his pockets for his phone. The face of his silver watch caught the light, blinding Jack with a flash of reflected sun. Jack's head balanced like a watermelon on his neck as he shook it from side to side.

"Need...home," he managed. He struggled to all fours, determined to crawl home if he had to.

The Sorleys didn't go to doctors. They had too much magic inside them. What if the doctors asked questions? Instead they relied on his middle brother, Glen, whose healing abilities rivaled anything modern medicine had to offer.

Doyle put his hand on his hip and frowned at his phone before scanning the water.

"Son, you've been missing for over two weeks. You need a hospital." He waved his phone in the air, searching for a signal. Jack's jaw dropped and he got a mouthful of river water. Two weeks? His mother was going to kill him!

"Douglas. He's...cop. Please." His strength was failing. The edges of his vision dissolved into fuzzy, white spirals. Sheer stubbornness kept him from passing out.

"You mean Officer Sorley? He'll be informed." Doyle moved away in search of bars. "Why won't this damned thing work?" No sooner had the words left his mouth than the distant shriek of a siren shattered the peace of the woods. Doyle spun around. "How in the hell...?"

A black and white cruiser sent gravel flying as it skidded to a stop a short distance away. Douglas Sorley, white-faced and wild-eyed, flung open the door. His badge glinted as he vaulted a dilapidated wood fence to reach them.

"Jesus, Jack!" He all but knocked the Sheriff aside as he scrambled to pull Jack into his arms. There was a weighty thud as the harp hit the ground. Douglas froze. With his nose buried in Douglas' jacket Jack couldn't warn him that Doyle could see the harp too.

There was an awkward silence in which nobody moved.

"I'll call for an ambulance." Doyle turned away with clipped efficiency, still studying his useless phone. Blinking back tears, Douglas shook his head and gathered Jack into his arms.

"It'll be faster if I take him." His voice was uneven.

"Wait...!" Jack let his arm fall, groping. Douglas bent to slide one arm beneath Jack's legs for a more secure grip. The movement gave Jack the opportunity to snatch up the harp. This time when his skin connected with it there was no sizzle of power, no bombardment on his senses.

"I should go with you—" Doyle began, but Douglas shook his head again.

"I've got it from here, Sir." Douglas straightened, his entire body trembling. Jack gave up the fight to stay awake and let darkness take him.

A POTHOLE SET OFF A firecracker in his skull that jolted Jack back to consciousness. He moaned. The tires squealed as the car lurched to a halt. He hissed as his head flopped from side to side. Douglas twisted in his seat.

"Damn it, Jack! Don't you ever pull another stunt like that again, do you hear me? We thought you were dead!" Douglas' voice sent splinters through his brain. Jack tried to look at him and explain, but his lids were gummed together and crusted with dried mud and sweat.

"Not...my choice." He groaned and shifted to get the seat belt buckle out of his kidney. Douglas coughed to clear his throat. Another sharp turn made the harp thrum in gentle reproof as it slid under the passenger seat. Jack groped for it, but just as the tips of his fingers brushed the warm metal, a violent cramp wrung his stomach like a dish rag. He went rigid and willed it to pass.

Two weeks, he reminded himself. Though it only felt like a day to his mind, his body had suffered every second of the missing time. The gnawing in his belly crawled up the back of his throat, strangling him. No matter how he struggled he couldn't keep his head above the drowning hunger and throbbing pain. In the end, it swept him under again.

He floated, distantly aware of the flurry of activity when Douglas pulled up to the hospital. It was hard to keep the kaleidoscope of voices, smells, and faces from dissolving into darkness as they rushed him through the stark white halls. He felt a pinch and cool fluids surged through an IV into his arm. Scissor blades skimmed up his belly to cut away the scraps of his filthy, mud-crusted shirt.

Gasps spiraled the room.

Jack forced his eyes open. His rib cage jutted from his chest like a mountain range. His skin stretched so thin it was nearly translucent across the veins and withered muscles. He fainted.

Hours or minutes later he woke to the prod of a metal spoon against his teeth. His lips parted automatically to let warm ambrosia slide over his tongue. Familiar healing magic engulfed him in a silver cocoon that was blinding even through his closed eyelids. Glen's strength poured into him, restoring what Faerie had leeched away.

Chopped carrots and caramelized onions lent their sweetness to the rich chicken broth. Jack gulped and tried to follow the spoon as it turned back for more. Someone supported his head as another spoonful pushed into his mouth. Nutrients raced to withered cells to renew and revive. His muscles swelled, regaining their former firmness. He inhaled deeply and opened his eyes.

All six of his brothers were arranged around the room. Keith occupied the padded seat to the right of the hospital bed. In a tall, green, glass vase he held a bouquet of primroses and St. John's Wort. 'Old Man, Keith' they'd started calling him when he turned thirty last year, but with the heavy bags bulging from the deep shadows beneath his eyes he looked ancient. Craig sat on the edge of the green couch by the window with his elbows on his knees. An iron disc the size of a quarter danced anxiously back and forth across his knuckles. Douglas stood watch at the door. Ross scowled at a flock of crows out the window with his back to the room. His shaggy brown hair was tied back at the nape of his neck. Glen sat beside him with the spoon in his hand while Logan lounged on the empty cot to Jack's left with his head propped on his fist. Jack managed a feeble smile and a wave.

"Hi."

A spasm passed over Keith's face. He pressed his fist to his forehead and took a deep steadying breath. Glen shot him a wary glance before hurrying to refill Jack's bowl.

"Logan's going to try and talk the doctors into letting you come home tonight. The less you look like a skeleton the easier it will be to convince them you're fine."

"What about my leg?" Jack slid his hand under the blanket to explore the extent of his injury. He touched bare skin below the hem of his boxers. Glen's doughy features tightened.

"What happened to your leg?"

Jack snorted. This side of the Otherworld, the answer to that sounded ridiculous. He lifted the blanket to see that there was no puncture wound where the dragon spike had speared him. There wasn't even a bruise. He craned his neck to inspect the back of his arm where the scorpion had stung him. There was no mark there either. Whatever wounds he received in Faerie had stayed behind. Here he only had to deal with two weeks' worth of starvation and dehydration. His hands trembled as he took the Tupperware container in both hands and guzzled the rejuvenating broth.

"Where's Mom? How freaked out is she?" he asked after swallowing the last of the soup. He coughed as a shred of meat went down the wrong tube. He thumped his chest hard, hacking to clear his airway. No one moved to help him.

The AC kicked on, sweeping cold air through the room.

"Now's not the time," Glen fumbled the lid back on the empty container. Jack sat up straight. They stared at him, six grim gargoyles. Only a year or two separated one brother from the next in age, except for the five years between Glen and Logan. Still, facing their haggard stares made Jack suddenly feel like a child in the company of wizened, world-weary, old men.

Instinctively, Jack knew he'd stumbled into another nest of scorpions. A hundred scenarios swarmed him, stinging with possibilities more painful than the last. Finally, Logan cleared his throat.

"When no one could find you Mom went looking herself, and—" His Adam's apple bobbed. Jack dug his fingers in the blankets, but Logan couldn't find the right words. That told him all he needed to know.

"She was found at Wildwood Park up the river from where you washed up. The official report says she slid down the bank and drowned," said Douglas. He covered his eyes and sank onto the couch beside Craig, who put a hand on his shoulder. "I saw the hoof prints on the bank. She went looking for the kelpie."

Jack heard, but he didn't understand. He pressed his palms against his eyes, refusing to believe his fae-fearing mother would do something so stupid.

"But why would she follow a kelpie?" His head pounded with disbelief. "Why didn't someone stop her?"

It was the wrong thing to say. The grief in the air ignited.

"You went out on All Hallows' Eve and showed every fae for a hundred miles what you are, and you're going to stand there and point your finger at us?" Ross rounded on him with bloodshot eyes. "You didn't even win! You came in last place!" Jack's swell of self-righteous indignation deflated in an instant. Last place?

"You're lucky they didn't wipe us all out. Not that it matters to you. You'd sacrifice each and every one of us if you thought it'd make you a star!"

Logan leapt off his cot and Craig shot to his feet to intercept him before he lunged at Ross. Keith signaled for quiet while Douglas sent a furtive look at the open door.

"We're just glad to have you back," said Glen after a moment. He meant the words, and not even Ross was angry or grief-stricken enough to deny it, but there was no antidote for the accusations poisoning the air.

LOGAN EXERCISED ALL of his persuasive charm to convince the hospital staff to ignore protocol and let Jack go home early. By the time he was done clouding the memories of the doctors and nurses into forgetting that Jack had been near starvation, the residue of his magic coated the painted powder blue walls in a sheen of platinum glitter.

The final doctor was just adding his signature to Jack's patient chart when they heard a low click from the doorway followed by a flash of light. Keith swore under his breath. He and Craig jumped to shield Jack from the reporter angling his camera phone for a better shot. The doctor, a clean-cut man in his mid-thirties whirled around with a scowl. Jack could only stare, stunned by the man's persistence.

"You've been front-page news for two weeks," Logan said with quiet anger. "They didn't get bad until Mom.... It was starting to look like a conspiracy and well—this is Straifield. What else did they have to write about?"

Puffing out his chest so that his badge caught the light, Douglas joined Keith and Craig at the door to form a barricade.

"My brother has nothing to say at this time—" but he might as well have said nothing. The reporter simply shouted his questions over their heads.

"Mr. Sorley, Todd Stevens, Channel 7. Where have you been? Did your disappearance have anything to do with your poor performance during the Battle of the Bands? Should parents be worried about their children's safety?"

Jack gritted his teeth and focused on tying his shoes. Keith braced his arms on either side of the doorway to block Stevens' access, and Craig balled his fists to show that he was seconds from erupting into violence.

"I don't know who let you in here, but if you aren't gone in the next five seconds Channel 7 will owe the sum of your next paycheck to the Linn County Police Department to cover your bail."

Stevens flinched and leapt back as Sheriff Doyle bore down on him. Taking one last haphazard photo of the Sorleys gathered protectively around Jack's bed, he bolted.

"I'd understand completely if you'd like to press charges," said Doyle, watching Stevens disappear down the hallway. He'd changed out of his civilian clothes into his leather jacket and brown uniform. His hair bore the furrows of a recent pass with a comb, and a fleck of blood dotted his jawline where he'd nicked himself shaving.

"I came by to see when you'd be accepting visitors and they told me you've already been cleared to go home. I had to see it for myself. No offense son, but this morning you looked like death, and now...." He took another step into the room and kicked the door shut behind him. "Care to tell me how that happened?"

Keith's face could have been carved from petrified wood. Caught off guard, Ross and Craig exchanged mystified looks that quickly solidified into distrust. Glen nearly dropped his Tupperware. Only Logan managed to maintain his composure. His green eyes grew watchful as his lips folded into uncharacteristic silence.

Jack didn't have the energy to erect a convincing mask of ignorance. He tried, but the moment his eyes met Doyle's direct gaze they darted away in hasty retreat.

"We appreciate your concern, Sir, but you didn't have to come all the way down here." Douglas glided in to intercept the Sheriff. Doyle's brow arched.

"I wish I could say it was just a social call, but I was hoping your brother could give me some leads about where his... 'kidnappers' might be." His eloquent pause confirmed that he was in no doubt who—or what—was to blame.

"Kidnappers?" Jack blurted out before he could catch himself. Keith's eyes sliced in his direction with all the subtlety of a backhand.

"Care to account for where you went after we parted ways at the fair?" Ignoring the semicircle of brothers arranged against him, Doyle turned to Jack and pulled a small yellow notepad from his pocket.

If he hadn't grown up in a house with Logan, Jack might not have recognized the subtle push of compulsion for what it was. His jaw clenched even as his mind raced around the realization that the Sheriff not only had Faery Sight but was fae-touched too.

"It's all a little fuzzy." Jack scratched the back of his neck and waited for one of his brothers to give him a clue what to do. Doyle huffed and lowered his notepad.

"Look son, you're not protecting anyone by staying silent. You think if you bury your head in the sand it won't happen again? Their next victim might not know they're in danger until it's too late. My condolences, by the way. I can only assume she let her better judgment be swayed by fear for your safety."

The blood drained from Jack's face so quickly he grew lightheaded.

"Our family's been through a lot and we're anxious to have Jack home," said Glen with soft firmness. "It was nice of you to stop by." Doyle shrugged, keeping his focus centered on Jack.

"It's my job to keep Straifield safe. No one else should have to go through what you have." If he thought his words would inspire cooperation, the Sheriff was disappointed. After a moments' silence Doyle sighed, gave a curt nod, and left the room without another word.

"Well that was interesting," said Logan into silence that followed.

Interesting was an understatement.

Chapter 5

"What. Is. That?" Keith stood on their front porch an hour later with his hands on his hips watching Jack climb out of Douglas' cruiser with the golden harp tucked under his arm. Jack tightened his grip.

"I don't want to talk about it," he muttered, trying to move past him into the house, but Keith flung out an arm to stop him.

"You stole from them? Jesus, Jack! What the hell is wrong with you?" Keith tried to snatch it out of his hands, but Jack dodged out of the way.

"I didn't steal it!" he shouted before catching himself. "At least, I didn't mean to."

"Oh, well if you 'didn't mean to' I'm sure they won't come looking for it." Keith added a flourish of air quotes to emphasize his sarcasm. Jack's mind swam with heat, and he reared back.

"You have no idea what I went through down there."

"You never would have gone through anything if you'd stayed home where you belonged!"

"Hey, hey!" Douglas stepped between them. "Jack's right. We don't know what happened. It's a little premature to judge him without hearing the whole story." Keith's nostrils flared, and he clenched his jaw. Fire burned the corners of Jack's eyes, but he gritted his teeth against the tears. Keith dug in his back pocket for the round tin of dip he always carried. It gave off a faint wintergreen smell.

Pacing up and down the porch he pinched some of the black grounds between his fingers and tucked in against his gums. Finally, he came to a stop back where he' started, stuffed the tin back into his pocket, and folded his arms.

"Alright, the last any of us heard, you'd found some girl on the side of the road, called Doug to come get you because—and I quote—'something weird is going on.' But by the time he got there both you and Bess were missing, there was no girl, and the only clues were footprints leading to that sewage drain behind the livestock tent." His words dripped scorn. Jack's vision swam, and he swayed slightly no matter how hard he tried to hold himself straight.

"Was it the girl?" Douglas prodded. Without meaning to he had slipped into his professional persona. His voice deepened with controlled patience as he tried to get all the facts to form a whole picture. Jack shook his head.

"Doyle and his son showed up and gave her a ride home. I went back to the livestock tent and saw that Bess had been taken. I'd only been gone a few minutes. I thought I still had time to get her back...." With his eyes on the ground Jack told them everything. He thought Keith might pop a blood vessel when he heard that Jack had tossed the mistletoe seeds into the water. Jack skimmed over the details of the Great Chamber and the music's effect on him.

"I still don't understand why the hell you would go near that thing," Keith muttered gray-faced when the story finished. "It's obviously enchanted." He shot the harp a black look. Jack's shoulders sagged with weariness.

"If it had been some exotic plant wouldn't you have moved in for a closer look?" It wasn't often Jack found common ground with Keith, but an undiscovered strain of plant held the same lure for Keith that a faery composition held for him. The harp had reached out for him and he'd reached back.

Keith's lower lip protruded mulishly.

"Fine, but you really think bringing that thing here is a good idea?"

"What else am I supposed to do with it? I can't just leave it on the side of the road. Doyle's seen it. He knows where it came from. This is the safest place for it."

Keith swiped a hand over his face and shook his head.

"You never think, do you?" he murmured more to himself than to Jack. "They had an Urisk and a dragon guarding it. Obviously, it's not something they wanted to get out. You really think they'll just let you keep it?"

"They can't come here. Winterthorn swore no fae would ever set foot on our land uninvited."

"He also promised that no fae would ever harm a member of our family, and yet both our parents are dead."

"What do you plan to do with it?" asked Douglas, trying a different tact. Jack shrugged.

"I'm not going to take it on a world tour if that's what you're worried about."

One corner of Douglas' mouth twitched in the ghost of a smile.

"It's on you," said Keith seriously. "If you suspect for even a moment that it's a danger to us, I want it gone."

"Of course," Jack said with utter sincerity. Keith exchanged a weighted glance with Douglas before heading back into the house. Douglas watched him go with an unreadable expression on his face.

"Just be careful, Jack," he said in his low, even voice. "On the outside it might look like a harp, but nothing that comes out of the Otherworld is ever that simple." Before the weight of that warning could put too much tension in the air, he hooked Jack's neck in the crook of his elbow and pulled him in for a hug. "I'm glad you found a way back."

RATHER THAN JOIN THE rest of his brothers in the kitchen, Jack sought refuge in his room. Family pictures lined the wall along the stairs. The weight of his missing weeks grew heavier with each glimpse of his mother's face. At the top of the stairs hung one of her laughing with the sun shining behind her. Jack nearly missed the step seeing her bathed that way in the golden halo. She looked like a willowisp.

The ground eroded beneath his feet as the horrible truth pressed down on him. The denial he'd summoned against Keith's accusations didn't work against the voice whispering in his mind. He pictured the little fireball racing and twisting to break free. 'Give me back my baby!' He ran his hands over his face and up into his hair to force the memory away.

His bedroom was the first door on the right, but he stared at the closed door at the opposite end of the hall. Denial stiffened his spine. If he opened that door he'd find his mother reading in the afternoon sun. She would look up, smile, and ask if there was anything wrong. Against his better judgment, he walked up the hall and opened the door.

The room was like a carousel, old world and ornate with whimsy and wonder worked into the wainscoting. Above each of the three arched windows carved roses were clustered in elaborate swags. It was the only room in the house that was uniquely feminine. Flowers from Keith's garden always filled the crystal vase on the bedside table next to the book of poems Logan wrote as a Mother's Day gift a couple years back. Jack inhaled deeply, searching for the smell of peppermint tea.

But there was nothing.

Someone had taken down his mother's long, lace curtains. The pastel blue walls had been painted a harsh tan. Gone was her vase and perfume bottles, her makeup and brushes. The only thing that remained of hers was the vanity with its tri-fold mirror lovingly carved with roses by their father years and years ago.

Jack's brain couldn't comprehend what he was seeing. It was as if he'd stepped out of his handcrafted home into a stark suburban house. Why? When their father died his brothers hadn't packed up his things and steamrolled over his memory.

He nearly stormed downstairs to demand an explanation, but stopped after the first step. Even if everything was returned to the way it was his mother was gone.

Shuffling back to his own door he half-expected to find his room empty too. They'd have hell to pay if someone sold off his guitars....

But everything was just as he'd left it down to the dirty laundry on the floor. The only difference was his father's guitar folded over its old stand in the corner. No one had tried to repair it, but clearly, they didn't have the heart to throw it away. The purple flyer for the Battle of the Bands hung off the corner of his desk. He wanted to rip it into shreds.

He ground his fist against his eyelids. Two weeks in real time—one day in Faerie—yet the place felt as alien now as the Great Chamber of Muirias. The posters belonged to a stranger, an innocent kid who'd never set foot beneath a faery hill. The framed compositions were the doodles of a five-year-old compared to the music scribbled into his mind by faery bells and pipes.

Wearily he set the harp on the edge of his desk and sank onto his bed. With any luck he would close his eyes and sleep for days, but the moment he closed his eyes he was back in the rocky tunnel, wedged in place and unable to move. Though his body lay still as a corpse, his skin prickled under invisible scorpions swarming out of his memory. His heartbeat pounded against his eardrums like thuds of the Urisk's fist. A particularly vivid sensation slithered against his rib cage. His eyes flew open and he shot up in bed, but there was nothing there. Shuddering, he kicked the blankets to the floor. He couldn't stand the thought of monsters lurking beneath the covers where he couldn't see them.

Automatically his eyes jumped to the harp standing regally across the room. Just the sight of it banished some of the terror clawing through his head. It was the only good thing that had come out of that trek to hell.

A simple, soothing string of notes danced across his mind. His fingers flexed, eager to play, to turn the nervous energy into something beautiful.

The door opened with a slow creak. Fear leapt into the back of his throat.

Logan stood in the doorway waiting for permission to enter. Still rigid with fear and ashamed of being frightened, Jack said nothing. Logan poked his head in first, waited as if he expected Jack to throw something at him, and—when no projectiles flew—stepped fully into the room. He twisted his silver watch absently around his wrist.

"Keith told us how you made it back."

"And?" Defiance hardened Jack's voice. His defenses were as fragile as spun sugar, and if Logan started in on him too they would dissolve under the flood of emotion he was desperately trying to hold in.

"And I don't blame you if you hate me."

Jack blinked. For the first time, he noticed the bags under Logan's eyes.

"I never should have left you there alone." Logan wiped his hair out of his face. "I drove off with Daisy, and I didn't even make sure you had a ride home. I mean, I knew your phone wouldn't work. Your phone never works, especially not when you've been playing.... We broke up, by the way. She didn't take it well—keyed my car, slashed the tires...everything. I deserved it though. If I'd been there I—"

"You never would have made it past the girl in the car," Jack said around a lump in his throat. To his surprise he heard himself chuckle. "You'd have taken one look at her and ditched me anyway—faery or not." Jack shivered at the sudden chill that invaded his bones.

"What's wrong?" Logan's tentative smile vanished.

"Doyle knew what she was...." He got up and strode past Logan, who frowned.

"Where are you going?"

"The girl was fae—at least I thought she was at first. That's why I called Douglas, to get a second opinion, but Sheriff Doyle showed up first." By that point he was at the top of the stairs with Logan stumbling after him.

"So?"

"So...after spending some time in Faerie, I'm not so certain she was fae. But he still thinks she is." Jack jumped the last three steps and swung around the corner into the kitchen. To his relief only Glen and Douglas were sitting at the counter.

"You should be resting," Glen scolded. Jack ignored him.

"I need you to take me to Sheriff Doyle's house," he said to Douglas. Douglas lifted a sardonic eyebrow.

"And why would I do that? Glen's right. You should be in bed."

"That girl from the fair, I think she might be in danger."

For a moment, it looked like Douglas wasn't going to help him, but he sucked in a long, low breath and exchanged a grim look with Glen.

"I don't see how she's your problem, but I can't say I'm not curious to find more out about him." He drained his mug of coffee then jerked his head toward the door.

THEY TOOK THE CRUISER. Static crackled as occasional calls came across the radio. Douglas' knuckles were white on the steering wheel, and he kept scanning the trees as if he expected something to jump out at them.

"So, what's the deal with the Sheriff? Is he fae-touched too?" Jack asked finally. Douglas tilted his head to the side, thinking.

"I've never gotten a sense of magic off him before, but he must have Faery Sight. It explains why he's suddenly so interested in us."

"What do you mean?"

"He's been leading the charge to find you. Apparently, you told him we were brothers. He called me into his office the day after Halloween and wanted to know if he could talk to you about that girl's accident. I told him I hadn't seen you. He might have left it alone if he hadn't been the one to find Mom. When you didn't turn up for the funeral we had to declare you missing to keep him from asking too many questions."

"Do you think he's dangerous?"

"I don't know, but he's got way too much interest in our family for my taste."

Sheriff Doyle lived on the outskirts of Straifield. A wrought-iron gate opened onto a long, winding dirt drive up to a lodge-style house. An orange and white tabby lounged on the front porch as they pulled into the yard.

"You feel it don't you?" Douglas leaned forward to peer at the house. Jack nodded. There was a buzzing in his chest.

"There's magic here. Strong stuff too."

"I'm going to have a look around. Go knock on the door."

With his stomach sinking to his toes, Jack climbed out of the passenger seat and started up the front steps. The tabby hissed at his approach. Jack jumped back and silently scolded himself. Cats were notorious for their ability to sense magic. Once upon a time, when people still believed in the fae, cats were one of the few ways those without the Sight could detect them. Whether this one knew he was fae-touched or sensed the lingering traces of Faerie that clung to him, it arched its back and scuttled away on its hind legs, ears flat to its head.

"Funny, Hamlin usually loves people," said Aiden through the screen door. Jack nearly tripped over the last step. With everything that had happened he'd completely forgotten that Aiden was Doyle's son.

"Uh, your dad stopped by the hospital and said he wanted to talk to me about something. It seemed important." They spoke through the screen, eyeing each other with more than a little dislike. Aiden wore a sleeveless black workout shirt with basketball shorts.

"I heard he found you washed up in the river." He braced an arm against the door frame waiting for Jack to explain. He didn't.

"So, can I talk to him?"

"He's in his workshop."

Jack lifted his brows expectantly only to frown when Aiden didn't elaborate.

"So, I should just wander around until I find it or...?"

"No. He never lets anyone back there." Aiden seemed to take pleasure in being as unhelpful as possible.

"Are you planning to go get him anytime soon?" With Douglas scoping the place out it was probably smarter to keep Aiden distracted, but his vague answers were getting under Jack's skin.

Heaving a long-suffering sigh, Aiden pushed open the door to let him in. No sooner had Jack put one foot across the threshold than the buzzing in his chest became a hive. Aiden released the door so that it slapped against Jack's shoulder. He picked up a white, cordless phone hanging on the wall to the left of the door.

"Hey, that guy you found earlier just showed up and says he wants to talk to you. Want me to send him back?" He was silent a moment, nodded, and then hung up.

"He says he'll be up in a few minutes."

Jack nodded, and another awkward silence fell. Aiden glanced over his shoulder, clearly wishing he could go back to whatever he'd been doing. With every passing second Jack liked him less and less.

"So, how's Eira's car?" he asked. It surprised him how easily her name rolled off his tongue. Aiden's jaw flexed and his hard, brown eyes bore into Jack.

"The whole town's been looking for you for weeks. Where did you go?"

"Around." Jack shrugged. He could give non-answers as easily as the next person.

With a loud zap, every light in the house cut out. The air hummed as they flicked back on a moment later. Electricity surged through the air, and the fine hairs at the nape of Jack's neck stood on end. Aiden frowned, glanced at the window, and did a double-take.

"It's snowing!"

Jack made a face, annoyed Aiden thought he was that gullible.

"It was clear a minute ago." It had also been warm enough that he'd only worn a thin, long-sleeved shirt. Aiden's eye twitched.

"Well it's snowing now."

Jack joined him at the window. They kept enough space between them that their shoulders didn't touch in the narrow space, but they both pressed their noses against the glass to watch as the tiny white flecks got bigger and fell faster.

Weird as the freak snowstorm was, it was nothing compared to the sudden sucking sensation in Jack's chest. He dropped the curtain and rubbed a slow circle over his heart. A knot formed, grew hotter and coiled tighter. Blood surged through his veins at a double rhythm. He took a step back, shaking out suddenly clammy hands. Something called out to him—screaming in a voice just beyond his range of hearing, but he felt it like a sledgehammer to the gut.

Though he tried to hide it, his breath came in short, sharp gasps as panic threatened to drown him. Dancing quicksilver spirals whirled in front of his eyes so that his vision dimmed.

"Are you okay?" Aiden held out a hand.

Jack couldn't answer because at that moment pain barreled into him so hard he stumbled and fell, knocking his forehead against an old radiator. The burst of stars blinded him.

Hands held his arms. He couldn't feel his legs. He couldn't see—he couldn't breathe!

Power rolled over him like a tidal wave. His mind flew back into his own head. The darkness cleared to reveal Aiden kneeling over him. His hand hovered just above Jack's shoulder as if he was too freaked out to actually touch him. There was genuine concern on his face. Jack pushed away from him and crawled to his feet.

"I should go." The words were lost in a gasp. His mind tore itself in two and he clapped both hands to the sides of his head as if that would hold it together. He staggered toward the door, but Aiden beat him to it.

"Are you having a stroke or something?"

"No! I just...I just need some air." Before Aiden could stop him, Jack dashed outside. Snow fell in blinding sheets now. The smothering nature of it unnerved him. Hugging his arms across his chest he stumbled around the front of the house looking for Douglas. Just as he rounded the corner, Douglas barreled into him at a full sprint. He grabbed Jack's sleeve and yanked him toward the car, but not before Jack caught a glimpse of Doyle dragging a large black shape toward the trees lining the yard. Oily black smears streaked the ground behind him, swallowing the white flakes that landed in its trail.

"Go, before he sees you!" Against the pale gray sky, it was hard to see that Douglas had masked himself with a soft silver mist. Anyone without Faery

Sight would look past him as if he wasn't there unless he did something to draw attention to himself. Not for the first time Jack thought Douglas had gotten the most useful gift from the fae.

They ran to the car and jumped in. Douglas took off before Jack could buckle his seatbelt.

"I don't know how he's doing it, but he's catching fae. He killed the kelpie." The last was said in a low voice wavering between horror and satisfaction.

Before he could examine his own feelings about that, Douglas slammed on the brakes so hard Jack's head hit the dashboard with a loud thump that brought more stars to his eyes. Dazed, he looked up to see an enormous silver stag standing in the middle of the road. Its crown of antlers was enormous. It pawed the ground and blew a jet of steam from its nostrils. Red flames burned in its dark eyes. Jack felt the heat of that gaze scorch through him like a laser.

"Hang on!" Douglas threw out his right arm to pin Jack to his seat while his left spun the steering wheel hard to veer around the Otherworldly creature. The stag didn't so much as twitch as the car swerved within inches of its flank. Its head swung around to watch them pass. As Jack watched, the animal dissolved into a whirl of driving snow. Just as fast, the blizzard became a white-out.

How Douglas kept from driving into the ditch on either side of the road Jack would never know. The storm chased them. As the nose of the car dipped down the long road leading away from Straifield, ice spiderwebbed cross the wet asphalt in front of their tires. There wasn't time to hit the brakes before they were skidding and sliding down the steep hill. Jack latched onto his door handle for dear life, praying Douglas could keep them on the road.

When they hit the bottom, the back end fishtailed around so that they spun out. Douglas turned the wheel hard and just managed to get control before the rear tire slid off the drop. The sudden grab of traction shot them off to the left. An avalanche roared down the hill after them.

Their turn was just up ahead. Douglas hunched over the wheel, speeding toward it as fast as the engine would carry them. The moment the tires turned off the main road the wind and snow thinned to a simple shower of flakes.

"You okay?" Douglas flicked his eyes sideways.

"I'm having one hell of a day."

One by one Jack unclenched his fingers from around the door handle as Douglas let out a shaky laugh. "That was him, wasn't it? That was Winterthorn?"

"Yes, I'd say it was." Douglas looked over his shoulder to be sure the faery bounty hunter wasn't following them.

"But he swore he'd leave our family alone." Jack's voice rose. "Why was he there?"

"I don't know, Jack." There was an edge to his voice that suggested Douglas did know, or at least suspected something. After a moment, Jack sat back against his leather seat.

"You think it's me. You think he's come for me."

"You stole from them. Name me one story in which the Fair Folk don't take offense when humans mess with their things."

"I told you, I didn't steal it!"

"Well someone seems to think you did," Douglas fired back. "And clearly he wants it back."

There was one last steep hill to their house, and now that the worst of the blizzard had eased, Douglas took his time navigating the white-blanketed road. The air between them simmered.

Douglas pulled into the driveway.

"Go inside. There's going to be a lot of accidents tonight. Tell the others not to expect me until late." He didn't look at Jack as he waited for him to get out.

Suddenly furious, Jack threw open the door and an eruption of goosebumps exploded along his skin. The dive into the car had been too quick and adrenaline-fueled for him to register just how cold it had gotten, but in the ten steps it took for him to climb the stone steps to the door, icicles formed in the snot running from his nose.

Glen was waiting by the front door with a blanket fresh from the dryer. Through chattering teeth Jack passed on Douglas' message then made his way up to his room. He was so tired he had to pause halfway up the stairs to brace a hand against the wall for support.

"I'll send Logan up with some food," said Glen, watching from the landing.

"Don't bother. I'm going to bed." Jack closed the door behind him, and as soon as he did the harp's presence reached out with a soft, welcoming hum. Swaying, Jack took it off his desk and brought it to bed with him, where he laid down to admire its intricate pattern of leaves, flowers, and vines. If the Wild Huntsman had come to collect his prize he wasn't going to get it.

Chapter 6

That night Winterthorn buried the town beneath a mountain of snow and ice. When Jack's radio alarm clock sounded the next morning, rather than music he woke to hear the accounts of numerous accidents emergency crews had their hands full trying to deal with. All around Straifield, people were trapped in their cars and homes. Nearly three and a half feet of snow fell over the course of one night. According to the DJ, the paramedics had been bombarded with reports of severe frostbite and broken bones, but thanks to how suddenly the storm had appeared the plows were overwhelmed and couldn't clear the roads fast enough before black ice encased the streets.

With a sick feeling in the pit of his stomach, Jack flipped off the radio and tucked the harp between his mattress and the box springs. Dragging a hoodie over his head, he went downstairs to breakfast where he nearly ran into Keith on his way to the front closet. Grumbling about the effect on his plants, Keith shrugged on his heaviest winter coat and stomped out back to his garden. If he noticed Jack he gave no acknowledgment.

Glen and Logan were in the kitchen where Glen patiently listened to Logan complaining about having to miss a date with some girl he'd met at the convenience store. Glen smiled wearily at Jack and pushed a bowl of hot oatmeal down the counter to him.

"Did Doug make it back last night?" Jack asked. The smell of cinnamon made his stomach growl, but he didn't move to pick up the spoon his brother slid him. Before Glen could answer, a toilet flushed upstairs. Considering Craig and Ross rarely showed their faces before ten-thirty, Jack had his answer.

Abandoning his breakfast, Jack took the stairs two at a time. The door across the hall from his mother's stood open, and Jack rapped his knuckle against the frame. Douglas stood with his back to him, thumbs hooked under the waistband of his boxers. Seeing Jack, he groaned and peeled the red shorts down his legs to threw them at him. Wrinkling his nose, Jack batted the underwear aside, refusing to be driven off. Douglas sighed and pulled a fresh pair of boxers from his dresser.

"Make it quick, Jack. I'm beat."

"You said Doyle's torturing and killing faeries behind his house. He thinks Eira is a faery. What if he tries to go after her?"

"I'm not sure what you want me to do. I can't accuse the Sheriff of an attempted kidnapping if he hasn't done anything. For all I know if she is a faery the cops that go to investigate might not be able to see her."

"Aiden saw her, and I'd bet every guitar I own that he doesn't have an ounce of Faery Sight." He would never have fallen for Logan's trick so easily if he could see the magic pushing him to make a fool of himself.

Douglas groaned and rubbed at his bloodshot eyes once more. "What was her name again?"

"Eira," said Jack at once. "Eirawen Rothchild."

"Hmmm, Rothchild. That name sounds familiar. I'll look into it after I get some sleep. And you should be resting too. You just survived a trip to Faerie, not to mention you've got two weeks' worth of school to make up. You've got way more problems to deal with than some girl who may or may not be a faery."

Rather than argue, Jack left and went down the hall to his own room. School. Right. Like he was going to waste time worrying about that right now. He'd never been one to pace, but a half hour of wandering back and forth wore trenches through his carpet. After forty-five minutes, he contemplated plugging in his electric guitar and blasting heavy metal at the dividing wall, but an angry Douglas was an uncooperative Douglas.

"I'll call you if I find anything."

Jack nearly jumped out of his skin. Douglas stood in the doorway, his expression wryly amused. Jack opened his mouth to insist on going with him, but realized that he would only draw attention if someone saw him rifling through records down at the station. Double-tapping a fist against the doorframe, Douglas left.

Immediately the restlessness returned. Pacing hadn't taken the edge off. Jack needed something else. Really only one thing in his room had the power to take his mind of what was happening, but it was the last thing he needed to be thinking about.

His willpower lasted all of two minutes before he closed his door and pulled the harp out from under his bed.

The musical library inside his brain threw open its doors. Centuries worth of faery music had been generously donated to his already impressive repertoire. His fingertips itched. Just one. One song would be enough to distract him from the craziness that had taken over his life.

He chose something simple, a faery waltz that would let him feel out the instrument's capabilities—he had never played a harp before, and while his fingers instinctively knew which notes to play, their dexterity left something to be desired. For the first time that he could remember, he fumbled over keys. Each time he messed up he went back to the beginning so that the song became hypnotic with its repetition. By the time the phone rang three hours later he was so focused on practicing that when Logan came in to hand him the phone, Jack barked at him to leave him alone.

"You rat bastard!" Douglas shouted when Jack finally got on the line at Logan's urging. "I drove all the way down here through three feet of snow and black ice to do you a favor, and you couldn't even be bothered to hear what I found?" Jack winced and held the receiver away to spare his eardrum.

"Sorry, I... uh, got distracted." He glanced at his bed where the harp was stuffed haphazardly under his pillow. "Did you find her."

"No."

"Did you check public records?"

"Thanks, I hadn't thought of that." Sarcasm hung from the words like icicles. "I'd have to go to town hall to get those, and oddly enough they're not open during the worst blizzard in over a decade." Jack ground his teeth.

"This is serious, Doug. She could be in trouble. I have to warn her."

"I know it's serious, but I can't just go poking into people's private files just because you're paranoid."

"Who's going to catch you? No one'll see you." His magic-enhanced stealth was the reason Douglas had gone into law enforcement. Eventually he wanted to become an undercover officer, but their mother had begged him not to move away.

"Not. The. Point." Douglas bit out each word, clearly irritated with the wild goose chase.

"What about school records?" Jack tossed out before Douglas hung up.

"Those would be at the school—another place that's been shut down because of the storm. And now that I'm in the office I have real cases to work on that involve crimes that actually happened and aren't just what if's in your head." His brother's annoyance traveled over the phone lines with the dial tone.

Sulking, Jack hung up and stared at the collage of black and gray outside his window. Their family's protection from magic kept the worst of Winterthorn's storm away, but even so, several inches buried the roots of the surrounding trees. He couldn't explain his obsession with finding Eira. It made no more sense than why the thought of getting rid of the harp left a bitter taste in his mouth.

He dug the instrument out from under his pillow and studied it. The peace he'd found in its music before was lost. He was sure if he tried he could recapture it, but he needed a place where he wouldn't be disturbed.

His father built his workshop off the back of the garage. After he died the place became little more than a private museum showcasing the unfinished masterpieces the world would never see. Their mother insisted everything be kept exactly the way he left it. Only when someone needed a tool or work cloth did any of them dare venture inside.

Glancing over his shoulder to make sure none of his brother watched from the windows, Jack pried open the rusted latch and slipped inside. The beaded chain that hung from the overhead light tickled his ear. He gave it a light tug, but in ten years the bulb had burnt out and no one saw a need to replace it. Cracking the door to let in enough light to see, Jack let his eyes adjust to the gloom.

Tadgh Sorley had thrived in chaos. Jack remembered scraps of wood scattered across the lawn when his father pulled his three-legged stool into the yard so he could watch his sons play while he polished a rocking chair or made a bookshelf. His half-finished pieces were stacked against the back wall. His tools lay scattered along the waist-high shelf or hung on the hooks jutting from the back wall. Under the worktable Jack spied the red, tin tackle box that stored his father's favorite tools. The top came off and the inside lifted on either side to reveal storage space within. Letting his backpack slip from his arm, Jack unzipped it to pull out the golden harp. His fingers traced the intricate carvings through their seasons, the bare branch of winter through the cluster of flowers in spring to the leafy summer garland and then the withered fall leaves. He doubted even his father with his fae-enhanced talent could have created something so fine.

Carefully, Jack laid the harp inside the toolbox and reassembled it. It was an awkward fit, but eventually he managed to get it closed. He sneezed. The lingering smell of wood shavings and polish called up shadows of Tadgh Sorley. Unexpected tears sprang to Jack's eyes that he blamed on the dust stirred by his feet.

A chance encounter with a faery woman changed his father's life. What advice would he give his youngest son who faced the same dilemma? Eira was in danger, not from warring faery kings as his father's faery had been, but by humans who knew too much and not enough about the Otherworld. The weight of everything he'd been through collapsed on top of him, and Jack felt as weary as if he'd gone years without sleep. He took one more glance at the harp to make sure it was really hidden before he crossed to the door, headed back to the house, and went to bed.

Jack had a vague awareness of his brothers coming to check on him, calling him down for dinner, and when he didn't come, bringing him a plate of food. But the sleep he had missed during his two weeks in Faerie came for him with interest. He slept through the night, waking just long enough to use the bathroom around three.

He woke the next morning feeling worse than when he'd gone to bed. Knots in his neck and shoulders forced him to remember the glowing red eye that had watched him stumble through his dreams of smoky figures dancing in a cave, reaching for him and chanting a single, foreign word—*Uaithne*. He scrubbed his face with his hand and rolled stiffly out of bed.

The smell of maple syrup drew his attention from his disturbing dreams. Saliva pooled in his mouth at the thought of his mother's buttermilk pancakes before reality cuffed him for forgetting. Glen's pancakes tasted great, but they weren't the same.

"Have I told you today how happy I am that you're my brother?" Logan was saying around a mouthful of pastry when Jack padded barefoot into the kitchen a few minutes later. Glen rolled his eyes as he flipped a pancake with a toss of the pan.

"Great, if you're so happy then you can do the dishes."

"Let's not get carried away now," said Logan, waggling his finger in gentle reproof.

"It's not like you have anything better to do," said Keith from the end of the island without looking up from his plate. He wore thick overalls over a plaid, wool shirt.

Logan laid a dramatic hand over his heart.

"Are you kidding? Someone has to manage our little celebrity's image." He waved a hand toward Jack. "He's hot stuff right now. Every news channel, paper, and radio station for three counties wants to know where he's been." Jack groaned, which made Logan frown. "This is exactly the sort of publicity you need if you ever want to get your career off the ground."

"He's not going public with his story," Keith's teeth clenched around his fork with a decisive click. Logan raked his hair back off his forehead with a pained expression.

"Do you think I'm stupid? It's a classic bait and switch. We get them in the door thinking they'll hear an update about what happened after the fair, and he'll distract them by showing off what a musical prodigy he is. I'm telling you, he'll be bigger than the Beatles by Christmas. I've got it all handled—at least I will if I don't have to spend my morning cleaning up this mountain of dishes Glen's building."

Keith slurped his coffee loudly to illustrate his interest in Logan's argument. Logan slanted a glance sideways to where Jack was dragging a steaming pancake onto his plate. "Besides, Jack here hasn't done any chores for two weeks."

Jack's fork froze in midair.

"Really?" His eyes went flat with disbelief. Keith shrugged.

"Fine, both of you do them." He crunched a stick of bacon in half and gave them a closed-lipped smile. Logan slapped Jack on the back.

"Welcome home, buddy! Did you miss us?"

DESPITE ALL OF LOGAN'S complaining, it only took forty-five minutes to restore the kitchen to Glen's standards of pristine.

"I didn't want to say anything while the others were here, but you've already got an offer," said Logan, wiping his hands on a linen dishrag. Jack frowned.

"An offer?"

"A talent scout heard you playing at the fair. He said he'd be willing to listen if you sent in a CD with some of your music." A slow smile spread across Logan's face. Jack gaped. A talent scout wanted to hear from him? He couldn't decide whether to be ecstatic or terrified.

"Are you serious?" he managed hoarsely. Logan put a hand on his shoulder.

"You know I hate to say, 'I told you so,' but seriously, what did I say?"

Fog filled Jack's brain. What songs should he send in? Should he submit a variety to show off his range, or channel his energy into one instrument? Did the scout want original pieces or covers of other songs? Without realizing it, his fingers began picking out a series of notes in midair. Logan laughed.

"Come on, let's go get your guitar."

The phone rang. With Jack too distracted to notice, Logan turned back to answer.

"Sorleys. Yea, he's right here. Her, who? Really...?" He waggled his eyebrows suggestively at Jack, who snatched the phone from his hands.

"Did you find something?"

"Guess who just walked in the station," Douglas said in a low voice, clearly trying not to be overheard on his end.

"You're sure it's her?" Jack ignored the way Logan's head reared with interest. Douglas grunted. "Whoever she is, she's throwing off some kind of glamour that's keeping anyone outside of five feet from noticing her. Everyone inside that circle is giving her plenty of attention though. I thought Dobbs was going to fall out of his chair when she walked past his desk." Jack turned his back so he wouldn't see Logan lean closer to eavesdrop.

"Why's she there?"

"Considering she just walked into Reynold's office, I'd say she's filing some kind of report. I'll see if I can catch her before she leaves." Douglas hung up before Jack could ask anything else.

Jack took his time returning the receiver to the cradle. Logan loudly cleared his throat.

"Woman troubles?" He lounged against the counter, waiting for the story. Reluctantly, Jack told him about his concerns that Doyle would target Eira, mistaking her for one of the fae. When he finished, Logan canted his head to one side.

"And you're making this your problem...why?"

Jack opened his mouth to answer but eventually closed it when he realized he didn't have one. Logan held up his hands.

"I get the protective instinct. She's a pretty girl and all—trust me, been there done that—but you're talking changelings, immortal bounty hunters, and Faerie conspiracies. You don't want to get involved with all that."

The phone rang again. Jack snapped up the excuse to escape the conversation.

"Something spooked her. Get Logan to give you a ride." Douglas sounded out of breath.

"What happened?"

"Don't know. One minute she was sitting outside Reynold's office, the next she turns white as a ghost and practically runs out of the building. She's not going to listen to me if I try and talk to her so get down here and we'll go after her together."

"Logan will give me a ride," Jack confirmed, not giving him a choice. Logan went to the window over the sink to check the sky. Dark clouds loomed in the distance, but patches of blue could be seen here and there. His mouth twisted.

"She better be worth it," he warned.

DOUGLAS' CRUISER IDLED in the parking lot when Jack hopped out of the Mustang a half-hour later. A torn statement form graced with long, looping letters in blue ink sat on the passenger seat. She'd filled in her name, street address, and the first three numbers of her phone when she'd stopped.

"She lives over by the park," he read aloud as Douglas put the car in drive. "She was going to file a complaint. Do you think Doyle tried something?"

"If he did she's got guts to go after him head on like that," Douglas murmured, pulling out of the parking lot.

In less than five minutes they had driven down Main Street, turned up the road that led to the park, and were cruising slowly down the white gravel road where she supposedly lived. They leaned forward to read the brass numbers on the mailboxes. When they finally found hers, it was not what either expected. Jack had seen sheds bigger than the white, aluminum-sided house. The small square yard was boxed in with a white picket fence that all but disappeared beneath rosemary hedges and St. John's Wort flattened by snow. Cement blocks served as steps to the weather-beaten front stoop. To the right of them lay a giant, rust-colored dog with its back to them. A horseshoe was nailed over the door.

"A faery girl with faery wards," Douglas murmured as they pulled alongside a rusted brown Pinto. "Interesting."

"Her grandmother must've put them up."

As soon as Jack spoke, the dog's pointed ears rose and twisted in their direction followed by its head. A ring of yellow flames rimmed the unearthly, brown eyes. Black lips curled back in a snarl.

"Don't look at it!" Douglas hissed, snatching the back of Jack's neck and forcing his head down. "Stay here." After a deep breath, he undid his seatbelt and got out of the car. With slow, stilted steps he approached the stoop. The wolf's lips pulled back even further, but it shuffled back, maintaining the distance between them. Douglas trained his eyes on the door. His hand gave a betraying wobble as he raised it to knock

"Miss Rothchild?"

The wolf sheathed its teeth, but its hackles rose in a red ripple of menace, making the already monstrous animal appear even bigger. On all fours it stood as tall as a Great Dane. Afraid for Douglas, Jack rolled down his window and waved to get the beast's attention.

Suddenly, the bushy tail tucked. Its great head swung toward the park. Jack looked around.

His pancakes threatened to make a comeback.

He stood close to seven feet tall with a crown of antlers at least five feet wide. He walked upright, but he was midway between a transformation of four-legged animal to two. Dark skin blended seamlessly into brown-gray fur, and a long, straight nose merged with a human mouth to form a snout.

Their gazes locked and Winterthorn's went flat and hard. He bent at the waist, and before Jack's eyes the lingering traits of humanity melted into the incredible form of the stag.

Jack fumbled for his seatbelt and only just managed to squirm into the driver's seat before the giant buck hit the car at full speed. The cruiser rocked, and Jack's heart nearly flew out of his mouth. The great stag dipped his head until his antlers caught the lip of the car, lifted it onto two wheels only to slam it back down. Jack bounced, nearly losing an eye on the gear shift. One flailing hand landed on the horn, and the honk startled the stag back several steps. Jack mashed the horn again. The faery hunter snorted and drove his antlers beneath the car.

Jack groped for the door behind him. It swung open, and he fell hard on the white pebbles. Across the underbelly of the car he saw hooves as big as a Clydesdale's. The curved tips of those antlers had a firm grip under the car now and the stag grunted as the car rose onto the driver-side tires. Jack kicked free, but the skitter of stones alerted the stag that he'd gotten out.

The stag stepped back from the car. It rocked onto all four tires with a groan of metal.

Jack didn't wait to see what Winterthorn would do. Flipping onto his stomach, he pushed to his feet and ran. He started for the house, but one glance at the red wolf and her white teeth sent him skirting the house and making a break for the park. At any moment he expected antlers to run him through or the wolf's jaws to take a chunk out of his calf.

A glance over his shoulder two blocks later confirmed that he wasn't being followed, but when the sky darkened and white flakes started to fall, he knew he wasn't going to escape the gathering storm. The temperature dropped as fast as he ran. He'd catch hypothermia before he made it back to Main Street.

An engine whirred behind him, coming up fast. The horn bleeped twice. Without slowing his pace, he turned to see Daisy Rowe—Logan's ex, the one who'd carved her namesake into the gas cap of the Mustang—guiding her cherry-red car along the curb. She rolled down the window.

"Want a ride?" Dressed in a snug, cream-colored sweater, skin-tight jeans, and brown knee-high boots, she looked like she belonged on the cover of a winter fashion magazine. Mistaking the reason for his perusal, she drew a shoulder up to her cheek and tossed her runway-worthy blond curls over her shoulder to give him the best view. Jack hesitated, but a frigid gust of wind made his decision for him.

"Thanks," he grunted, sliding into the front seat. He held his hands out to warm them on the hot air blasting from the vents. It circulated her sugar cookie scented body spray around them until the small car smelled like a bakery. She cranked it up to full blast and puckered her lips in a pout when he refused to meet her eye.

"Relax. I may have gotten a little crazy when things with Logan went sour, but trust me, I'm over it. I knew what type of guy he was when I asked him out." She fluttered her lashes as if that was supposed to convince him of her sincerity. He fixed his gaze on the side mirror, watching for any sign of the silver stag. Heat crept up the back of his neck as he felt the weight of her stare.

"So, where to?" She flashed an over-bright smile that told him she wasn't as blasé about her breakup with Logan as she pretended.

"Home," he said reluctantly. Her eyes lit up.

"You got it." She hit the gas with a little too much force, throwing him back against his seat. Quickly, he fastened his seatbelt.

"Oops," she said with a giggle. He shrugged as if it didn't matter, but inside he reconsidered his odds against the weather.

They rode in awkward silence. Jack stared fixedly at the radio hoping she would take the hint, but she just swerved down the country road that led away from town. They passed the intersection near Doyle's house. Through the bare trees his wrought iron property fence could be seen. Jack scooted lower in his seat.

"So, what were you doing at Eira's place?" Daisy asked finally. His leg twitched.

"You saw me?" What exactly had she seen? How did those without Faery Sight account for the car tipping onto two wheels?

"Looked like you couldn't get away fast enough." She lowered her lashes and sent him a teasing look. "Don't tell me...cold feet?"

"What?"

She fluttered a hand at him.

"I get it. She's sweet. Smart. Gorgeous. You probably can't help but be in love with her, right?"

"No," he said flatly. "That's not it at all." She laughed, though it came out sounding forced.

"Right...."

Her car hit a patch of ice at the base of the final hill leading up to his house. The tires spun. Jack latched onto the door.

"You can just let me out here. I don't want you getting stuck."

Frowning in concentration, Daisy gunned it. The smell of burning rubber filled his nose, and Jack sent her another sidelong glance as the tires caught. She leaned over the steering wheel to scan for more ice.

"I always wondered what this place looked like," she said as she pulled alongside the driveway to let him out. It didn't shock him that she'd never been to their house before. There were too many Sorleys for Logan to bring a girl home and expect to get any privacy.

The Mustang was parked to the right of the garage. The flower scratched into the paint was prominently displayed along the side. Jack winced.

"Thanks Daisy, uh...."

She waved her hand again.

"Don't worry about it. I can see he's home." Whew. "As for your little problem, try writing her a song. You're one of the few guys who could pull off a move like that. I doubt even he could do that." She jerked her thumb toward the house.

"Thanks for the advice, but it's really not like that."

"Of course not." She waved a dismissive hand to shoo him out. With one last lingering look at the house, she maneuvered a three-point turn on the snow-covered road and drove off.

Logan wasn't the only one home. Keith's Land Rover stood next to Craig's Camaro, and Ross' green F150 parked on the street. The only car missing was the Cruiser. Jack would rather take another trip to Faerie than tell them about Winterthorn's attack. Blowing warm on his hands, he skirted the house and headed for the workshop.

The toolbox came apart much easier than before, and when he saw the gleaming instrument inside he breathed a little easier. He glanced over his shoulder to gauge the distance to the house. He should be far enough that no one would hear. Settling his hip against the workbench, he tucked the harp against his chest and drew a haunting rendition of 'Greensleeves' from the strings. The familiar melody enveloped him. Haunting, beautiful, and completely human, it was just the tune to unravel his nerves after his close encounter with the leader of the Hunt. The time for analyzing the significance of Winterthorn's attack would come later—it promised to be a loud, heated debate with plenty of pointing fingers, but not yet. Just a little longer....

The growl of an engine broke his concentration. Jack lifted his head in time to see the Cruiser charge up the road like a bull. He sighed and stilled the strings with his hand.

Two car doors slammed. Jack froze.

"Where are we? I thought you said you'd give me some answers."

Jack's jaw dropped. Hastily, he stuffed the harp back into the toolbox, rearranged everything just as it had been, and raced across the backyard.

Seven pairs of eyes swung around when he pushed through the storm door into the kitchen. At the sight of him, Douglas collapsed onto a stool and covered his face with a moan. Keith slammed Jack's cellphone on the counter.

"Where have you been?"

Jack didn't hear him. His world narrowed to the girl who sat stiff-backed at the end of the counter. A silver sheen illuminated her fair skin in spite of the gold hue of the overhead light. She looked even more fae than before. The angles of her face were sharper. Flecks of diamond glinted in her wide blue eyes, and purple and green hues made her dark hair shimmer like a raven's wing. That anyone could look at her and think she was human was laughable. And yet....

When she saw him her eyes narrowed, and she squeezed the coffee mug so tightly he was surprised it didn't break.

"I heard you disappeared," she said in velvet accusation. Her gaze sliced into his before he thought to look away. Suspicion illuminated the deep shadows in her eyes. There were scratches on her face and hands. She raised her chin in a show of bravado, and he saw a thin, red line skiing down the slope of her neck. His knees buckled. She flinched and dropped her gaze, shaking her hair forward to cover the mark.

"I'm sorry about your car," she mumbled unexpectedly.

Douglas uncovered his face.

"That dip at the bottom of the hill turns my stomach every time I go over it too." His eyes darted meaningfully around to the rest of them. Jack scratched his chin. Ah. Their property had wards that kept the fae out. She'd gotten sick when she'd come onto their land. Eira was human enough to be allowed in, but there was enough fae in her that she couldn't come without a cost. She massaged her temples.

"Can someone please tell me what's going on? Why did you bring me here? Who are you?" A slight whine threaded her voice.

Glen took her cup to refill it while Logan reached out to take her hand. Her eyes darted down, but she allowed the contact without pulling away. It annoyed Jack that Logan would try to put moves on her when there were more important things going on, but he ignored him to watch Glen pull a small glass jar from the cupboard above the sink. After a furtive glance to make sure she wasn't looking, he shook a sprinkle of dried, four-leaf clover into her tea.

"This will help," he said quietly, pushing it back into her hands. Eira took the cup automatically, but didn't drink. Douglas leaned toward her.

"Tell me more about the men that attacked you. Could you describe them?" Jack's head snapped up.

A shudder rippled over her, but she lifted the mug and took a deep gulp. Glen murmured approval under his breath. Eira frowned at the badge on Douglas' chest before she started to speak.

"I'd just got home from work and was about to make dinner when someone jumped me from behind. They must've been waiting for me otherwise I would've heard them come in. I never got a good look at them." Her forehead creased.

"I don't know what they wanted. I thought it was just a break in, but then one of them grabbed a knife off the counter and..." She covered the cut on her neck with her hand and scowled. The tension in the room mounted. Even Ross' face looked grim.

"Did they hurt you?" Jack couldn't stop himself from asking. The longer he stared at the slash on her throat the angrier he got. She shook her head slowly.

"The more I think about it the more I think they were just trying to scare me. Nothing they did made any sense. They just grabbed me and tied me up. One of them broke a window, and I thought they were going to—but they must have heard someone coming because they dropped me and were gone before I could roll over. They didn't even take anything—not that I have anything worth taking. It all happened so fast. There were at least three of them but I never saw them." Rather than the fear one would expect to hear in her voice, there was nothing but cold fury that someone had broken into her home and taken her by surprise. No one knew what to say. Craig cracked his knuckles.

"She can't go home until those creeps are caught."

"She should stay here," said Logan predictably. Ross snorted.

"And since there's no extra beds you're more than happy to share yours, right?" Even Eira's lips went white. Slowly Logan removed his hand from where it covered hers. He shot Ross a withering look.

"She can have my room," Jack said abruptly. "I'll sleep in the basement."

Now that Keith had taken over their parents' room, he and Jack were the only ones with rooms of their own, and Jack knew Keith wasn't about to give up the master suite to a girl who may or may not be fae.

Eira held up her hand.

"Wait! I'm not staying here. I appreciate you're just trying to help, but I can take care of myself." She half-rose from her seat before Douglas put a hand on her shoulder to stop her.

"You live alone, right? You told me your grandmother died in September. I'm not trying to scare you, but if those guys know that they might try and come back. At least stay for one night just to be safe. I'll take you back in the morning."

By morning the effects of the four-leaf clover would kick in, and if nothing else Eira would be able to see her attackers if they returned. Had the clover been fresh it would already have taken effect. Jack was certain that the ones who'd tried to kidnap her had definitely been fae. How else could three of them have wrestled her to the ground and tied her up without her seeing a thing?

He pushed away from the railing, practically vibrating with restless energy. Eira's eyes stalked him. Though she hid it behind a wall of bravado, her desperation beat at him. Shrugging off an unexpected rush of guilt, Jack left the kitchen to tidy up his room for their guest.

Chapter 7

Even with two floors separating them, Eira's uncertainty battered at Jack. It was close to midnight, and although she'd gone to bed hours ago he knew she wasn't asleep. He hadn't told any of his brothers about the strange link between them. He wasn't even sure if Eira sensed it. They'd kept their distance from one another all evening.

Covering his head with a pillow, turning on the old box TV, sticking headphones in his ears—none of it worked to drown out her emotions. Her fae essence was a magnet repelling the magic in him. Did his brothers feel it too? Surely, they would've said something. Neither Keith or Ross ever passed up a chance to complain.

Jack slept on his mother's old, bean-shaped futon. The Styrofoam stuffing rustled with his every move, and the cushion smelled strongly of dust, but it was better than trying to sleep on the same floor with the faery girl that had turned his world upside down.

Did he want her to leave? After hearing about her break-in, he didn't want her out there on her own, but what was the alternative? She was being hunted—the Wild Hunt had literally camped outside her door.

He covered his face with his hands. He needed a distraction. Jack fished under the futon for his sneakers. For all he knew one brand of faery magic might cancel out the other.

A DISTANT SCREAM WOKE him. Jack leapt up. His foot landed on a rake that swung up and nearly took out his left eye. Disoriented, he stumbled around until he came up against his father's red toolbox.

He'd fallen asleep in the work shed. The harp gleamed on the workbench behind him, suggesting he'd had enough presence of mind to set it down before nodding off. Quickly, he stuffed it back into its hiding place, making more noise than he meant to because his fumbling hands were completely numb. He kicked the rake out of the way and ran for the house.

Bursting into the kitchen, he found Glen standing with his back to the stove and his eyes on the ceiling. He scratched at the thinning patch of hair on top of his head.

"The clover must've finally kicked in."

Footsteps stomped down the stairs and disgruntled voices steadily grew louder. Jack sank into the seat closest to the back door, eyes trained on the landing.

"Women," grunted Ross as he stepped into the kitchen, blinking in the florescent light. Keith came next, echoing Ross' sentiments, but Craig and Douglas exchanged amused glances as they headed for the plate of toast. Predictably, Logan came last, his arm around Eira's shoulders.

"You really don't see anything different?" She held her hand up and stared with such fascination at her fingers that she walked into the doorframe. Craig snorted.

"Something wrong with your hand?" Glen asked, holding out a sky-blue mug with hydrangeas painted across one side.

"It's just...." No one said anything, waiting for her to say it. "It's glowing."

Though they'd all seen the tell-tale light of magic radiating from her the night before, it shone undeniably brighter now. On Halloween Jack hadn't noticed it until he saw her face, but now it was strong enough to challenge the overhead light. Was it the effect of the clover or was her awareness enhancing the effect?

It puzzled him that she had never seen her true self before. Surely a changeling—which was his latest guess about what she was—even one that had spent nearly twenty years separated from Faerie, retained their faery senses.

"How do you like your eggs?" Glen interrupted her inspection of her palm. She jumped.

"You don't have to do that. I can—"

"What's one more?" He waved his spatula at the six men gathered around the table. Eira sighed.

"Whatever's easiest." Nodding, he grabbed his mixing bowl and started cracking eggs. She blinked when a wisp of silver light followed the yolks into the bowl.

Having emptied the egg carton, Glen swirled his spatula through the mixture until a faint glow illuminated the yellow liquid. Eira's did a double-take to watch him pour the eggs into his cast iron skillet. A crease appeared between her brows. Logan coughed to hide his grin, but Jack elbowed him in the ribs with a shake of his head.

"Would you mind watching this while I grab the bacon?" Glen turned the cast iron skillet toward her. After a slight hesitation, her hand closed over the metal.

"Ouch!" she yelped and yanked her hand away. "I'm such a klutz," she muttered red-faced, and looked around for an oven mitt. Keith lowered his coffee mug. Even Jack sat forward. So, iron did affect her.

"Thanks, I've got it now," said Glen, gently taking her place. He checked her hand for burns, but the skin was pale and unblemished. As soon as he took the skillet, the eggs fluffed, perfectly scrambled. Eira stood stock still, frowning at the pan.

"Yes?" he prodded, but she just pursed her lips and shook her head.

Jack scowled at Glen for toying with her. Her rising anxiety pounded in his temples, and she was clearly too practical to believe in magic. Gritting his teeth, he studied the ivy leaves carved into the crown molding.

"Looks like there's fresh snow on the ground," said Logan loudly. "After breakfast, we should take a walk." Eira nodded, but she looked as eager for a walk in the snow as a patient prepped for a triple bypass. Glen shot him a pained look over her head, but Logan grinned around a bite of toast and rested his gaze on Eira's skeptical face. Keith cleared his throat to intervene, but Logan held up a hand.

"Trust me. There's some cool stuff around here I think you'd like to see." As if on cue, a wave of brown hair trickled into his eyes just so he could shake it back with a winning smile. A silver glow illuminated him, and Eira nodded with a frown. Jack bit into his toast. It tasted like cardboard.

Eira pushed her eggs around her plate and pretended to ignore the way they watched her every move. Annoyance radiated from her, and when Logan pushed his plate away ten minutes later she surged to her feet, eager to escape. Craig nudged Douglas in the ribs and jerked his head toward the living room. They took their plates, and Jack wondered why they hadn't left sooner. Keith harrumphed and headed upstairs while Ross sidled outside.

"Here. Wear mine." Logan offered his thick, peacoat before he hesitated, frowning into the front closet. Jack and Ross shook their heads watching him, waiting to see how long it took him to remember that the peacoat was the only winter jacket he owned. An uncharacteristic blush spread over his cheeks as he floundered to cover his mistake. Without a word, Jack reached for his own jacket hanging on a peg by the back door and held it out to her.

"I need to talk to you." Eira caught his wrist before he could pull away. The moment her skin touched his, energy arced between them. She jumped and a hundred questions filled her eyes, but Jack's skittered away.

"Um. Okay." Apprehension churned the eggs in his belly. Before he could think of a more eloquent reply, Logan stepped between them to take her jacket and hold it up for her to slip her arms in. Eira's smile looked more like a grimace. Her eyes flew back to Jack, begging him to come with them. Before he knew what he was doing, Jack pulled a spare coat from the rack.

Ross leaned against the deck railing when they filed outside. Jack, Logan, and Eira emerged from the house in time to see him raise his right arm straight out from his side. A falcon swooped out of the trees to land on Ross' wrist. Eira gasped and snatched Jack's hand.

Ross and the falcon gazed into each other's eyes. The snowy backdrop made it difficult to distinguish the swirl of magic from the gray clouds formed by his breath. Murmuring, Ross prodded the bird's wing. It ruffled its feathers and flexed its talons in reply. Satisfied with his examination, Ross lifted his arm, and the bird took to the air with a whoosh of its black wings.

"Did you train him to do that?" Eira asked, following the bird's flight. Jack flexed his fingers, aware that she still gripped his sleeve. Ross shook his head. His face hardened at the idea of domesticating a wild bird.

"You mean that was a wild falcon?" She ducked, scanning the trees. Ross' lip curled.

"All animals are wild. You can't tell me you've ever met a 'tamed' house cat."

"I'm not much of a cat person," she said ruefully. "And they don't like me."

Genuine amusement tightened the corner of Ross' mouth.

"No. I guess they wouldn't."

Logan chose that moment to pull her away. He swept his hand across the large backyard to encompass the herb garden, greenhouse and work shed.

"Dad designed and built everything himself."

She looked over her shoulder at the two-story house skeptically.

"You're saying he built all of this by hand?" Jack moved past her to rest his elbows on the deck railing to face the yard. He didn't have to look at the house to understand why she didn't believe it. His father built the house before he realized it would become his prison. The summer he finally mustered up the courage to ask Edna out he spent all of his free time building her a castle in the woods. It came complete with mermaid statues in the bathroom, forest scenes etched into the wood paneling, and a rose motif masterpiece carved in the master bedroom, sanded until each petal was paper thin.

"He had a gift," Logan agreed. "There wasn't anything he couldn't build. Over there is his workshop. You never knew what you'd find him working on in there. One day it might be a bedroom suite, the next a one-of-a-kind mantle. He was on his way to becoming a household name in the furniture industry when he died. Drunk driver." Jack breathed a sigh of relief when Logan turned away from the shed to point out Keith's garden.

"He and Craig plan to expand the greenhouse next spring. That ought to be something to see. Craig's about as good with metal as Dad was with wood. Too bad they didn't get around to it this year. I don't think Keith's going to be able to salvage much after these storms, but you never know." Only a few wilted stalks poked through the snow covering Keith's vegetable garden. Just days ago, rows of beans, peppers, pumpkins, and squash stretched across the gentle slope down to the river marking the edge of their yard. A thin layer of ice coated the water's surface thanks to Winterthorn's storm.

Eira made all the right sympathetic noises over the state of Keith's plants, but her eyes fastened on the frosted stream. Ignoring Logan as he went on about the potential benefits of a greenhouse, she strode away from them, headed for the water. Jack and Logan exchanged confused looks while Ross rotated a finger around his ear to illustrate his opinion.

"Has it ever frozen completely?" she asked, tapping the white edge of the water with her toe. It cracked but didn't break. Logan scrunched up his face and tugged on his ear as if he could shake the information loose from his memory.

"Not that I remember, but Keith said when he was thirteen there was one winter where they got five feet at one time. It probably iced over then." Jack frowned at the water.

After Tadgh Sorley made his deal with the fae, Straifield had seen nearly a decade of the worst winters imaginable. They set record lows for the nation four years straight. Then, according to his brothers old enough to remember, the harsh winters just stopped. People chalked it up to climate change and other theories that didn't account for such a dramatic shift in such a short period of time.

"Oh good, you do have neighbors." Relief resonated in Eira's voice. "I was starting to think you guys lived out here all by yourselves." Confused, Jack and Logan followed her gaze to the opposite bank where a figure clad in shades of gray knelt beside the river's edge.

The slow creep of comprehension rooted Jack to the spot. Eira leaned forward, squinting at the gray lady.

"Who is she? I think I've seen her before..." but before she could finish the question, the Washer Woman began to sing.

"Wander. Awaken. Turn winter to spring.
Give back the gift that was granted.
Low may they lay thee
Though steadfast ye be.
Into the darkness go sinking.
Wander in shadow. Shed blood and bone.
Fall to the Soul-Keeper's reaping.
Down through the earth,
Step willingly
Into the Steel-Maiden's keeping."

The eerie song sounded even worse delivered in her hoarse croak. Jack recoiled from the message of death and exchanged horrified looks with his brothers. Whose fate had she foretold?

Eira took a step toward the gray lady, her eyes unfocused.

Logan and Ross lunged for her, but Jack was closer. He caught her from behind, clamping a hand over her mouth and an arm around her waist. Awareness returned to her instantly and she fought.

"Shhh!" he hissed, but it was too late. The Washer Woman lifted her head and stared straight at him. Red-rimmed gray eyes sunk deep into sockets eroded from weeping for those whose fates she foretold. The endless wash of salt tears gave her the face of a corpse left to decay in the sea. As soon as her eyes met theirs she opened her mouth and wailed.

The scream that erupted from her made Jack want to stab a razor through his skull. Her keening was shrill enough to drive them all to their knees, but his gift amplified the attack until his mind felt as raw as infant bared to a sandstorm. Jack dropped Eira to cover his ears. His legs buckled and his world splintered as the banshee's voice rose.

Images flashed before his eyes, scattered and disjointed—terrible, grotesque scenes of the dead and dying—a man thrust head-first into flames until his skin blistered, bubbled, and peeled from his bones—snapping jaws tore open an exposed human throat—smoke rose from iron chains bound against pale, faery flesh—Eira sprawled lifeless on a white sheet of snow.

The banshee's mouth stretched impossibly wide, as if her jaw was on a hinge that could open a full hundred and eighty degrees. Eira collapsed, squeezing her head between her hands. Her fear shattered through the visions filling Jack's brain.

He pried his eyes open to see her rocking from side to side. He folded his body around hers to block what noise he could as he tried to drag her back. The screaming intensified. His eyes rolled back into his head until he couldn't see. Warm liquid trickled down both sides of his neck.

A hand grabbed the back of his jacket. Ross leapt in front of him, scooped up a large stone, and lobbed it at the banshee. It thudded against her chest, knocking her over backward. Her cry choked off. With a screech of its own, Ross' falcon shot from the sky, talons stretched toward her eyes. They didn't stay to witness what came next.

Scrambling on all fours, the four of them raced for the house. Logan was in the lead. White-faced, he snatched open the storm door to wave them through. Eira's foot slid out from under her on a thin sheet of ice, and she skidded to a stop.

"What was that thing?"

Jack and Ross collided with her, but she refused to budge, bracing her arms on both sides of the door frame to demand an answer. Ross gritted his teeth and swung his eyes back toward the water. Jack wiped his nose on his sleeve and it came away slick with blood.

"That," panted Logan, jerking his thumb over his shoulder, "was a banshee, and unless you want to hear an encore you need to get inside now." Eira didn't move.

"A banshee? You mean the witch that tells you when you're going to die?"

"She's not a witch," Jack corrected grimly, pinching the bridge of his nose and tipping his head back. "She's a faery. And so are you."

The time for gently introducing her to the world of Faerie was gone. The fae had never come so close to the house before.

Eira's mouth fell open, but Ross shoved her into the house before she could speak.

"Who punched you in the nose?" asked Glen, dropping the dishrag he was using to wipe off the counter.

"You want to help me out?" Jack wheezed, trying not to bleed all over the linoleum. He shuffled aside so Logan could usher Eira onto a stool. Ross scowled in the doorway with his hands on his hips. Glen went to the pantry to get a plastic bag while Logan told him about the banshee.

"What was she doing this close to the house?" he asked after Logan finished.

"I'll give you three guesses," muttered Ross with a pointed look at Eira. Her back was to him so she couldn't see, but she whirled around bristling with irritation all the same.

"You don't seriously believe that was a faery that just tried to kill us."

"You were there, weren't you?" Ross bared his teeth, squaring off like an angry bear.

"That's stupid! There's no such thing as faeries. Oh wait. Is this the part where I clap my hands?" She widened her eyes in mock horror. Jack snorted, spraying flecks of blood.

"They are real, Eira." Glen held a washcloth out to Jack. "Only people who have Faery Sight can see them."

While he came around the counter to check Jack's nose and ears, Logan slipped out of the kitchen to get the others. Eira bit her lip, watching him go. Her jaw clenched.

"So that's what you guys are? Faeries?"

"Like hell!" Caught in the act of tugging off his boots, Ross spluttered and jerked upright.

"We aren't faeries," said Glen as he ushered Jack onto one of the empty stools. "A long time ago our dad found a faery in the woods who needed his help. Logan, you're the storyteller, you tell it." Logan had just returned with the others in tow. He puffed out his chest with importance.

"Once upon a time—" He held up his hands in mock-surrender when everyone groaned. "There was a faery trapped in an enchanted tree. No one knows how she got there, but one day our father found her...." He dropped the sing-song tone and continued in a normal voice. Jack tipped back his head so Glen could clean the blood from his neck while he listened.

"Dad was hiking with his dog when she got loose and ran off. He chased her to a clearing where he found a woman tangled in the roots of a tree. She was under an enchanted sleep, but as soon as he pulled her out she woke up.

"To thank him for breaking the spell, she promised that he and his line—her words, not mine—would forever have her blessing. And just like that my dad became one of the best woodworkers in the world. There wasn't anything he couldn't build. All he had to do was get a picture in his mind, and the wood practically shaped itself. But the thing about faery gifts is they come with a cost." He gestured for a glass of water, and Douglas stepped forward to pick up the story while Logan drank.

"By setting her free Dad messed with something he didn't understand. Someone locked her away for a reason, and when they found out she had escaped they sent the Hunter to bring her back."

"Who?"

"Winterthorn." Logan dropped his voice to a sinister whisper. "He goes by a lot of names: The Green Man, the Lord of Holly, some even call him the Hoarfrost King. Whatever you want to call him, he's the leader of the Wild Hunt. It's his job to harvest the souls of Faerie's enemies and take them back to the Otherworld. He came looking for Dad."

"Dad didn't know a whole lot about the fae back then. He wasn't as careful as he should have been about looking over his shoulder. Winterthorn kidnapped my mom—this was when she and Dad were still dating. He said he'd exchange her for information about where his lady had gone. But Dad didn't know where she went after he set her free. Since he wasn't sure how that would go down with Winterthorn, Dad made him swear that if he told him what he wanted to know no faery would ever come after him again. So Winterthorn wove a spell around our property. No magic but ours could get in uninvited. No faery can get within ten feet of us unless we approach them first, and we're immune to their spells. He gave Dad his promise in good faith, and Dad did the dumbest thing he could've done—he lied."

A shudder went around the room as the Sorleys shifted in their seats, ashamed by what their father had done. Glen clicked his tongue as he applied the glowing pads of his fingertips to either side of the bridge of Jack's nose. The burning sensation in his sinuses cooled, and Jack winced as the lining of his nostrils regenerated. He pulled away and blew a rust-colored glob into the rag Glen had given him. The sight made him queasy. Logan was still talking.

"Faeries can't lie—for some reason they're physically incapable of doing it. But humans can, and Dad did. He deliberately sent Winterthorn off on a wild goose chase off somewhere in England, and as soon as Winterthorn left, he couldn't get within ten feet of Dad or talk to him again. Let me tell you—never piss off a faery.

"Winterthorn couldn't attack Dad directly thanks to his promise, but the fae are good at bending rules without breaking them. Dad died a few years ago in a head on collision with a drunk driver. The man was hopped up on faery wine. There was so much alcohol in his blood he should have been dead twice over from alcohol poisoning. To this day he swears he doesn't remember drinking a single drop. He's serving a twenty-year sentence, but Winterthorn's hands are clean. He didn't kill Dad. All he did was share some wine with a man driving the opposite direction Dad was."

"Okay, so not saying I believe you," Eira began in an uneven voice, "but what does all that have to do with me?"

"That we're not sure about yet." Douglas frowned in frustration. "The first time Jack met you he thought you were fae. You look like them—honestly in the twenty-four hours since you've been here you look more like them every second. You see it too. That's why you thought your hand was glowing earlier. The strongest fae are so powerful they radiate light. It's the same light you see when one of us uses our gifts. Only those with Faery Sight can see it."

She looked at each of them in turn and folded her arms. For a moment Jack thought she was going to demand a demonstration, but apparently the banshee's attack had opened her mind to the possibility of magic. Her eyes narrowed.

"What if I'm under a spell that makes me look like them?" After a second, she realized what she'd just said and scrunched up her nose and shook her head with force. "Don't answer that. I can't believe I'm listening to this." She pushed away from the counter. Logan stretched his arms in a nonchalant arc over his head that blocked her path to the door.

"Evidence suggests you're a changeling—a faery child left to replace a stolen human one," he said conversationally, as though he was guessing something as mundane as her astrology sign. "It's rare for one to go undiscovered long enough to grow up, but I guess your family saw they lucked out by getting one of the pretty ones and decided to keep you." He flashed a winning smile, but she covered her ears with both hands.

"This is crazy!"

"We're not the only ones who know what you are," Douglas said with quiet urgency. "That's why you were attacked. It sounds like the fae figured out you're one of them and tried to take you back. Or if it wasn't the fae it was someone who recognized you as one."

"If they weren't fae why would they care?" She bit the words out with her back to him.

"In the old stories, if you captured a faery they owed you a wish—" Logan was determined to remain charming in spite of her rejecting every word coming out of his mouth.

"Ha! The only wish I plan on granting is when I make those creeps wish they'd never been born. Fellas, you're all nuts! I'm not a faery! I have a human mother. Her name was Gwen Rothchild and she—"

"—was killed by the Wild Hunt," said Douglas with brutal honesty. "Now I remember why I knew your last name. Your mother's death has gone unexplained for almost twenty years. She, her boyfriend, and your great grandmother were mauled by wolves in the middle of a suburban neighbor-hood with no tracks leading in or out."

She shook her head hard as if she could shake loose everything they had told her.

"She died because she went into labor and couldn't get to a hospital in time."

"What about her boyfriend and your great grandmother?"

"Grandma told me Mom and her boyfriend fought a lot. He had anger issues and thought my great grandmother was turning Mom against him. When Mom died he snapped, and—."

"And you believe that her blood attracted a random pack of wolves who mauled him to death? Because that kind of thing happens all the time." Keith stuck out his jaw, daring her to try and defend the ridiculous theory the press had circulated all those years ago. At thirty-five, Keith was old enough to re-member the panic that had gripped Straifield at the inexplicable violence.

"Stop it," she ground out. Jack cringed. She was practically vibrating with anger now.

"No, you stop," he said heavily. "You woke us all screaming this morning because you looked in a mirror and saw yourself the way you really are. Glen's iron skillet burned you even though he could touch it with no problem. And yesterday you got sick the moment you crossed our property line. You're fae, Eira."

"So, what changed?" She rounded on him. "Why all of a sudden can I see these things when I didn't before?" In the face of her crackling anger Jack wasn't sure he was brave enough to tell her the truth.

"There was four leaf clover in your tea yesterday," Logan answered with nowhere near enough apology in his tone. He shrugged. "It's the easiest way to give someone Faery Sight."

Eira rocked back on her heels so fast that she nearly lost her balance.

"You drugged me? That's why I've been seeing things?" Her voice dropped to a scathing whisper. "You guys were the ones who came to my house, weren't you? So, what? Is this some kind of sick game?"

"Don't be stupid." Ross rolled his eyes as the conversation circled back nearly to where it started. Eira wasn't listening. She knocked past Logan's outstretched arm and ran from the room. A second later the front door creaked open and then slammed shut.

"Well that went well," Craig said into the stunned silence.

Chapter 8

"**S**omeone should go after her," said Logan as they sat staring at each other.

"Be my guest. You're the genius that told her we slipped something into her drink," grumbled Ross. "Good riddance, I say."

"You saw how close the banshee was. Who knows what'll find her once she makes it off our land." Jack dropped his ice pack. No sooner were the words out of his mouth than a clawing panic raked his insides. Without a word, Jack blew past Logan and raced for the front door. Chairs scraped as his brothers followed him.

"What is she, part wind-faery?" Ross grumbled as he peered around Jack at the empty front lawn. Logan ran back to get his keys.

"I don't see what all the fuss is about. She's not our problem," Ross complained even as he rushed back to the kitchen to grab his snow boots. Jack gritted his teeth. Deep down he felt responsible for what was happening to her. Things had gone steadily downhill since Halloween. The blame for his mother's death rested solely with him. Maybe he was the reason for Eira's problems too.

"She's not safe on her own—not until she knows how to protect herself." He jammed his arms back into his coat sleeves. Even Ross couldn't argue that point. Opening her eyes to their world, they'd essentially released a tamed bird into the wild. While Logan went to start up the Mustang, Jack and Ross ran outside. The others stayed behind in case she came back.

By the time they reached the top of the hill with no sight of her Jack was starting to believe Ross' theory that Eira had sprouted wings and flown away. The ditch at the bottom of the steep hill marked the northern boundary of their land. Skidding to a stop, they looked around for a sign to point out where she could have gone. The road was a mixture of frozen gravel and hard-packed snow too dense for her steps to leave an imprint.

"Can't you do something?" Jack snapped. The echo of Eira's fear was a living thing inside him battering against his bones in a desperate bid to escape. Ross gritted his teeth. It bothered him to ask the animals for help. Helping a human went against their nature, and though he couldn't override their free will any more than Logan could with people, unlike Logan Ross believed it was an abuse of powers to even ask.

A fountain of light poured out of him to seep into the ground. From a nearby tree, a flock of ravens took wing and arced off to the left over the forest. Ross jerked up his chin in a 'follow them' motion. The cold air burned through their lungs as they took off again.

A piercing howl split the air. The hairs on the back of Jack's neck stood up straight. Ross staggered to a stop, his mouth hanging open. Jack glared over his shoulder.

"Still think letting her go off by herself is a good idea?"

Weaving in and out of trees, he was quickly losing speed as a cramp sank its serrated teeth deep into his side. But a menacing bark just up ahead banished the pain from his mind. He put on a burst of speed when he caught sight of Eira standing motionless in the center of a clearing just ahead.

Above her on an overhang, feet braced, ready to spring was the red wolf. Rings of orange flames glowed in its dark brown eyes. Eira stood frozen beneath it, half-turned to run but glaring up at it with angry defiance. The wolf's teeth flashed white as Ross and Jack appeared.

Jack snatched Eira by the elbow and hauling her behind him. She struggled half-heartedly, as if her pride balked at being rescued like a damsel in distress. Ross blew past in a whirl of pumping limbs. He stopped just below the outcropping of rock and held up a hand in a staying gesture. A cloud of silver rose from his shoulders, and the wolf's head dipped slowly in submission—for a moment.

A growl bubbled up from its throat, and it shook its head hard. Jack's heart hammered in his chest. He'd never seen an animal break Ross' influence before. The wolf paced back and forth on the overhang, panting loudly. Ross tried again. He raised his hand, and the wolf's head started to lower before jerking out of the compulsion a second time. It snapped its teeth in warning.

"That's not just any wolf, Ross," Jack muttered, backing away. Eira flattened herself against his back.

"You think?" Ross snapped over his shoulder. He took a step forward, and the wolf retreated, keeping the same difference between them—no less than ten feet. A low growl vibrated deep in its chest. Its fur rose into stiff spikes along its neck. Jack tasted fear.

"Wait, Ross!"

Ross flipped him the bird.

"I don't tell you how to string your guitar, do I? Get her out of here and leave this to me."

The red wolf crouched low, muscles bunching. Her long tongue hung out. Then she glanced over her shoulder and whined.

"I've got this," Ross repeated through clenched teeth. "Get her back to the house." Jack grabbed Eira's wrist and spun. As soon as Eira moved, the wolf's head came up and her ears flattened. Ross dove to put himself between his brother and the angry animal. Jack shoved Eira to speed her up as they fled. Clumps of snow kicked up behind them. Ross' ravens circled overhead. Jack didn't understand why until the Mustang barreled through the lane between two trees. Logan threw open the passenger door.

"The Wild Hunt's after her," Jack shouted, pushing Eira into the passenger seat before diving in after her. Logan didn't wait for elaboration but threw the car in reverse. The wheels bounced over the uneven terrain, and Jack fell hard against Eira's side, smashing her into the seat back.

"Easy!" he snapped, bracing his hands on the roof and dashboard. At the first opportunity, Logan swung them around so they were going forward instead of in reverse. Within moments they were back in the Sorleys driveway. He switched off the engine and let out a long, shaky breath.

A gentle snow began to fall. Snowflakes drew a thin sheet across the windshield, closing them in. Eira covered her head with her arms. Jack and Logan exchanged a look. Neither knew what to say.

"We're not trying to hurt you," Logan murmured finally, sliding an arm behind her to touch her shoulder. "We just want to help."

A muffled groan escaped between her fingers.

"Ever since Grandma died everything's been falling apart."

Jack winced. Her grief was a physical hand wrapping its fingers around his throat.

"I know what you mean." If he could have gone back in time he never would have gone to the fair. Maybe Bess wouldn't have been taken. His mother would certainly still be alive. One night. One choice. His world would never be the same.

Eira started to cry—silent, self-conscious tears that made him turn his head away. The invisible fingers clamped on his throat slipped down into his chest to curl around his heart. She drew her knees up to her chin and pulled her elbows tight against her so she wouldn't touch either of them. Jack shifted his weight to give her what little space he could on the narrow seat while Logan reluctantly removed his hand from her shoulder.

With nothing but a low whistle for warning, a gust of wind barreled into the side of the Mustang with enough force to make it rock on its tires. The layer of snow on the windows shook loose, leaving a lace pattern through which they looked out. The towering trees around the house bowed nearly in half as another gust swept through.

"We should get inside," Logan murmured, wiping the rapidly fogging windows to peer out at the rising storm. Jack took a deep breath and pushed open his door. A furious wind tore it out of his hand and smashed the side mirror into the Mustang's white painted hood. Glacial cold poured through him, trying to freeze him from the inside out. Hunching against the blistering wind, he stood back to let Eira slide out. She hissed and jammed her hands beneath her arms.

On the other side of the car, Logan slipped on a sheet of ice and went down. He staggered upright, dragging his turtleneck up over his ears. Another howling gust crashed into them, knocking him backwards and slamming Jack and Eira against the car.

Ducking their heads against the snow and wind, they staggered up the sidewalk to the front porch. Before they could reach for the door handle it swung open and Craig reached out to pull them into the warmth and safety of the house. He called over his shoulder to let the others know they were back. Shivering from head to toe, they skimmed out of their wet clothes. Jack's hands shook so badly he could barely peel his socks down his shins. Eira blew on her fingers to warm them.

Keith strode past them, kicking aside socks, shoes, and coats to yank open the door. A wave of wind crashed into him and he flung up an arm to ward off the attack. The world outside was a whirling cyclone of snow and ice.

"Where's Ross?" He had to shout to be heard. He and Craig strained to shut the door against the gale. Jack closed his eyes. A wave of soul-sucking nausea swamped him at the thought of what would happen to Ross caught out in the storm.

"He stayed to distract the wolf." Jack reached for his wet boots, his movements slow and jerky with guilt. In his gut, he knew they'd never be able to find him in the storm. But before he could sink too deep into self-loathing, a heavy knock pounded the front door. Keith yanked it open again to reveal Ross shivering and stamping on the threshold. An orange and gray shape wound around his ankles before darting back out into the blinding white. The knot of shame in Jack's belly gave one final squeeze before unraveling. Ross must have called out to the local gray foxes to lead him home.

Hugging his chest, Ross stepped over the threshold and glared around at everybody.

"Thanks for coming back to get me, assholes," he growled through chattering teeth.

JACK DIDN'T SLEEP THAT night. Every time he closed his eyes the banshee's warning replayed in his head. 'The Soul-Keeper's reaping...' She had to mean Winterthorn, but who was he coming for?

The basement door creaked softly, and a knife of blue light cut across the floor. Jack lay quiet as a pair of feet padded down the steps. Eira. None of his brothers would go out of their way to not wake him. He waited, wondering what she was up to until he heard the quiet click of the washing machine door followed by a soft clump as she fed her laundry into the machine. He lay still, listening and feeling surer with every passing second that she knew he was awake.

"You can be as quiet as you like, but the moment you turn that thing on it's going to wake everybody in the house," he said finally. She sucked in a sharp breath and straightened so he could see the top of her head over the back of the futon.

"I thought you'd already be asleep," she lied. She walked over to the wall and flipped on the overhead light. Even the dim yellow glow of four dying bulbs was blinding after no light at all. By the time his eyes adjusted she had come around to the end of the futon. Hastily he kicked his foot to throw the end of his blanket over the column of the instrument lying against his leg. Eaten up by shame all evening, only the gentle strains of the harp had been able to distract him. With Eira standing over him pale-faced and shivering, the emotion was coming back again. Or was that her guilt he was feeling. He was starting to lose sight of where her feelings ended and his began. She shivered and rubbed her arms.

"Everywhere I turn I keep thinking I see them now. That banshee...?" She waited for his nod of confirmation that she'd used the right term. "I've seen her before, or something like her."

Alarm cut through him. He tensed.

"Where?"

"It was a long time ago when I was little. I saw her while Grandma and I were walking to the grocery store. I tried to say hi, but Grandma grabbed my hand and pulled me away. It seemed normal at the time. She was always telling me not to bother people, so I never gave it a second thought, but I swear it was the same woman. How could I see her if I didn't have Faery Sight until now?" There was still a challenge banked in her voice, as if she was baiting a trap in the hope she could prove everything that had happened was an elaborate prank Jack and his brothers were trying to pull.

"She let you see her," he said in a tight voice. "Banshees typically show up when someone close to you is going to die." Tension vibrated through him. Not too many people who saw a banshee lived long enough to see another. She frowned, trying to read in his face what he wouldn't tell her.

"The wolf was supposed to kill me." She said it matter-of-factly. Jack opened his mouth to tell her that the predicted death would have something to do with the banshee's song but thought better of it.

"You could have asked any of the others what the banshee's song meant. Why wait to do your laundry after midnight to ask me?"

She studied him in silence for a moment. She seemed to see him in a new light, as if her newborn Faery Sight revealed more of him than she had seen before.

"You were the first to show up after my car went into the ditch. The day after those creeps tried to kidnap me you turned up on my doorstep. And to-day, even after I ran out of your house and called you all liars you came after me and saved me from the wolf." Her blue eyes fixed bright and intent upon his face reflecting the same suspicion he'd shone her when she first arrived.

"Your accident was a distraction. While I was out helping you, the fae stole Ross' cow." But even as he said it a whispering voice spoke out of his memory. 'The child was alone and away from the protection spells the old witch wove on their house. Who knows when such an opportunity will rise again.' He frowned. "It was a trap."

"If you hadn't come along I'd have been alone and stranded. I wouldn't even have been able to see them coming for me. After the way I acted earlier I... I didn't want you to think I wasn't grateful." Her hands flexed at her sides, opening and closing as if it took a great effort to say the words.

"Don't worry about it," he said, trying to release the tension he felt coiling inside her. She grimaced and glared off into the corner of the room, annoyed with herself. It occurred to him that if she was a changeling then she was bound to the same rules of reparation the rest of the fae were. Like the pixies that stole Bess and left mistletoe in her stead, if the fae took something then their honor demanded they leave something of equal or greater value in its place. Eira stared at the edge of the futon as a line burrowed deeper into the skin between her brows. It fascinated him to discover which rules applied to her and which ones she could break.

"Well, if you really want to make it up to me you can give me your opin-ion on a song I've been working on." He didn't know why he suggested it. So far, he'd done his best to hide the harp from the others, hoping they'd forget he still had it. But he wanted to see whether the faery in her would respond to the harp's magic.

He fished the harp out from under the blankets around his feet.

"Whoa. Where did you get that?" Her voice deepened as she got a good look at the gilded details. She reached out to touch a delicate leaf that curled back from the strings. Before he could stop himself, he tightened his grip and pulled it away.

"I found it," he said, shifting so he could draw it against his chest and give her room to sit beside him. She quickly shoved her feet under the blankets, kicking his calf by accident. Rather than apologize, she burrowed her toes beneath his leg. Jack offered up his body heat, suddenly more aware of the thick fan of lashes that swept down from time to time to veil her eyes.

'Charm her.' Daisy's advice crept unbidden into the back of his mind.

He glanced sideways at Eira. She was already dazzled by the harp's appearance. Her eyes traced the vines and leaves as they transitioned through the seasons. A thousand songs bubbled up from the well in his brain. As he rifled through them, his fingers glided up and down the strings, not enough to pluck a note, but just enough to make them hum. Eira's eyes rolled closed as she pillowed her cheek against the plump cushion.

"Play," she murmured. The song that answered her gentle command was ancient and slow. Low dripping notes that lightly melted away before giving ground to deep, strong chords. It was a winter song, written eons ago for Faerie's High King. All this the harp told him even as it guided his hands through the dance of the strings.

"What are you doing playing at county fairs?" she asked when the song came to its eventual end. He barely heard her over the sound of his heart thudding in his chest. Magic, he'd felt real magic surging in and out of him as the harp fed the notes and melodies to his hands. Suddenly he wanted Eira gone. He wanted to give himself over to the music's power to see what it could do. He didn't know whether it was using him or the other way around, but together he knew they could create something incredible.

"It's too dangerous," he mumbled. The familiar excuse tasted like ash.

Eira snapped upright, frowning.

"So, you're just going to hide out here in your basement where no one will ever hear you? No, Jack! That's such a waste."

"There are faeries who prey on artists and musicians. If they caught me they'd drain every ounce of my talent away. If they took my music...." He shivered. Eira didn't look convinced.

"But no one will ever know how great you are."

"You'll know," he said with a rueful smile and a shrug. They both knew it wasn't enough.

THE CREAK OF FOOTSTEPS woke him. Blinking in the semi-darkness it took a moment to remember what the warm weight was pinning down his ankles. Eira's head curled against the opposite end of the futon. Her hair hung over the side, dusting the ground. She had her knees drawn up to her chest so that she took up as little space as possible, but sometime in his sleep he'd stretched out so that her hip settled against his feet.

Not wanting to wake her, Jack tried to inch himself free. However, just as he cleared enough space to swing his feet to the floor, she stirred.

"Mmm, did I fall asleep?"

Deciding the answer was obvious, Jack fished around in the blankets for the harp. A dull ache throbbed in his temples.

She watched him lift the edge of mattress cushion to hide the instrument.

"I don't like when they mess with my stuff," he said in answer to her unspoken question.

With a dubious look she shrugged, stretched, and got up. A second pair of feet joined the first clomping overhead. Eira pulled her laundry out of the dryer while Jack headed for the steps. Depending on which brothers were awake, things might get awkward if they came up at the same time.

"...had his throat ripped out.... Blood everywhere...."

Two rooms away the low murmurs were difficult to catch, but a few phrases were impossible to miss. Jack cocked his head to listen.

"Who was he?" asked Keith in his gravelly, before-coffee voice. Jack tiptoed up another step so he wouldn't miss the answer. The floorboards creaked.

"What have I told you about eavesdropping, Jack?" Douglas raised his voice. Caught, Jack stepped out where they could see him and shrugged under their disapproving stares. Dressed in a decade-old pair of striped pajamas that had shrunk in the wash until they showed two inches of pale ankle, Keith moved to the top of the kitchen steps.

"The Wild Hunt killed a man last night—a man named Curtis Hobbs. Do you know anything about him?"

Jack started to shake his head when the accusing tone registered.

"Should I?"

"He worked at the police station," Douglas said in a soft voice. "He and Doyle go way back—been best friends since high school, maybe longer. I wouldn't be surprised if he helped Doyle—" Douglas broke off, glancing sharply at Keith. Neither of them had told Keith what they'd discovered about the extracurricular activities Doyle conducted behind his house.

Eira climbed the stairs with a laundry basket balanced against her hip, but Jack leaned his shoulder against the door jamb and made a subtle staying motion to keep her back. Douglas cleared his throat.

"Apparently Doyle specifically requested me for this case." He steepled his fingers with a thoughtful expression. "This might be a good opportunity to find out what he knows—or thinks he knows—about us." Keith immediately shook his head.

"I don't want him poking around our family any more than he already has. He can cause more trouble for us than we can for him." Douglas didn't respond. He checked his watch and muttered about having to get dressed for work before he shuffled out of the kitchen. There was a long stretch of silence as his feet tramped up the stairs. Finally, Keith rubbed his knuckles in the slow way that meant he was about to deliver bad news. He looked at Jack.

"I don't know if the girl staying here is such a good idea." Embarrassment that Eira could hear while they talked about her rushed to Jack's head. Keith was as predictable as a morning glory, perfectly content to show up when things were going well but the first to curl up and hide the moment things took a turn for the worst. Jack cut his eyes at his oldest brother, truly seeing him for the first time.

"If we send her home she'll just be the next crime on Doug's list."

Keith clenched his jaw. Eira's safety meant next to nothing to him when the fae were literally at their door.

"I don't believe in coincidences where the fae are concerned, and everything about her is one big coincidence wrapped up in a pretty little bow." He glanced uneasily at the ceiling where he still thought Eira was upstairs asleep. Anger and resentment beat at Jack. Keith was such a wuss.

"What are you worried she's going to do? Her whole life she's believed she was an ordinary human girl. How is she any more dangerous than any of us?

"For starters, she's not an ordinary human girl; she's a faery. And just because she's never used magic before doesn't mean she can't figure out how to use it now. Power corrupts, Jack. She might seem like the girl next door now, but maybe that's what she wants you to think. Have you thought about that? It's what her kind are designed to do—lure you in with a pretty face and then suck the soul out of you. For all you know she's already started. You've certainly been different ever since she showed up."

Jack's face flamed as Eira's cool rage simmered at his back.

"You have no proof that she's even dangerous but you're treating her like she's here to murder us in our sleep."

"Jack, she's fae! How much more proof do you need?" His voice cracked with strain. He sent another furtive glance toward the ceiling. Jack clenched his teeth.

"You're a coward. If Dad were here he'd be ashamed of you."

Keith stared at him for a long moment, and then his lip curled,

"Pull your head out of your ass, Jack. Dad wasn't some crusader waging a one-man war against the fae. He got involved in something he shouldn't have, and when Winterthorn came calling he weaseled his way out of punishment with a lie. He wasn't brave—he was clever. And being clever is what got him killed. Just like you were being clever when you went off to play in that stupid fair." *And got Mom killed.* Keith didn't say it, but he might as well have shouted it. Jack flinched as though he'd been slapped in the face. Some of the heat went out of Keith's face, and he took a deep calming breath.

"Look, I can tell you like her, but that girl is a real threat. Maybe not Eira herself, but the attention she draws. Winterthorn wants her, and he's going to keep coming until he gets her." The lash of guilt still burned in Jack's mind, but it wasn't enough to shake him from his course.

"She's not going anywhere."

Keith made a disgusted sound in the back of his throat and stalked out of the kitchen. Eira climbed the steps until she and Jack were on a level. Her features were pinched with self-righteous anger. Jack had no words to apologize for what she'd overheard.

The TV in the kitchen was on, and in the silence, they could hear the report that had started the argument.

"...Reports say the victim received multiple lacerations to his arms and upper body that looks to be the work of claws. Probable cause of death is a torn jugular, which further points to the work of a wolf. Officials say the recent winter storms have driven the animals to seek alternative food sources. Police urge everyone to secure their doors and cover any garbage that contains food...." Fortunately, the news station had nothing more interesting to show than a headshot of Hobbs, who was in his mid to late thirties with a hairline that started so far back it looked like someone had skimmed a razor straight down the middle of his head.

"This has something to do with that attack yesterday, doesn't it?" Eira's eyes speared him, daring him to deny it. Jack felt a small current of tension radiating from her at what his answer might mean. He wanted to lie to her, anything to take that stark look off her face. Undoubtedly, she was picturing herself torn to shreds by the Red Wolf.

"There's something you should know," he said heavily. "A few days ago, Douglas and I went to see the Sheriff at his house about—I'm not even sure why I went. I knew he wanted to expose the fae for what they've done, and I guess I thought I could talk to him. Anyway, while we were there Douglas discovered that Doyle is capturing and killing fae. That's why I had Douglas help me track you down. I knew Doyle saw what you were that night at the fair, and I wanted to make sure he didn't.... If Hobbs was an old friend of his maybe he was in on it and Winterthorn found out." She shifted her gaze over his shoulder to where an antique mirror hung on the wall. Her features sharpened.

"I guess he was asking for it, then."

Jack did a double-take. For a moment, she looked as heartless and cold as the Ash Queen. The resemblance was so strong that he shivered. She meant it. The man's throat had been ripped out, his body shredded by wolves, and she didn't care. He didn't know how he felt about that. She lifted her chin, daring him to judge her.

"If he's working with Doyle to help kill fae then he'd have killed me too. Do you think I should feel sorry he's gone?" She leaned into his personal space. A shadow shifted across her blue gaze, a movement so quick that he glanced over his shoulder half-expecting to see one of his brothers sneaking up behind him. There was no one there, just their reflections in the old mirror. When he turned back, Eira studied his face through narrowed eyes.

"Well, Jack?"

Searching for the uncanny shadow he'd glimpsed in her eyes, he didn't answer for a long time. Finally, when he could find nothing more than the flecks of silver inside the forget-me-not blue, he lifted his chin in a slow slice to the left. If Hobbs was stupid enough to try hunting the fae, then he only had himself to blame that he became the Hunt's prey.

Chapter 9

"Logan..." Eira purred his name as she glided into the kitchen where he and Jack were still eating breakfast an hour later. Logan lifted his head to respond and missed his mouth with his spoon by several inches. Jack's toast froze halfway to his mouth, forgotten. Her hair was damp from the shower and it hung in wild black tangles over her shoulders. She wore a snug, lilac sweater that was either a size too small or designed for someone with less assets to conceal. Realizing he was staring, Jack found sudden fascination in the melted butter on his cinnamon sugar toast.

"I was wondering if you could give me a ride into town." She came to stand beside Logan's stool and cocked her head inquiringly. The movement caused the slick coils of her hair to pour over her shoulder like black ink.

"Where do you want to go?" His husky answer came without hesitation. Jack choked on a laugh. Eira glanced at him and an attractive blush rose in her cheeks when she realized that he saw through her coy act. But Jack wasn't the one with the car, and Logan greedily drank up the 'come hither' look glittering in her eyes.

"I've got to be at work in half an hour. I'm the only one with the keys to open the shop." She batted her lashes, and Logan practically dissolved at her feet.

He jumped up, abandoning his oatmeal to run for his jacket. Eira smiled after him looking pleased with herself and only a little disappointed at how easy he'd been to convince.

"You're playing with fire," Jack warned quietly. Her head swiveled around, and she tested out an expression of wide-eyed innocence. He shot her a bland look, insulted that she thought he was that susceptible. She sighed.

"Look, I get all the reasons why I shouldn't go, but I don't have much choice. I can't afford to call in sick. Money's tight enough as it is." She wouldn't look at him, and Jack was suddenly reminded of her fury at finding all four tires slashed on Halloween and how bitterly she'd announced that she couldn't afford to tow her car home. His sympathy went out to her.

"I can go with you. You know, as backup?" She snorted. When he didn't understand why it was funny she lifted her shoulder and said, "I suppose I could use an extra hand."

It took several nudges to remind her not to stare as they rode into town. Fae lurked everywhere. Frost faeries hung upside down like bats from branches coated in hoarfrost, ice gremlins jumped from tree to tree trying to snap the brittle wood under their weight. A wind faery glided alongside the car for a little while, her translucent body made entirely of fog.

"I still don't understand why you brought a backpack," Logan complained for the fifth time since leaving the house. His griping had more to do with Eira's announcement that Jack was tagging along than because he cared what was in the bag.

"I brought some sheet music in case inspiration happens to strike. I need some new material for that tape for the talent scout." He closed his fingers around the strap of the black bag next to his leg. But it wasn't the sheet music Jack wanted to keep with him, it was the instrument. Through the cheap material he felt the outline of the faery harp against his calf.

"Do you want me to grab some coffee?" asked Logan as they swerved onto Main Street. By then, Eira was paler than Jack had ever seen her. Her nails dug into her seat and she stared straight ahead.

A brown gremlin dropped out of a nearby tree to land on the windshield as they rolled to a stop at the traffic light. Eira's hand jumped up to seize Jack's where it rested on the shoulder of her seat.

"It's weird knowing they've been around but you just couldn't see them, huh?" he asked, squeezing back in a subtle request for her to loosen her grip. The gremlin scratched at the glass, and Jack had the uncomfortable sensation that it was trying to get to him. He let his gaze slide over it and saw its red, slitted eyes fastened on him intensely as its lips peeled back from sharp, pointed fangs.

Logan cursed under his breath and flicked on the windshield wipers. A jet of clear fluid splashed the gremlin in the belly, and the black wipers batted him off to the side. Eira's nose wrinkled.

"I hate those things," Logan said as the light turned green.

They pulled into the gas station.

"He really doesn't have to do that." Eira watched Logan step inside the Stop N Go, wave 'hi' to Stevie at the counter, and head up the aisle housing the coffee dispensers.

"He's pulling out all the stops," Jack observed, sliding out to pump gas. Eira's brows puckered. Jack sighed, not sure whether explaining would help Logan or hinder his chances with her.

"He's been trying to impress you since you walked through our door."

She got quiet, probably rethinking the tactics she'd used to convince him to bring her into town. Jack concentrated on unscrewing the gas cap. Most girls were happy to find out they were Logan's flavor of the week. When it was their turn for attention they forgot or forgave him for dumping their best friends, cousins, and sisters. Jack hoped Eira was above that, but he didn't want to be disappointed. He kept his back to her and stared off up the street.

The rhythmic chug of the gasoline pump was hypnotic. He let his mind drift as he scanned the frozen remains of a front yard beyond the crosswalk. Neighborhood kids had built a snow woman. They'd tied a red, crushed velvet, Halloween cape around her neck. It was a novel departure from the classic stovetop hat. He did a double-take when honey-colored eyes glared out from beneath the raised hood. His heart slammed against his ribs.

"You know what, why don't I just walk? I can see the store from here." Eira's voice startled him, and he spilled gasoline across his shoe. The fumes made his head swim. He turned to see her pointing out a shop several doors down before she walked off. Jack whirled back to the snow woman. She was gone. The yard stood completely empty.

"Where'd she go?" asked Logan when he returned a few minutes later holding a large Styrofoam cup in one hand and a handful of sugar packets and creamer cups in the other. A small bag of donuts swung off his wrist.

"You're coming on too strong," said Jack, replacing the gas cap. Logan rolled his eyes.

"Right, like I'm going to take advice on women from you." He laughed. Jack looked him in the eye.

"Don't make it weird. She's staying with us."

"How could I forget?" Logan sighed dramatically, dumping the donuts in the passenger seat before climbing in.

Eira stood wiping off the jewelry display cases when Jack and Logan arrived. The place had the strong chalky smell of dust mixed with the heavy rose scent wafting from a potpourri basket on the front counter. Jack sneezed the moment he walked through the door.

"Sorry, it's been a while since I vacuumed." Eira blushed as she skirted around him to a supply closet hidden behind a room divider printed with cherry blossoms. She wrestled an ancient, industrial vacuum cleaner through the narrow door.

"I've got this," said Logan chivalrously, all but yanking the vacuum out of her hand. His foot tangled in the extension cord, and Jack and Eira looked on in amusement as he fought to free himself. A soft noise, like the purr of a cat caught Jack's attention. After a quick glance around he nudged Eira's side and threw a pointed glance toward the far corner of the room where a six-inch brown elf sat on an overturned shoe watching Logan's antics with a grin. Logan deflated without so much as glancing at the brownie.

"Do you run this shop all by yourself?" Jack asked, his voice over-loud. Eira shook her head, trying her best not to look in the corner where the brownie sat. Her wide eyes held his gaze, silently asking whether or not they were in danger. He couldn't blame her for being afraid, but brownies were one of the few fae who wanted nothing more than to care for the humans they adopted as pets. He wasn't sure how to relay that information to her without alerting the brownie that they knew she was there. The best he could do was maintain a reassuring smile and hope she got the message that everything was alright.

"Trudy and June help out a lot. Oh! They've probably been worried sick about me!" Eira's rushed to a wall-mounted phone. The brownie skipped up to the counter, directly in front of her.

"Don't!" Jack called out as Eira reached for a phone book to squash the little creature. Her head jerked up, and he held up his hand. "Don't feel guilty," he said in a much gentler voice. "You've had a lot going on. I'm sure plenty of people have missed you." He indicated the brownie with a thrust of his chin. The strain in Eira's face eased, but only slightly.

She flipped on a round blue stereo beneath the register. The final chorus about a gentle death via guitar music faded into a morning radio program. Just as Eira prepared to dial one of her two coworkers, Logan switched on the vacuum. The mechanical roar drowned out the boring disc jockeys. Pinching her lips, Eira set the phone down to wait until he was finished. She had to put a stop to his cleaning about a minute later though when he nearly tore the frills off a hideous blue blouse using the extension wand. Clucking angrily, the brownie hopped down from the counter and produced a needle and thread from thin air to repair the damage.

"You know, there's no reason for both of you to stay." Eira flashed an overly bright smile. "I'm sure you have better places to be than watching me run an empty store." Though she addressed both of them, her blue eyes fixed on Logan. Color invaded his cheeks as he took the hint. He straightened slowly and set the vacuum down.

"Uh, sure. Okay. Just call if you want a ride home. I'll uh...I'll just go then." He scratched the back of his neck looking lost. It was probably the first brush-off of his life.

Assuring him that she would call at the end of the day, Eira ushered him toward the door. Logan allowed her to steer him out, shoulders rounded in humiliation. Jack hid a smile. He'd pay a hundred dollars to watch that again.

He didn't expect the little shop to be very busy—it was a consignment store after all—but within half an hour at least twenty women in their mid-forties or older stopped by to check on Eira. More than one offered to let her stay with them, assuring her that with the weather turning foul so early in the season things could only get worse, and it was no time for a young girl to be living on her own.

"Thanks for the offer, but I'm staying with some friends of mine." She waved a little desperately in Jack's direction. He'd been doing his best to make himself inconspicuous in a corner with his sheet music in his lap. Several eyebrows rose in scandalized surprise.

"You're staying with the Sorleys? Now? After Edna—"

Anger leeched the color from Jack's face. Not only was the casual mention of his mother's death a punch to the gut, but he'd never heard anyone pack so much disdain into one word the way these women said his last name. While the ladies' opinions of his family didn't matter to him, he saw Eira recoil from the revelation that her reputation had taken a direct hit. An elderly lady named Mrs. Keller tied her fuzzy green scarf around her chin, sniffed, and tilted her nose in the air with the regal pronouncement that she had 'other errands' to run. Eira's mouth fell open as she watched her go.

"What, does she think that just because I'm staying at your house I must be sleeping with one of you?" She came to stand beside him, seeking refuge from the sideways glances. Jack opted not remind her that the ladies were probably taking Logan's reputation into account too.

"Jean-Marie says she saw the police over at your house the other day," said Mrs. Summers, a local piano teacher with chin-length, brassy hair. The column of Eira's throat flexed before she plastered a rueful smile on her face.

"Oh that? That was just a friend stopping by to give me a ride."

"I thought that's what it had to be. As soon as she told me, I said, 'Eira's not the sort of girl to get herself mixed up in any kind of trouble.' Winnifred raised you better than that." Eira gave her a polite, brittle smile. Over the piano teacher's shoulder, Jack mimed shooting himself in the head. Eira's lips pinched, and her eyes snapped back to Mrs. Summer's face, but not before the woman followed her gaze.

"Why Jack Sorley! What are you doing here?" Her gaze bounced between them, and her lips curved in a knowing smile. Jack scratched his ear, deliberately avoiding the eye of the imp the size of a cockroach that sat on her shoulder. It tugged on her earlobe and poked its entire head inside her ear where it whispered suggestions of what she should say next.

"What instrument are you banging around on these days?" she asked. Unease slid down the back of his throat like an ice cube. Years ago, his mother persuaded her to let him perform in her spring recital, and he'd outshone even her most seasoned students. Afterwards, several parents came up to him and asked where he took lessons and whether his teacher was accepting new students. From the lemon pucker of her lips, Mrs. Summers still hadn't forgiven him for that. Still, she wasn't the one who wanted to know about his latest musical accomplishments.

"Guitar mostly," he lied, scratching the side of his nose as the imp jerked its head from her ear and bared its teeth. It hopped from her shoulder to the crook of her elbow where the chain-link strap of her purse rested.

"Jack!" Eira called in a high-pitched voice. "There's some boxes in the back that need to be sorted. Could you help me out?" She sounded panicky.

The imp leapt for him, but Jack stepped to the side, and it went head-first into the wall with a thump that made Mrs. Summers jump.

"Did you hear that? It sounded like it came from inside the wall. I hope you don't have rats."

"I doubt it," said Jack, stepping on the little creature. It squished beneath his foot like a tick. Imps attached themselves to their unsuspecting victims and siphoned off the energy from their negative thoughts. Sometimes they whispered to their hosts, sowing seeds of paranoia and discontent for a better harvest. Only by getting rid of the imp could the person return to normal.

Mrs. Summers clapped a hand to her temple with a hiss. Jack gave her space.

"If you need me, I'll be in the back." Shuffling his feet, he dragged the limp body beneath his shoe to the back of the store where he picked it up between his thumb and forefinger and flung it out the window into a snow-covered bush.

The bell over the front door jingled. Jack fished his backpack out from under the farmhouse table where Eira had been dumping the new clothes for consignment. After the imp's no-so-veiled threat Jack suffered an undeniable needed to check on the harp.

"Aiden, what are you doing here?"

Jack whipped around to see the tall boy standing at the counter, a bulging white trash bag resting against his leg.

"My dad went through his closet and found some of Mom's things she left behind after the divorce. We've been meaning to get rid of them. That's funny. I didn't know you worked here."

Jack rolled his eyes. Sure he didn't. Eira's mouth quieted as if she didn't believe it either.

"I own the place." She tossed her hair over one shoulder. Jack's stomach dropped as her back arched, and she leaned her forearms across the counter. Aiden grinned.

"You do? That's awesome! Oh, well I guess not, I mean... this place was your grandma's wasn't it?"

"It was ours. I practically grew up in this shop." She looked around wistfully.

"You guys must've been close, huh? I mean, last summer you made it sound like she never let you out of her sight. She even homeschooled you, didn't she?"

"Yea." Stiffness settled in her shoulders at the mention of her grandmother, but Jack was surprised by the undercurrent of resentment he sensed bubbling beneath her surface.

"I didn't mean to make you sad," said Aiden quickly. "It's just all you could talk about last summer was how happy you were that she let you join our youth group. All that time together. You must miss her." Eira grimaced at the pathetic picture he painted of her.

"I try to take things one day at a time. It's strange how you can live in the same house with someone and never really know much about them until they're gone."

"Yea, I know what you mean. My dad's like that. All he ever wants to do is go hunting or fishing with his buddies when he's not putting in extra time at the office. I think football is the only thing we have in common, and even then, he never makes it to any of my games."

"He doesn't take you hunting with him?" Jack had to hand it to her, she was subtle. Aiden had no idea she was pumping him for information. He shook his head.

"Nah. He's got a group that he goes out with. I asked to go once, and he told me I'd just get in the way so I haven't asked again. I mean, I don't need a neon sign to tell me he doesn't want to hang out with me."

She made a softly sympathetic noise and looked down her nose in a silent invitation for Aiden to show her what he'd brought. He jumped at the reminder of why he was there. Fumbling, he set the bag on the counter so she could untie the yellow handle strings to look inside. Her eyebrows shot up and her lashes fluttered as she pulled out the first item.

"This was your mothers?"

Aiden's shoulders lifted in a shrug. As far away as he was, Jack saw color tinge the rim of Aiden's ear.

"I don't ask questions I don't want to know the answer to," he mumbled. Eira lifted out a blood-red, leather and lace corset.

"Interesting...." She held it against her body, looking down with a wicked smile. Jack's mouth went dry. Aiden whistled.

"Looks like it's about your size."

She threw her head back.

"Ha! Nice try."

Aiden leaned his elbow on the counter and crossed his feet at the ankles.

"You could wear it on our date—if you'll go out with me, that is."

Jack's eyebrows shot up. Wow. And he thought Logan was cocky. Eira snorted and covered her mouth with her hand. Abandoning his hiding place, Jack stalked up to the front counter and snatched up the plastic bag before she could pull out anything else—like matching panties.

"Should I sort through these too?" His voice came out rougher than he meant for it to. Eira's eyes widened in an unmistakable reprimand while her nostrils flared. Turning back to Aiden and running her fingers through her hair, she waved Jack away.

"Yea, sure. Whatever. Take them to the back."

Disbelief burned hot and left Jack cold as he snatched the heavy bag and hauled it to the back room. Deliberately he crinkled the plastic so he wouldn't have to hear any more of the flirting happening at the front counter.

His efforts weren't enough to completely mask the murmur of voices though. Eira giggled girlishly, and Aiden gave a throaty chuckle. Jack felt like an idiot.

A few minutes later, the front bell jingled. The creak of uneven floorboards heralded Eira's approach. Jack didn't want to face her. He'd acted like a jealous ass, and he had no intention of apologizing or explaining himself. Snatching up his backpack, he ducked out the back door before she reached the inventory room.

A fist of icy wind sucker-punched him the moment he opened the door. Regretting his decision to abandon his jacket, Jack was torn between going back to face Eira, or seeking refuge across the street at Lou's Diner where Glen worked. When a second gust drove him back, he wrapped his arms around his body and hurried around the side of the building into the alley. Between the bank and the consignment shop, he saw Lou's Diner gleaming like a polished Airstream lit with neon lights.

"Where's your coat?" Glen asked from the flat top grill the moment Jack seated himself on one of the stools at the counter.

Jack hid behind a menu and mumbled that he'd forgotten to wear one. Glen turned his back on the patty melt he was preparing. He raised his spatula incredulously.

"It's five degrees outside. How could you forget?"

"I'll have the special." Jack pretended not to hear him. After a moment, he sighed. He really had made an idiot out of himself. "Make that two."

He swiveled his seat around to look at the consignment store across the street. Aiden's truck was still parked out front. Exhaust billowed from the tailpipe, but his parking lights were on. Why hadn't he left yet?

A heavy hand squeezed the tendon connecting Jack's neck and shoulder so tightly his fingers went numb. Batting his attacker away he looked up to see Craig standing behind him in a slate gray bubble jacket.

"I'd hate to be in your shoes when Keith gets ahold of you." Craig gave a mock shudder and slumped down on the stool next to him. "So, how's the babysitting?"

A passing waitress with a nose ring and dark purple highlights stopped in her tracks and beamed at him.

"You're babysitting? That's so cute!" At fifteen, Indira was on a constant lookout for her next big crush. Her brown eyes lit up at the thought of Jack taking care of a small child. Jack hunkered down in his seat, eying her warily. Craig grinned and clapped him on the shoulder.

"Don't get your hopes up, Indy. His heart's already taken." Rather than discourage her, Indira's interest doubled.

"Oooh, who's the lucky lady?"

"How's that chili coming?" Jack called a little desperately toward the kitchen.

"Table five's order's ready." Indira's older sister, Maria, ran the kitchen with Glen. She could not have looked more bored with their topic of conversation as she set the plates on the serving tray to go out. Giggling at Jack's discomfort, Indira glided away to serve her customers, but Craig wasn't so quick to let it go.

"Seriously, when was the last time you devoted this much attention to someone other than yourself?"

"What's that supposed to mean?"

"Aw, there's nothing to be embarrassed about," said Indira, returning from her table. "Whoever she is, she'd have to be crazy not to go for a sweet guy like you." She fluttered her false eyelashes at him and rested her hand on his knee. Jack jumped to his feet.

"I'll take that order to go!"

Chapter 10

"Look, I'm not saying you're self-absorbed or anything, but music is pretty much the only thing you ever think about," said Craig, walking beside Jack to block the worst of the wind on the way back to Eira's shop.

"No, it's not." The denial was automatic, a reflex developed over the years to hide any ammunition his brothers could use to tease him with.

"It's no big deal. You're an *artiste*. Half the reason you're so good is because you're passionate about it, but...."

"But?" An edge crept into Jack's voice.

"But there's more to life than music is all I'm saying. I think it's cool you're into—"

"I'm gonna stop you there," said Jack dryly. "I'm not into anyone. She's in trouble. We're helping her out. That's it."

"Right, and the secret to Keith's vegetable garden is Miracle-Gro." Craig hunched his shoulders against a particularly frigid blast of wind. "Geeze, this weather sucks."

They were just coming up the handicap ramp to the shop when the bottom of the brown paper bag tore. Jack rammed his chest into the wooden railing to catch the food from falling.

"You could help, you know," he complained as Craig stood by and watched. Craig held up his hands to show the plastic wrapped silverware and packets of crackers he'd brought with him.

"I am helping." He turned to the store window, no doubt hoping Eira was watching. "This place looks dead. Is she even here? The lights are all off."

Jack's head came up and the two bowls of chili nearly spilled out of his hands.

That's when he felt it, the tingling, creeping cold of winter magic at work. Icicles hung like gaping jaws over the door. Craig reached for the handle. He hissed and jerked his hand back as though he'd been burned.

"It's locked. Hell, it's frozen shut!" The round knob stood encased in a square block of ice. Alarms clanged in Jack's mind.

"Break it!" He ordered.

"What?" Craig looked at him like he'd grown a second head. "I'm not breaking down the door."

"Something's wrong. Break it!"

Glancing around to make sure no one was watching, Craig dug into his pocket for his Swiss Amy knife and brought the metal handle down on the ice cube. It took two more swings before he chipped enough away to turn the handle. The hinges whined as the door swung open. A cloud of crushed rose and cedar perfume made their eyes water.

Silence hung over the store like a black veil. A layer of gloom clung to the dusty racks.

"Eira? Eira!" No answer.

Their breaths rose like ghosts in front of them as they exchanged a worried glance. Craig flicked the light switch, but nothing happened. Not even the heat was on.

Dumping the food on the counter, Jack made a quick circuit of the narrow shop.

"I don't think she's here," said Craig uncertainly. All humor was gone from his broad face. Jack barely heard him through the storm of guilt raging around him. How could he have left her alone?

A boot from the window display sailed across the room to slam against the wall. Craig whirled with his fists raised. Jack saw the brownie's small figure dash past the trifold mirror near the changing area. Needing no further directions, Jack ripped the curtain off the bar above the first doorway and found nothing. He tore the loops off the second, and pulled so hard on the third that he brought the shower rod down with it.

Eira lay face down on the carpet. Her sweater was discarded on the floor beside her. Instead she wore the blood-red corset over her black lace bra.

Jack flipped her over. The corset was laced so tightly he could see the seams straining against her rib cage. He tore at one little ribbon, but the moment he touched it, the lacy wriggled like a snake and pulled even tighter. A hoarse grunt left Eira's throat as the air wrung itself out of her lungs. Blue veins marbled her face.

"What the hell?" Craig skidded to a stop behind him.

Eira made another croaking sound, but she couldn't suck in any air. Veins stood out in her neck as she fought to breathe. Craig dropped down beside them and pried at the bows too, but his thick fingers couldn't get beneath the straining laces. His efforts only made the corset cinch even tighter. They heard a crack and Eira's eyes flew open. She slapped the ground, tried to sit up, and fell back with a whimper.

Craig flipped open his pocket knife. He wedged the blade between her hipbone and the leather and sawed up toward her ribs. They heard a loud ripping noise. His arm jerked wildly as the knife sliced up to her armpit like it was skimming through butter. The corset sprang open. The moment it was off her he flung it into a far corner before it could wrap around him next.

Eira knelt on all fours, panting. She still had on her black lace bra and jeans, but Jack snatched an outdated dress hanging up in the stall and threw it over her. Angry red grooves outlined where the corset bones had bit into her. There was even blood in places where the material tore her skin. Jack put a hand behind her back but didn't dare touch her. Unable to think of anything else to do, Jack hummed softly. The shop lit up with the glow of his power. It didn't take any of her pain away, but she relaxed a little, and her breathing grew more controlled.

She sank low over her knees, alternating between great choking gasps and low, broken whimpers. Cursing softly, Craig fished his cellphone out of his back pocket. He hit speed dial, waited, and edged away from Jack before trying again. Glen answered on the third try.

"Get over here now!" Craig didn't waste time explaining.

Eira's eyes darted around, touching every inanimate object. Her fear raked at Jack, but it was nothing compared to the guilt clawing at his belly. Why hadn't he stayed with her? She squeezed her eyes shut and jerked her head from side to side. She clenched her teeth so hard they heard the molars grinding in her jaw. The makeshift blanket slipped and they saw a growing blackberry bruise spreading across her side.

"Is he coming or what?" Jack snapped. Every gasp and wince were like knives in his chest. Her hand came up to wrap around his bicep, the fingernails digging through his sweater and long-sleeved shirt. At long last the front bell tinkled and heavy footsteps announced Glen.

He took one look at Eira crouched on all fours and pushed Jack aside. Eira wheezed and reached for Jack's hand as Glen's fingers lightly traced her side. Suddenly she flinched and tried to roll away only hiss with pain on the other side as well.

"Gah! I can't—! It hurts!"

Jack glared at Glen. Why wasn't he doing something? Glen sat back on his heels looking grim.

"There's at least one break, possibly more. How did this happen?"

Craig pointed to the corset lying innocuously on the floor. They knew what had happened but not how, and Eira was in no shape to tell them.

"Bring it. We've got to get her someplace where she can lie down. I'm sorry, Eira, but before I can try and heal you we're going to have to move you, and it's going to hurt."

"You can't do anything for her?" Jack asked incredulously.

"I can't just knit bones back together. That kind of damage takes time." His pudgy face glistened with strain, and he pushed his hair out of his eyes.

"But at the hospital you caught me back up on two weeks of malnutrition with one pot of soup."

"And Keith boosted every vegetable to give them as many vitamins as possible. I'm on my own with this one and I don't have a lot of practice resetting bones." It was true. Despite the odds against seven brothers running wild in the woods without any serious incidents, their fear of the fae made them too cautious to take unnecessary risks.

"My car's at the shop getting an oil change," Craig mumbled. Glen sighed.

"I caught a ride in with Doug, and I suppose Logan drove you guys in. Who knows where he's at right now. Ross is probably our best bet."

While Craig stepped away to call Ross, Glen helped Eira to get up. She tried to sit first, but stopped midway and fell back with a cry. Jack could actually see the bones moving beneath her skin. Her teeth sank into her bottom lip and a tear leaked through her thicket of eyelashes.

By the time they got her up, clothed, and to the door Ross was there. Between the five of them they managed to help her into the middle of the bench seat of his truck. Ross' jaw clenched in an 'I told you so' kind of way, but his face paled at the sight. Glen had to go back to the diner to give an excuse for why he wouldn't be back, and Craig decided that he'd only get in the way, so he headed back to the mechanic shop at the end of the street where he worked.

"Why would Aiden's mother have something like that?" Eira asked as they waited for Glen to come back. Her voice was barely a breath of sound, but Jack heard it as clearly as if she's spoken into his head. It was a fair question. Assuming Aiden's story was true and the corset had belonged to his mother, why would she have had something so dangerous? Had Aiden known what he was bringing into the store with him? As much as he didn't like him, Jack couldn't see Aiden being that deceptive. He seemed genuinely interested in Eira. Then again, his car had been parked out front for a long time....

"Eira, did Aiden come back inside after I left?"

"It wasn't Aiden's fault," Eira said with an absolute certainty that grated on Jack's nerves. The facts didn't exactly agree with her.

"Let's go," said Glen, climbing into the backseat. He blew on his hands to warm them before latching his seatbelt. Ross muttered under his breath as he backed out into traffic.

They were almost to the end of Main Street when Jack spotted the black cruiser tailing them. He slid down in his seat and squinted into the rearview mirror to make out the driver. They turned the corner onto the road that would take them out of town, and when the cruiser made the same turn he was able to read the word 'Sheriff' printed boldly across the side.

"Ross, he's behind us," he whispered. "You've got to lose him." Ross looked at him as though he'd lost his mind.

"Who are you, James Bond? I'm not going to 'lose him.' We'll just circle around for a while until he gets bored."

"He doesn't know where you live?" Eira asked. Her fingers squeezed Jack's hand as if she was trying to crush his bones as payback.

"The protection spell doesn't just keep the fae away. It's hard to find your way to the house unless one of us leads you in."

"What's the worst he can do?" She lifted her chin bravely. Jack thought of the kelpie Doyle tortured and killed in his shed.

"You want me to pull over and find out?" asked Ross dryly. They circled the roundabout and drove back down Main Street. Straifield only had one main street that quickly faded into long rows of houses. Too much driving around might give Doyle an excuse to pull them over for suspicious behavior.

Ross pulled a U-turn right in front of Doyle and Jack's heart slammed into his ribs as he looked over and saw the sheriff staring straight at him through black tinted shades. Jack leaned forward to shield Eira as best he could. His foot kicked his backpack, which gave a soft hum.

"What was that?" Ross looked around sharply, but Jack pretended not to hear. "All right, hang on." The truck sped up and Jack twisted to watch Doyle close in. They came to the traffic light just as it switched from yellow to red. Ross pumped the gas to shoot them through the intersection. A green sedan turned onto the road between them and Doyle, and Jack breathed a sigh of relief. Already it had its blinker on to pull into the parking lot behind the pizza parlor.

Silver light illuminated the truck cab.

"Please boy, give me a distraction," Ross muttered, taking his eyes off the road to look at the sidewalk. Following his gaze, Jack saw a golden retriever trotting docilely beside a girl in a bright pink snowsuit. The dog's ears pricked up at Ross' words. It dug in its heels, yanked its leash out of the girl's hands, and dashed straight into the road.

Jack clenched every muscle in his body as brakes squealed behind them. The girl squealed. The dog woofed.

Crunch!

He whipped around. The police cruiser rear ended the sedan that hit its brakes to avoid the animal, who had turned back at the last moment from darting into the street.

"Well, that ought to keep him busy for a while," said Ross. His voice came out shaky from watching the near-miss.

"Is the dog okay?" Eira asked in a small voice. Ross pointed to the sidewalk where the girl was alternating between hugging her dog and scolding him with a finger in his face.

"Good boy," Ross murmured with more respect than Jack had ever heard him show a human. The dog's tongue lolled in a grin, before it jumped up to lick the girl's face.

With the fender bender behind them, Ross sped off for home.

By the time they pulled into the driveway Eira was hiccupping through her tears from being bounced over the uneven road. All three brothers were gray-faced. Jack thought he was going to be sick.

Getting her out of the car was almost the hardest part. She fought them. Between the bitter cold and the way each movement forced her to bend and shift, she was ready to barricade herself inside the cab rather than let them lead her into the house.

Glen fetched bandages from the medicine cabinet while Jack and Ross supported her upstairs. Her face glistened, and with her bone-white skin and the dark shadows under her eyes she looked like a walking corpse. When Glen hurried back with his arms full of bandages Jack fled before his brother got to work manipulating her bones back into place.

He took his time going out to the truck to collect his backpack. Hugging the black vinyl against his chest he pressed his forehead to the metal door-frame. A muffled cry from his upstairs window made him flinch. Glen was the best doctor Eurasia could hope for. He might not be able to fuse the bones back together, but he could reduce the damage to the surrounding tissues. It would hurt though. Another shout rang out, and it flayed Jack's spirit like the lash of a whip.

Desperate for a distraction, Jack fished out the white plastic bag where he'd stashed the remains of the corset. Carefully he picked up the scrap of shredded leather. In seconds, it changed shape before his eyes. It grew thinner and darker until it turned into to a dark brown belt. He dropped it.

WHEN JACK FOUND THE courage to venture back upstairs, Eira lay under his covers staring up at the ceiling with vacant eyes. He stopped in the doorway. Hot tea sloshed over his hand. She barely acknowledged him.

"Glen told me this will help you sleep and deal with the pain," he said, clumsily walking toward her with his eyes on the cup to be sure he didn't spill any more. Her lips pinched in a tight line of gratitude, but she jerked her chin toward the bedside table.

"Apparently in addition to coming alive and trying to eat people, that corset can also change its shape. I touched it for a second and it turned into a plain, brown belt." She paled. At that point, any reaction was better than her silence. Her fingers curled around the edge of the comforter and she brought it up to her chin.

Jack sighed.

"Eira, I shouldn't have left you by yourself. I knew better, I just..." He stopped talking before he admitted that her flirting with Aiden had turned him into an insecure jerk. She already knew that.

"What if the Sheriff comes here?" Her voice shook a little.

"There's only one of him and seven of us. We can hold him off. My brothers are pretty scary when they get angry." He coaxed a smile out of her, but it didn't last long.

"Why is he doing this?"

He didn't want to scare her, but he wasn't sure Doyle was the only one to blame for the attack. The store had been coated in a layer of ice so thick it could only have been put there by a supernatural force. Still, it didn't seem like Winterthorn's style to use an enchanted object to kill his victim when he could just sic the Hunt on them. Eira watched him, her eyes hot with accusation. Jack pushed his hair out of his eyes.

"There's no way something that powerful has just been lying around Doyle's house."

"Aiden said it belonged to his mother. Do you think she's one of them?"

"No." Not only would Aiden be much more in tune with the magic around him if he was part fae, but Doyle's hatred of them ran too deep to believe he'd ever fall for one. If he'd so much as suspected he'd been tricked into marrying one of them she'd have gone the way of the kelpie, and Jack had overheard Aiden bragging in class that his mother was sending him to Europe for the summer as a graduation present.

"Shouldn't you warn people how dangerous they are?"

"That creates more problems than it solves. People will just tell you you're crazy or worse they'll believe you and start poking around trying to see faeries for themselves."

She made a humming noise, but he could see that her eyelids were growing heavy. He nodded toward the mug in her hands.

"Finish it. You'll feel better after a nap." She drained the cup and handed it back. When their fingers brushed he felt the charge of electricity he was growing accustomed to. It was stronger now, so much that he expected to see an actual spark fly between their skin. Smiling sleepily, she sank back against the pillows and closed her eyes.

He stood for a long time feeling his heart hammering in his chest and blood rushing through his veins. He liked her. It was terrifying the feelings that barreled through him as he admitted it to himself. He wanted to keep her safe, wanted nothing more than to sit beside her and share faery tales while she looked at him like he was her own private knight in shining armor. He stared down at the dregs of her cup. But he wasn't her hero. He was the reason she needed one.

Downstairs, the front door banged open. Keith was home. Judging from the raised voices coming from the kitchen he'd heard about what happened. Eira flinched but didn't open her eyes. Resigned, Jack closed the door behind him and went downstairs. Keith was so angry that the potted lavender above the sink swayed from the rush of magic pushing it to grow an extra two inches.

"I told you she wasn't supposed to leave the house! Does she even know the danger she's put us in? Ross said the Sheriff saw you with her. You're going to pack her up and get her the hell out of here—now!"

Jack's fingers clenched around the mug until he thought it would break.

"She almost died. She's not going anywhere."

"She was attacked by a fae object! I don't care if Doyle's son did give it to her, the fae are involved now."

"The Sheriff's been catching and killing them in his backyard. Don't you think it's possible he's collected some things he'd want to get rid of?" Keith's head reared back and Jack remembered too late they hadn't shared that piece of information with him yet. Several spears of lavender shot up through the soil in the small clay pot. Jack glanced at the waving plants that seemed to be trying to get his attention to tell him to shut up, but he was ready to have this out.

"Why are you so paranoid?"

"Because I don't just think about myself, you little shit!" Keith slammed his fist on the counter. "Are you really that naïve that you think that thing just happened to show up in her shop today after everything else that's been going on? Maybe you're right and he did steal it off one of the fae he's captured, but I'll be damned if he didn't know it was dangerous when he sent it to her."

"He had Aiden deliver it. Do you think he's so hellbent on getting to her that he'd put his own son's life in danger?" They stood toe to toe, glaring. Neither wanted to admit the valid points raised by the other. Keith cracked his neck with a movement like a cobra preparing to strike.

"I want you to ask yourself something, and I want you to think hard about the answer. If Doyle sent that thing to suffocate her then why were the doors and windows frozen shut?"

He didn't wait for an answer. Digging in his pocket for his tin of dip, Keith stomped past Jack and headed up to his room. His work boots left a trail of dried dirt on the otherwise spotless linoleum.

Jack set Eira's mug on the counter and snatched up the black backpack from the front hall. He needed to lose himself for a while, and there was only one way he knew how. Without a backward glance, he pushed through the back door and headed for his father's workshop.

Chapter 11

Jack was just coming back inside with his head still ringing with otherworldly strains when Logan skidded into the entryway. His face was white.

"Is she okay?" He moved toward the stairs before Jack could answer, but stopped with his foot on the bottom step. The calm Jack had found, evaporated.

"She's got a couple of broken ribs, but Glen took care of the bruises and swelling."

"Why didn't anybody call me?"

Jack frowned.

"Why would we?" It never occurred to him to fill Logan in on what had happened. "How did you even find out?"

"I stopped by to see if you guys needed a ride home. The whole place was iced over. So, I went to the diner to ask Glen if he knew what was going on, and Indira told me he'd left early because of some family emergency that no one thought I should know anything about. So, what happened?" The last words were practically a growl.

Putting a finger to his lips to warn Logan not to wake her, Jack ushered him into the music room and told him everything. By the time he was finished Logan was pacing the length of the room with his hands curled into claws.

"He can't get away with this! She could have died!"

"I know, I was there."

Logan rounded on him.

"And you! I can't believe you left her alone with that loser."

"What was I supposed to do? She made it clear that she wanted some privacy." As much as his guilt gnawed at him Jack couldn't help the resentment that reliving her dismissal in front of Aiden conjured up.

"Well you can just sit on your ass if you want, but I'm taking the fight to them." Logan's face flushed with anger. Jack watched him storm up and down with a bland expression.

"And how do you plan to do that?"

"Maybe it's time one of his pets gets loose." From the startled look on his face, Jack knew his brother hadn't thought about it before he'd answered, but after a second Logan's eye lit with a speculative gleam. Jack glanced at the door, half-expecting Keith to burst in and rip them a new one for even thinking about going over to Doyle's house. But Logan's fervor was contagious. Maybe it was time Doyle got a reality check and remembered just how powerful the forces were that he was waging his war against.

"When do you want to go?"

"Tomorrow. When he leaves for work we'll sneak in and poke around in his workshop. If he's got any fae trapped down there we'll see if we can strike a bargain."

Jack knew deep down that what they were doing was stupid, but like Logan, he couldn't just let Doyle get away with a direct assault on Eira. It was bad enough he was rounding up the fae and torturing them with no thought for the consequences that might bring down on the rest of the town. Jack was amazed the fae hadn't moved against him yet. Surely, they were aware of what he was doing.

That night another ice storm ravaged the town. Sheltered from the worst of the wind by the towering trees and steep hills, nevertheless when the Sorleys woke in the morning it was to find the foot of snow on the ground tripled. The road was scattered with broken limbs, and the evergreens sagged beneath swags of ice that dripped like diamonds. He half-expected Logan to call off the plan, but he didn't count on the galvanizing effect Eira would have on him when she fell trying to get out of bed to go to the bathroom.

Jack and Logan, who were eating cereal in the kitchen, stumbled up the stairs one after the other at the sound of her harsh cry. Jack skidded to a halt when he saw her lying on her side, her face twisted in a grimace as she groped for the bed to drag herself up.

"What are you doing?" Logan scolded, swooping down to pull her upright with his hands under her armpits. She hissed and pulled away.

"I don't need your help. I was...I was just...." She clapped a hand to her side and doubled over. She seized a fistful of Logan's shirt to keep from falling. His arms came around her to support her, but the moment she felt his touch she shoved away from him.

"I can take care of myself. I don't need you all to keep babying me!" Still hunched forward, she backed away from Logan toward the door. Quickly, Jack stepped aside to let her pass. When she noticed him there, her blue eyes stabbed into his with fierce defiance, as if she expected him to try and coddle her too. He held up both hands in a gesture of surrender and stepped back. The dark purple shadows made her already large eyes seem enormous in her sunken face. He wanted to wring Doyle's neck for doing that to her.

Staggering, she walked to the bathroom unassisted. Neither brother was brave enough to offer to help when they heard the toilet flush. She yelped and there was a soft thud, but seconds later the door opened, and she walked stubbornly back into the room.

"What? I'm not going anywhere. You can stop watching me like you're expecting me to try and climb out the window." There was a flicker of fragility behind her eyes, no matter how hard she was trying to put up a brave face. Jack couldn't completely blame her. She was scared and it was easy to pin all of her troubles on them.

"Come on, Logan," he mumbled, ducking his head.

ROSS HAD HITCHED HIS plow to his truck and cleared the road by the time Jack and Logan were ready to go. Dressed in thick padded jackets with plump nylon gloves, they slid grim-faced into the Mustang.

"Did you see her?" Logan asked in quiet fury. "She's terrified."

"Are you sure you want to do this? If he's actually got a faery trapped down there there's no guarantee that if we free it it'll be on our side."

"They can't touch us."

Jack watched Logan out of the corner of his eye as they rode cautiously through the wilderness created by unfamiliar formations of ice and snow. He'd never seen Logan so worked up about anything before. Dramatic, Logan was usually all talk. But this was different.

"You really like her, don't you?" Jack said without thinking. Logan flinched.

"What's not to like? She gorgeous. She's brave. She's smart...."

"She's in trouble." Jack suspected that Eira's impossible situation played a big part in his brother's attraction to her. Logan wasn't overly chivalrous, but she was an undeniable damsel in distress, and it had evidently roused Logan's romantic instincts. Jack scuffed his shoe on the floor mat. His calf brushed his black backpack and the harp thrummed faintly.

"Why did you bring that thing?" Logan asked irritably.

"Keith's on the warpath. I don't want to leave this lying around. If he finds it when I'm not around he'll throw it away."

"So?"

"So, after everything that's happened I don't think leaving faery artifacts lying around where just anyone can find them is such a good idea," Jack snapped. That was only part of it though. Now that he'd had time to practice, he'd started to really get the hang of the instrument. The music it pushed into his mind was unlike anything he'd ever conceived. It was wild and unstructured, alien and beautiful.

Logan let it go, but he cast the bag a suspicious glance.

Jack directed Logan to the end of Doyle's long driveway, but instead of turning down the dirt lane, he continued down the road where a cluster of trees hid the car from direct view of the house. Jack leaned over the center console to get a better look at the dark building that stood out in the sea of white.

"Do you think he's home?" It was a stupid question. Half of the windows were lit and smoke curled from a chimney tucked somewhere in the back.

"His kid's there too," Logan said, pointing to where Aiden's red truck could be seen parked beside a detached garage. Jack was quickly losing enthusiasm, but Logan seemed to come alive with each obstacle. He rubbed his hands together.

"So, where's his torture chamber?"

Jack arched an eyebrow at the description, but Logan wasn't paying attention.

"Around back."

"Good. We'll be able to use the cover of the trees. And lucky us, it's snowing again." There were equal parts relief and irritation at the last observation. "Geeze, I've seen enough snow to last me a lifetime."

Jack slid the straps of his backpack over his shoulders while Logan unclasped his seatbelt. Anxiety fluttered in his chest as he surveyed the dark house. Tucked against the trees with the sea of unblemished snow licking against the front steps it looked like an impenetrable fortress.

Even though the house was over an acre away, Jack carefully closed his car door behind him as if he was afraid the sound might alert Doyle to what they were doing. It wasn't until that moment that he realized they were trying to break onto the *sheriff's* property. If they were caught....

The freezing weather sucked what little courage he had out through his nose.

"Logan, this is crazy." But Logan already had one leg swung over the wrought-iron fence.

"You coming or what?"

He dropped with catlike grace onto the balls of his feet on the other side. Reluctantly, Jack tightened the straps of his backpack and moved around the nose of the car. Snowflakes flew in his face like gnats. Wind licked down the back of his neck, and his foot slipped on a patch of ice. He fell against the hood. The harp hummed in gentle reproof.

Before he looked up he knew someone was there who hadn't been there before. A sudden malevolence poisoned the air. When he lifted his head, he saw a cloaked figure standing between him and the fence. It wore a long, black cloak with a deep hood that concealed its face in shadows. Only when the creature reached out to him with a long, blistered hand did Jack realize who it must be.

Another gust of wind blew back the hood to reveal the full horror of what lay underneath. Every inch of his skin was raw, angry, and red. The eyelids were gone along with the lips. Paralyzed by terror, Jack could only stare as the mutilated figure that had once been Odhran, the Faery Harper, stalked toward him.

Without warning, a snowball flew from the other side of the fence to smash against the back of the faery's head. He lurched forward and swung around with a hiss that promised retribution. Seizing his chance, Jack scrambled up and ran for the fence. Odhran lunged for him with preternatural speed.

Jack was in the process of swinging his leg over the fence when the faery grabbed his ankle in a bone-crushing grip.

Flames ignited beneath his skin and his world went white. Forgetting where he was and what he was doing, Jack let go of the iron posts. The faery's scream mingled with his own. The pressure around his ankle vanished, but it still felt as though his foot was roasting over a pit.

A hand clamped over his mouth.

"Shhh! He'll hear you!" Logan knelt beside him, twisted around to look at the Sheriff's house. Blinking, Jack saw that he'd fallen over the fence, and the Harper knelt clutching his arm on the other side.

"You can't hide forever. I will take back what you stole from me!" And in a rush of scorching fumes his form wavered like a mirage before vanishing. Where he'd stood was a melted circle in the snow.

"Okay, I don't know what you did to piss him off, but that guy was seriously creepy. And it looks like things are about to get even better. Get up! Doyle's coming." Fumbling, Logan pulled Jack to his feet. They looked toward the house where a figure stepped out onto the porch. The Mustang was mostly camouflaged against the snow, so they scrambled for the cover of trees. Neither brother wanted to chance the Harper waiting for them on the other side of the iron barrier.

"I don't think he saw us," Logan said after watching Doyle stand on the edge of the porch for a few moments and then go back inside. "He must've heard you screaming your head off. What was that about anyway?"

Jack didn't say anything. He could still feel the ring of fire around his ankle where the burned faery had touched him. The outline of the harp was a comforting weight across his back.

Watching him out of the corner of his eye, Logan led the way around toward the back of the house. The tree line provided cover, but every step made Jack feel as though eyes were boring into him from all directions.

"Huh, that's not what I was expecting." A large silver camper was parked behind the house. At first, they didn't see it because the silver blended so easily into the snow until flash of light glinted off its side.

"There's a window. Do you want me to give you a boost?" Logan offered. Honestly, Jack didn't want to know what was inside that camper. A deep throbbing pain built in his temples, warning him from going any closer. Logan was relentless though.

"I'd look myself, but I know you can't lift me. Come on, don't wuss out on me now." Somewhere along the way he seemed to have forgotten that this trip was supposed to be in retaliation for what Doyle had done to Eira. Now he seemed more concerned with satisfying his curiosity.

Jack allowed himself to be bullied into approaching the whale-shaped drift of snow. A black square stood out like a porthole about five feet above his head. Without checking to see if he was ready, Logan wrapped his arms around Jack's waist and lifted him straight into the air.

"Whoa!" Jack flailed for the window ledge, and as soon as he had a secure grip, Logan let go and ducked down so Jack could rest his feet on his shoulders. Jack grimaced. The pain in his head doubled until his skull felt trapped between heavy metal gears. Trying to ignore the pain, he pressed his nose against the glass and looked in.

At first the interior looked exactly how he expected the inside of an outdated camper to look. There was built-in bench seating around a small rectangular table just below him. A small kitchenette stood on the opposite wall. The thick shag carpet was a deep burnt orange. But the harder he looked the more he saw things that didn't belong. Stains in the carpet looked like muddy footprints at first, but they were haphazardly pooled in wide rust-colored puddles that arced and streaked in haphazard lines. In the corner stood a three-legged stool with a metal triangle where the seat should have been. At the sight of it, a crushing weight pressed against his temples until moisture leaked from his eyes.

"Do you feel that?" He ground his palm against his temple to force back the pain.

"Feel what?" Logan panted trying to hold still. Unease slid down the back of Jack's throat. Why we're his senses screaming and his brother didn't feel a thing? Had his trip to Faerie changed him somehow? Was that why he had a connection to Eira that no one else did?

Thick silver chains looped over the ends of the small breakfast table ending in manacles that hung open like jaws. What he'd first taken for a cabinet leaning in the corner upon closer inspection turned out to be a metal sarcophagus. He had the disturbing sensation he'd seen something like it before, and he knew in his gut that he didn't want to remember where. Mounted on the wall were guns, knives, and hunting equipment he'd bet his guitar weren't intended for tracking down deer.

"Well?" Logan strained to support his weight.

Apart from the silver chains on the table, nearly every metal surface in the camper was iron. Symbols hung on the wall, pentagrams, crosses, and older designs Jack didn't know.

"I'd be happy to give you a tour if you're that curious," said Doyle from the end of the camper. Logan jerked and Jack's face slammed into the window before he fell straight down.

Jack and Logan turned and ran. Doyle called after them. They heard his muttered curse before he gave chase.

Although they ran flat out it was next to impossible to gain any real speed with the snow up to their shins and nothing but slick leaves beneath that.

"Wait! Boys, I just want to talk!"

"Don't stop!" Logan panted.

By that point Jack was so turned around he half-believed they were being pixie-led around the property. Doyle was gaining on them.

The road snaked between the trees just up ahead. Jack slid down the embankment, prepared to take off the moment his feet hit level ground, but he wasn't counting on the patch of ice that sent his legs skidding out from under him. The harp slammed into his back so hard it felt as though it fused to his spine. Logan turned back for him, his face white as he looked up to see Doyle bearing down on them.

"Get up, get up, get up! What the—?"

Before Jack could look, white light exploded around them. It was so intense that even covering his eyes with his hands Jack's retinas burned from the intensity. A sickening perfume of lilacs assaulted his nose until he thought he would be sick.

By slow degrees, his eyes grew accustomed to the figure bright as a fallen star that had landed in the snow between him and Doyle. In the middle of the platinum brilliance was a woman. She towered over them, nearly seven feet tall. He couldn't see if those billowing white arcs fanning up above her were wings or just her billowing sleeves, but it gave him the impression of fragile beauty and strength. Her head turned, and he saw blue eyes and dark lashes amid the blinding light. Her gaze centered on his backpack with a look of possession. Blue flames leapt in her eyes and she raised her arms over her head to summon a spell.

Doyle skidded to a stop and reached into his back pocket to withdraw what looked like a can of pepper spray.

Jack didn't wait to see what would happen next. He scrambled to his feet and took off running up the road. An explosion rocked the ground. There was a yell from Doyle followed by an inhuman scream. Jack kept running. He didn't dare look back. Logan stayed right beside him.

Without warning, the sky unleashed a torrent of driving snow. The wind howled. Jack covered his ears to block the snarls and growls that could only belong to the Wild Hunt. Their ghostly bodies massed together in a whirling cyclone of teeth and fur. It barreled past them, streaming toward the faery woman facing off against Doyle.

"Get in!" Logan yelled, diving into the driver's seat. Jack was already in the passenger side. The snow fell in buckets. Wind pounded the car. Jack expected dents to appear in the metal sides. Each gust jerked them this way and that, caught like a leaf in the current during a raging storm. His knuckles stood out as he clutched his seat for dear life. Logan gunned the engine and took off.

"Slow down!" Jack yelped, when the car lurched again. He couldn't see anything outside the windows but swirling white, certainly not the road.

"The hell was that?" Logan shouted over the piercing wind. There were so many things back there Jack had questions about that he couldn't begin to guess which one his brother was referring to. At that moment, he only cared about getting out of the storm.

They hit the main road and the wind released them. The windshield wipers scraped furiously to clear the white blanket laid down between each sweep. Ignoring the cold, Logan rolled down his window to keep the edge of the road in sight.

"What was that?" He asked again, breathless this time. Jack shook his head, hugging his backpack to his chest. The outline of the gold harp was little comfort to him now.

"So, this stays between us, right?" Logan clarified. "Whatever just happened, Doyle brought it on himself. If anyone asks, we were never here." Jack imagined Keith's face and paled.

"Agreed."

Chapter 12

Jack and Logan tried to forget what they'd seen at Doyle's house, though they both managed to be present for the evening news. They wanted to hear whether the Sheriff had been found dead at his home, but his name wasn't among the list of those trapped or missing. They waited, certain it was only a matter of time before his name cropped up. Then around eight-o-clock Douglas got called into work. Doyle wanted to see him.

Jack debated whether or not to tell Douglas what they'd done, but in the end, he decided it would be easier for him to deny it if he knew nothing about it. He spent the evening picking out lullabies for Eira on the harp. The music put her to sleep quickly, but she tossed and turned and each jerky movement jostled her ribs.

For the next couple of days Douglas came home from work complaining about the close eye Doyle kept on him at the station. But he said nothing to imply that he knew.

Jack's curiosity gnawed at him. How had Doyle escaped the Wild Hunt? It occurred to him that Doyle was playing with him, waiting to see how long it would take before Jack's self-restraint cracked. He wouldn't give in. Not only did Jack not want to give Doyle the satisfaction, but there were other threats waiting for him to step off his land. Odhran's attack was still fresh in his mind, and Jack wasn't eager to see him again.

In the meantime, he filled his days playing nurse to Eira. A steady stream of Glen's herbal tea kept her shielded from the pain in her ribs. She was not the easiest patient. Even Ross wasn't as prickly about letting someone take care of him. But she wasn't sleeping well, and no amount of sugar or honey disguised the tea's flavor enough for her to enjoy it.

"Seriously? Again?" It was late Wednesday evening when Jack knocked on the door.

He tried to smile for her. He was as tired of it as she was. Each time he saw her she looked paler and smaller than the time before. Constant bedrest was only making her more irritable, but Jack took it as his due to bear the brunt of her displeasure.

"You know it'll make you feel better."

"It gives me weird dreams." She wrinkled her nose when he held the drink out to her.

"Glen can give you something for that." He grinned, and she rolled her eyes to stare out the window.

"He has something for everything, doesn't he?"

"Just about."

When she turned back to him, her eyes pleaded for conversation rather than sleep. A bowl of water sat on the bedside table with ash leaves floating across the surface, an old protection charm Keith sent up as a 'get well soon' gift. Jack scooted it aside to set the mug down and made himself comfortable on the floor.

"What do you dream about?"

"I keep imagining there's someone after me." She studied her fingers where they lay on top of his mother's hand-stitched quilt. She rolled her eyes with a faint half-smile. "I guess all this faery stuff has made me paranoid, but every time I close my eyes she's just there. Even after I wake up I can feel her anger reaching for me."

Jack stilled. She?

"What does she look like?" But Eira wasn't listening. She stared at the wall as if a movie played across the faded blue paint only she could see. Her delicate features contracted with horror. She covered her cheeks and dug her nails into the sides of her face. Concerned, Jack caught her nearest hand.

"Eira, stop! What is it?"

The moment their skin touched his body seized up, locking him in place. An explosion went off inside his head, sending his vision dark. He blinked to bring back his sight. It came slowly, but when it did he was no longer looking at the same scene as before. Eira still lay on his bed, but he saw her now through a square plane of glass set in a metal frame. It wasn't a mirror because she was silhouetted against tall, snow-covered, blue pines.

"No!"

The vision was from the perspective of the speaker so he couldn't see her face, but she tried to lift her hand toward the window. Jack saw thick, black metal rings encircling each long, slender finger. The once pale flesh puckered red and shiny where the metal ate through her fae flesh.

"If I must suffer then so shall you! He will pay for his transgression with your blood!"

The connection snapped like a rubber band, flinging Jack out of the vision so abruptly that he nearly fell over. He steadied himself on the edge of the bed, but the bounce jostled Eira, who moaned.

Instinct told him to put distance between them, but she reached for his hand before he could pull away.

"You saw it, didn't you?"

Shivers coursed through her. His heart beat at a double speed, but he drew in a deep breath and nodded.

"Have you always been able to do that?" he asked. "Share your dreams with people?"

"I don't know." Her hand clutched his so tightly that her knuckles stood out like knots in a strip of bleached driftwood. It was on the tip of his tongue to ask if she knew he felt her emotions, but her wild-eyes warned him now wasn't the time.

"It's okay," he said, bringing his free hand up to cover hers. By slow degrees she relaxed. "I know what will keep the bad dreams away." Before she could ask, he left the room. The faery woman's hatred sizzled in his veins, choking him with its venom. What was her connection to Eira?

"How is she?" Glen asked as Jack strode through the kitchen and pulled his jacket down from its peg. Jack didn't answer. He went outside and climbed the apple tree that grew a few feet from the back deck. Bare hands burning with cold, he hauled himself into the forked branches and shimmied higher and higher until he reached a green cluster of mistletoe. He broke off a small sprig. He held it up, studying it. Mistletoe had started this whole mess. Perhaps it would do something useful for a change. Glancing down to judge the distance to the ground, he dropped.

"Mistletoe?" Eira wrinkled her nose when he presented it to her. Ignoring her skepticism, Jack reached into his desk drawer and found a long red ribbon to tie around the end so he could secure it over the bed.

"Does this mean you're going to kiss me?"

His hands slipped. His eyes jumped to her face. She was smiling slyly. Heat climbed up the back of his neck and burned in his cheeks.

"It wards off bad dreams," he said into the awkward silence. She reached over to pick up the now lukewarm tea.

"Sounds like one of Grandma's old wives' tales to me. Are you sure it'll work?"

"Positive. Mistletoe is powerful stuff." His mouth twisted with wry self-depreciation. "Still, let me know if it happens again." He didn't want to tell her that the things she'd been seeing weren't dreams. The attack in her shop had forced her to accept their help and guidance as far as the fae were concerned—that didn't mean she was happy about it. She took a deep sip of tea and grimaced.

"If you could go back to not knowing about any of this would you do it?" She swished the mug, watching the dregs swirl.

"No," he said without hesitation. "Knowing is what has kept us alive."

WHATEVER MAGIC ENABLED him to share Eira's dream lingered with him long after he left her side. That night he had another nightmare—this one more vivid than the last. In a chamber deep underground Odhran, burned and twisted, bent over a flat surface projecting from the wall. Jack couldn't see what the Harper was doing, only the red and angry flesh that covered his bare back. Firelight glistened on some of the deeper burns that still oozed clear pus.

Odhran twisted to reveal another golden harp, but it was nothing like the stunning instrument Jack now possessed. This one was smaller, less ornate. Odhran's blistered fingers plucked at the strings, but instead of haunting beauty it sounded like a cat having its claws torn out.

With a roar of rage Odhran lifted the harp over his head and smashed it on the granite floor. He breathed so deeply that his flayed skin cracked and bled.

"He has no right! You chose me!"

Jack couldn't tell who he spoke to, but Odhran cocked his head as though a voice answered him. His body tensed. With a hiss, he covered his lidless eyes with both hands.

"No! I will not believe it! I will find you, and I will use his guts for your strings!"

Hot on the words Jack was assailed by the gruesome sensation of long fingers curling around his organs. Magic gripped his intestines as if squeezing sausage from its casing. Pain exploded deep in his belly. Jack woke with a cry and fell face-first off the futon. He clutched his stomach to hold in the guts the phantom harper was determined to tear out.

The basement door creaked open.

"Everything okay down there?" Craig sounded like he was trying not to laugh.

"Fine." Jack checked the time on his phone and saw that it was six-thirty. With the door open he could smell the tart scent of blueberry muffins. Saliva filled his mouth, but a hollow pit opened in his belly. Every Thanksgiving for as far back as he could remember he'd woken to his mother's blueberry muffins. Glen's would taste better, but it wouldn't be the same.

Thanksgiving was a big deal for the Sorleys. Keith and Craig went into the woods to gather firewood and swags of evergreens to hang over the doorways. It made the house smell like sap and smoky pine. Douglas went from room to room setting homemade candles in the windows. They put Ross to work prying open chestnut burrs to roast later for a snack.

In the kitchen Glen manhandled a twenty-six-pound turkey into a sagging roasting pan. There was something mesmerizing about the thick butter squishing between his fingers as he massaged it into the pale skin. Though he moved around the kitchen with confidence, his frantic energy betrayed his anxiety. This was the first time he'd prepared the meal without their mother. It was obvious that he meant to keep her memory alive by recreating her menu down to the last pinch of salt. With eight people to feed, Glen recruited every spare hand he could find. Even Eira, supported down the stairs between Logan and Jack, was put to work peeling potatoes.

The four oldest brothers took over the living room to watch the football game. Between them they made enough noise for an entire stadium. Jack hovered in the kitchen to devour any scraps Glen left in his wake. Eira watched quietly, drinking in their family with the longing of someone who'd never had one.

"Careful little brother. I think you're drooling," whispered Logan, coming up behind Jack with a stack of their mother's linen napkins.

By the time dinner was served the table groaned under the weight of the turkey, stuffing, casseroles, potatoes, corn, cranberries, and fresh bread. Eira sat next to Jack dressed in one of his mother's sweaters that Douglas had dug out of a box in the attic. When she took his hand during the prayer, the now-familiar current passed between them. Their eyes met, and Eira looked away first.

"May I say something?" she asked swiftly before they tore into the meal. All eyes fixed on her, and she flushed.

"I know I haven't been particularly grateful for what you've done for me. It's all been a lot to take in, and even when I had proof I didn't want to believe any of this was real." She laid her hand against the wrappings hidden beneath her sweater with a faint frown. "But thank you. For...everything. I don't think I could have made it through the past few weeks if you guys hadn't taken me in." She spoke with her eyes on her plate. Her cheeks glowed rose gold from the light of the candlesticks.

"It's our pleasure." Logan speared a marshmallow-slathered yam on the end of his fork. "I'm just glad I'm not the only face worth looking at around here anymore." And with the inevitable groans and rolled eyes, the serious atmosphere broke open. They dove into the sea of food, every man for himself. Beneath the table, Jack took Eira's hand. Her fingers curled against his and the glance she flashed his way sent heat lightning arcing through him.

They ate and laughed, and for a moment it was easy to forget that a deranged faery wanted his harp back, a mysterious fae lady wanted Eira dead, and Winterthorn circled them all biding his time to strike.

After dinner, while Craig and Ross stood shoulder to shoulder at the sink washing dishes, Glen unveiled two pies left to warm in the oven. Logan moaned as the smell of spiced pumpkin and flaky crust filled the kitchen, banishing the turkey grease smell permeating the house.

"I don't think I could eat another bite," Eira laughed, reaching for a crystal plate.

"Jack, grab your guitar," said Keith. His weathered face was creased with pleasure as he took the first thick slab of pumpkin pie. Feeling as though his skin was stretched thin across his swollen belly, Jack was more than happy to put off dessert until later.

The family shifted from the kitchen into the music room where Jack kept his guitar collection. However, when Jack joined them he carried the harp in his hands. Keith eyed the instrument with distaste. Craig flopped onto the couch against the far wall and tilted his head back on the soft cushion with a groan of contentment. Douglas took a seat in the corner, while Ross, Glen, and Logan lounged on the floor. Jack took a seat at the foot of the wicker rocking chair in which Eira sat.

"Any requests?"

"Play Greensleeves," said Eira. "Your version is so pretty." His brothers groaned, but Jack ignored them. The haunting holiday melody felt perfect. He nestled the harp against his chest and began to play. There, surrounded by his family, the song took on a life of its own, becoming more than the familiar tune. Jack let the variations play out as they came to him, and soon it was a different song altogether. His eyes slid shut as magic moved through him, igniting the strings so that they blazed with power. Invisible fingers guided his hands. A honeyed voice whispered the right notes in his ears.

Power seized his wrists and forced him to keep going. Jack's eyes flew open. His family sat frozen, their eyes vacant and mouths slack. Magic invaded the room like carbon monoxide, poisoning them before they even realized it was happening.

With a start, Jack flung the harp to the ground. His fingers curled as if they didn't want to let go.

"I think I'll turn in," he said, shooting to his feet. Craig jerked upright, looking around disoriented. Eira yawned so deeply that she winced. Douglas' half-lidded gaze swept the room for the dregs of his dream. Suspicion hardened Keith's features, and he narrowed his eyes at Jack.

"Aren't you forgetting something?"

Jack turned back to where the harp lay on the ground. The thought of touching it turned the feast in his stomach to glue. But Keith was watching him, and the last thing Jack wanted to do was provoke another argument when everyone was happy and full.

The gold was warm to the touch. Tucking it into the crook of his arm Jack knew he carried a living thing. Power radiated from it, taunting him. *Your talent called to me. We are perfect for each other.*

Jack dropped the harp down the basement stairs. It bounced from one step to the next with delicate bell-like tones like laughter. He watched it tumble into the darkness and wished he could slam the door and bury it beneath the house where no one would find it again.

It is too late for that, Jack Sorley. You are mine.

Overhead steps creaked as his family went to bed. If he acted now they would never find out just how stupid he had been. Breathing hard, he resolved to give the harp back to the fae. He didn't want to, and that told him more than anything else how dire his situation had grown. With heavy steps he went down to retrieve the object of power he'd so foolishly believed he could wield with no consequences.

He waited until after ten to be sure everyone was asleep. All the while anxiety twisted him up in knots. The need to do something, to take back his freedom sent him pacing the room. Alone in the mildew-scented basement with the enchanted harp made him more aware of how vulnerable he was to its lure. Already his mind tuned to the melodies he knew those gold strings could play. Shuddering, he snatched up the pillar before he could change his mind.

He snuck up to the closet in the entryway and fished around for his coat. No matter how he groped he couldn't find it without turning on a light. He settled for Logan's instead. A floorboard creaked as he crept through the kitchen to the back door. The sucking sound of insulation prying loose from the frame made him cringe and hold his breath to listen for movement upstairs.

He didn't plan to go far, just to the river. Like Excalibur, the harp could go back through the water to where it belonged.

A wolf howled in the distance.

Jack's heart stopped. There was only one reason why the Hunt would come this close to the house. He ran around to the front of the house. As soon as he changed course the light breeze blew stronger, pushing against him as if trying to hold him back.

Tucking the harp under his arm, Jack broke into a jog. He felt it then, the thread thin as spider silk that tied his emotions to Eira's. Her fear triggered a vibration that fanned his unease into a panic. A path of footprints descended the front steps and cut a straight line up the road. What was she doing? He dropped the harp and ran for all he was worth.

"Eira!"

His shout shattered the blue glass night like a rock.

He found her by the overhang on the edge of their land. She was wearing his jacket. His breath whooshed out of him in disbelief.

The red wolf stood before her, separated by a mere three feet. Jack skidded to a halt and looked around for a weapon. When it saw him, the wolf's teeth snapped and it leapt between him and Eira.

"Jack, no!" Eira cried. His head came up furious to demand what she thought she was doing, when a figure behind her shriveled the words on his tongue.

It was no wonder he hadn't seen him at first. His silver coat blended too perfectly with the snow. The enormous crown of antlers encased in hoarfrost looked like the limbs of a small tree.

Suddenly the wolf was the least of his worries. Jack lunged for Eira to drag her behind him. The wolf snarled and snapped, but couldn't touch him. The stag reared and pawed the air with his massive hooves. Fear was a web of thorns caught in his throat, but Jack wouldn't back down. They were still on Sorley land and Winterthorn couldn't hurt them.

She's one of us now. He sent the message with his eyes. *You can't have her.*

The stag snorted, pacing this way and that like a caged predator behind the plexiglass at a zoo. His corded muscles bunched, but instead of leaping at them, he took one last look at Eira hunkering behind Jack and bounded away into the night. The wolf whimpered. Its tail drooped before it slunk away too.

"What were you thinking?" Jacks rounded on Eira and grabbed her by the shoulders. She shoved him away.

"Your stupid mistletoe didn't work! I thought I was going crazy with all those voices in my head. I figured I'd just get it over with and see what they wanted. I'm not like you guys. I can't hide out here in the woods for the rest of my life hoping one day it'll all go away."

"'You thought you'd see what they wanted'?" The words made as much sense to him as if she'd spoken in faery tongues. "You mean the faeries that've been trying to kill you?" She flinched, but her mouth thinned into a stubborn line.

"I know what happened with the faery your father saved. Her name was Credeilia and she—" She spit the name out so fast Jack didn't have time to ram his fingers into his ears to block it out. Was she insane? There was nothing the fae guarded more carefully than their names. To hand it over so easily meant the fae didn't expect Eira would live long enough to use it.

Jack was so angry he was shaking—or was it fear that had him in its teeth? The line between their emotions was blurring, and that didn't make him feel any better.

Turning his back on her, he stalked off for the house. Eira trudged after him, hugging his coat around her. Eventually they reached the harp glittering in the snow. Her eyebrows rose, understanding the fear that had driven him to drop it so carelessly. Jack snatched it from the ground and stomped back into the house. He'd have to wait for another moment to give it back. Eira's look told him she saw what it meant to him. He didn't want to explain why he had to throw it away. Besides, she'd ruined his plans bringing the Wild Hunt to their door.

Chapter 13

Winterthorn's attack gave new meaning to the phrase, 'Black Friday.' Although initially he'd had every intention of telling the others that the Wild Huntsman had come to the fringes of their land, Jack couldn't bring himself to put Eira in Keith's crosshairs again. However, he didn't count on Ross overhearing the Red Wolf's cry and going to the window to see their tracks in the snow. Keith nearly burst an artery blasting them with 'what ifs.'

They only gained a reprieve when Ross unwisely suggested using his gift to communicate with the Red Wolf to find out what it wanted. The clay pot of lavender exploded, overflowing with flowers. Judging by the pulsing vein down its center, Keith's head wasn't far behind.

"It's like he hopes something bad will happen just so he can say 'I told you so.'" Jack muttered as he and Eira slunk out of the kitchen.

"He cares about you," she said, tight-lipped and austere. "They did think you were dead for two weeks." The reminder loosened the knot in Jack's anger, but it didn't stop him from getting annoyed at the watch they put him under. Every time he so much as looked at the door one of his brothers would appear to ask where he was going. Somehow, by covering for Eira he'd given them the impression that he was the one luring the Hunt.

If he felt stifled it was nothing compared to the treatment they gave Eira. Although by Monday she said her ribs felt fine, Keith flat out told her at breakfast that morning that she couldn't go back to work if she wanted to keep staying with them. When she argued that she couldn't afford to lose the money, Craig promised to provide her with enough silver to keep her out of debt. She relented, but wasn't happy being dictated to.

"After what happened last time you must be crazy." Ross folded his arms over his green camo jacket. "Why don't I just drop you off at the Sheriff's house and save you both a lot of time playing cat and mouse?" Jack's eyes jumped to Logan, who took particular interest in coaxing his hair into his eyes.

Glen cleared his throat and gave a warning shake of his head. Ross flipped the brim of his hunting cap backwards.

"What? What's going to stop the Sheriff from walking right up to her register and arresting her for whatever he damn well pleases? You think anyone would take her side over his?"

Doyle had made the evening news the night before talking about the efforts the police and rescue teams were making to keep people safe from the abnormally harsh weather. With his silver-streaked hair and navy collared shirt, his charm reached through the television screen, twining viewers around its finger.

"I should talk to him," said Logan unexpectedly. Everyone turned to look at him. "I'm the only one who can get him to talk about what he's really up to. This weather is just the beginning. If he's seriously trying to start a war, things are going to get a lot worse before they get better."

As much as he wanted to, even Keith couldn't shoot his idea down outright. Jack stirred his cereal, thinking hard. How could Logan want to go back to the Sheriff's house after what happened the last time?

"Do you think he'd talk to you?" Ross cocked his head. Logan leaned his hip against the counter with a shrug.

"He'd be tempted. He obviously wants to know more about our family."

"Are you sure you want to do this? You can smell the magic rolling off that guy," said Craig. He dumped his dishes in the sink while Logan raked his fingers through his hair.

"Come on, guys. Do you really think he's a match for me?" Logan pointed at himself with a crooked grin. No one could think of anything to say.

JACK DREAMED AGAIN that night, but it wasn't about lidless-eyed burn victims or beautiful faery maidens. This time he stalked through the forest, moving surer and faster than he normally could. He leapt into the air and circled the treetops like a breeze. Only when he touched down again did he glimpse his large front paws.

He was alone, which was odd because he was never without the rest of the pack. A soft whine issued from his throat before he circled back. He recognized the fork in the river. The smaller stream cutting off to the left marked the boundary he could not cross. He stepped into the water. The liquid ice didn't faze him, though he registered its chill. He waded along the stream's course until human scents invaded the night. Baked apples, boiled potatoes, warm bread, and beef.

The wolf paused and looked up the steep hill where a gabled roof could be seen. He tried to step onto the bank, but the invisible barrier held him back. Anxious now, he lapped at the stream with a few dips of his tongue and tried again. He needed to reach the other side. His life and his future were at the top of that hill. He panted so hard that his sides heaved and his long, pink tongue lolled.

Enemy. Danger. Hunt. Retrieve.

The wolf didn't think in words but impressions. It read the night's sheet music and followed its cues, noting each shifting leaf and the nocturnal counter melodies of predators and prey.

Pack. Hunt. Danger.

Agitated, the wolf paced back and forth in the frigid water so close to the barrier the fur along its ribs brushed it with each pass. Then, in a fit of frustration, it threw back its head and howled to the stars.

The cry jolted Jack awake. Cold sweat stood out on his forehead. He wiped it away as if he could banish the echo of the howl, but though the dream was over the call went on. She had come for him. In the dream, he'd shared her determination to claim and retrieve. He was almost relieved that it had come to this.

Picking his way through the darkness he picked up the harp and climbed the stairs into the living room. He froze when he saw a figure standing at the back door.

She was mostly turned away, but he saw her reflection in the glass as she stared out at the yard. A bone-deep yearning drew salty tracks down her cheeks. One hand rested on the door handle, but for the moment she didn't move.

"Eira?" he said softly, climbing the steps to join her. She jumped and snatched her hand away from the door. Quickly she brushed at her eyes.

"You heard her too. She's so lonely. I have to go out there."

Jack didn't particularly care if the wolf was lonely. From the snatches of its mind that he'd seen in his dream she was nothing more than a hunter being denied its prey. Eira swung from the storm door and closed the distance between them in three quick steps. Her arms wound around his waist, and he set the harp on the counter where it would be out of the way. She pressed her forehead against the hollow of his neck.

"I can't shut her out," she whispered. "Every time I try she keeps coming back. What am I supposed to do?"

"I don't know," he murmured against her ear. Standing there with his arms wrapped around her and the smell of her hair in his nose suddenly felt more dangerous than opening the back door and welcoming the Wild Hunt into the house. His heart raced, but a strange calm stole into his mind.

Eira shuddered and stepped back.

"Sorry." She thumbed away another tear. Jack wanted to drag her back, but he dropped his hands.

"Tomorrow we'll see if Logan can't get some information out of Doyle. If anyone knows what's going on it'll be him."

"I don't see why we don't just kidnap him," she muttered. For a moment, Jack entertained the idea. Douglas could easily sneak in, and if Craig helped him they'd have no problem overpowering Doyle long enough to get him into a car. Jack sighed.

"I know what you mean." He moved to the fridge and poured himself a glass of milk while she went back to stare out at the yard. Starlight reflected off the snow, illuminating her face with an ethereal glow. His tongue swelled with words he wasn't brave enough to say. Words weren't his strong suit. But music.... She was music personified, dark keys and light, flighty as a piccolo but with a cello's deep strength. In his mind, where she couldn't see, he wrote her in notes. The tempestuous grace of it made his chest ache. Without thinking, he reached for the harp.

Play me.

The silent command was a splash of ice water. It startled him so badly that he spilled milk down his chest.

"New at that?" Eira threw a smirk over her shoulder as he hastily wiped up the mess with a dishrag. His eyes darted to the doorways in a vain hope the voice he'd heard belonged to one of his brothers, but no one was there. Dancing fingers tickled his mind, letting him feel the brush of retracted claws.

"Don't do anything you'll regret," he said quietly before heading back down to the basement with the harp tucked securely under his arm. The glint of gold guided his steps through the dark. He meant the words as much for himself as for her.

LOGAN RODE TO WORK with Douglas the next day. An air of purpose hung around him as he downed the milk from his cereal and followed Douglas out the door. Jack and Eira watched through his bedroom window as the Cruiser backed up and pulled away.

"Maybe I should talk to Aiden," Eira suggested. Jack's gut clenched, but he hid the reaction from her. "I'm sure he knows something about what's going on, and he knows me. He might even like me. Maybe he'll tell me what his dad's up to." He *might* like her? Of course Aiden liked her! He had all the symptoms of a guy under a faery's thrall.

"He doesn't know anything," he said a little too quickly.

"How do you know?"

"Because Aiden doesn't know what you are. And if he doesn't know that then he doesn't know why his dad would be after you, which makes him pretty much useless to us." Jack dismissed him, but she frowned.

"He's not useless. What if we could get him to come to our side? You could give him Faery Sight the same way you gave it to me, and then he could spy for us."

"You think if he had a choice he'd pick us over his dad?" Her, maybe, but definitely not Jack and his brothers. She lifted her eyebrow in a way that spelled trouble. Jack withdrew from the window and went to examine his collection of guitars hanging on the wall.

"You're awfully quickly judge him," she said, her tone changing. He shrugged.

"If his own father's keeping him in the dark I don't see why we should enlighten him." He backed out of the room before she could argue. Deep down he knew he was being harsh, but she definitely gave Aiden more credit than he deserved. For reasons of his own, Doyle was hiding his crusade from his son. That meant that whenever the truth came to light Aiden was going to be blindsided, but that wasn't Jack's problem.

His fingers flexed, needing an instrument to release his pent-up anxiety. Almost without conscious thought his feet guided him down to the basement where he pulled out the harp. Warmth radiated from its metal surface. His mind registered the strangeness, but his fingers reached for the strings. Music spilled out. His hands took on a life of their own, taking the song he had written for Eira and changing it into something dark and haunting. Frowning at the turn it had taken, he shook his head and stopped—except his fingers didn't stop.

Isn't it beautiful? You were born for this music. No one in a thousand years has the skill you possess.

Suddenly he was the instrument and the harp was playing him! Jack tried to tear his hands away. His hands held on, playing music so beautiful blood trickled from his ears.

Don't fight it. This is what she promised you. Music. Music such as the world has never known.

"Let me go!" he hissed between his teeth.

Abruptly, the harp flew out of his hands to land a few feet away with a heavy clang. Jack stood panting. Sweat plastered his shirt to his back. His body shook. He stared at where it lay innocuously on the ground.

"Forget that!"

Looking around, he yanked the pillowcase off the nearest pillow to use as a buffer between the metal and his skin. He scooped it up and tied off a thick knot. A noise like angry cicadas rattled in his mind. The harp wasn't happy. Good. Neither was he.

He took the stairs two at a time, holding the pillowcase before him as if it would explode. Miraculously, no one was in the living room or kitchen when he burst out of the basement. He paused just long enough to grab his jacket and boots from the front closet before storming into the frosty morning.

You think you can escape so easily? The silky voice poured into his mind like oil. Jack dropped the pillowcase.

"I'm going to dump you into the deepest pit I can find." Conviction lent his voice strength that fear threatened to take back. It gave a coy, flirtatious laugh, like a girl playing hard to get with a man she'd already chosen to take back to her room. He shook his head, trying to get its intrusion out of his brain. Tugging down his sleeves so that the cuffs covered his hands for added insulation, he picked up the pillowcase again and ran for the bottom of the hill.

With every step the harp whispered in his mind, teasing him, taunting him, telling him they were destined to be together forever. Jack wanted to hurl.

At the top of the hill he slipped on a sheet of ice and rolled his ankle. The thick padding in his jacket made it hard to keep from sliding, and with his hands caught in his sleeves he couldn't catch hold of a root or stump to stop his descent. He swallowed a mouthful of dirt, snow, and gravel as he skidded head-first on his belly. The salted road at the bottom stopped him like a brick wall. The breath exploded out of him, and soft laughter rang in his ear.

Scrambling to all fours, Jack swung the pillowcase around his head like a lasso and let it sail. It soared up, bounced off a tree, and landed pathetically not ten feet from where he stood. Officially it was off Sorley land, and that was all that mattered to Jack. He hoped the wolves dragged it away to their den. Maybe the red wolf would finally leave Eira alone. Was it using her to get to him?

He rubbed his hands against his jeans to remove the magical residue lingering on his skin. He turned to go. One step. Two. A sinking sensation settled in the pit of his stomach. Three steps. He couldn't do it. In his mind, he saw it lying golden and beautiful inside the dirty pillowcase, and he simply couldn't walk away.

I told you....

Against his will, Jack turned his head. Sunlight glittered on gold peeking through a tear in the pillowcase. His body turned. One foot stepped in front of the other. Each step carried him further from home and the protection of his family. At the edge of his property he dug in his heels, but it was like playing tug of war with a train. His muscles strained against the inevitable as it pulled him over the line.

He stood over the harp. Longing and loathing flapped around him with leathery wings.

You belong to me. I chose you. Now you are mine forever.

Jack fell on it like a wild animal. He shredded the thin pillowcase and tore at the strings until music erupted into the air. It burst up and out of him like a beacon, signaling to all who heard that he was claimed. He screwed his eyes shut against the harp forcing its way into his mind. But it was already there. With gleeful delight it used him, contorting his hands into painful positions, stretching his fingers to reach chords they weren't designed to play. The webbing between his thumb and forefinger tore. Jack sank his teeth into his bottom lip and bled.

The music was around him, inside me—it was him. It pounded him mercilessly, relishing his attempts to resist. He played until his fingertips bled. He played until fire ignited in his joints so that he thought he would go up in flames if the harp didn't release him. He played until the light gray sky darkened to indigo blue. The temperature plunged below zero, and still he played. Headlights washed over and past him as his brothers came home from their jobs. They didn't see him. He was too far from the road. His voice was encased in a thick block of ice. Despite every shout he willed to escape, his lips remained silent.

Inside he was screaming.

"I can't..." he panted, though whether he spoke aloud or merely thought the words he didn't know. The harp was merciless.

You must be conditioned.

His knees gave out and he sprawled on his back. Even then, he tucked the harp safe against his chest. Blood splattered the white snow. It formed an intricate pattern of speckles and streaks.

And when he thought it couldn't get any worse, a shadow of malevolence peered out from the trees. Jack sensed him and knew Odhran had come to reclaim what he'd lost. 'Take it!' he wanted to yell, but the harp held him silent. Lidless eyes watched him suffer, and in the distance, Jack heard a low, mocking laugh.

IT WAS NEARLY EIGHT by the time Ross, Craig, and Douglas found him. His hands glowed red with frostbite. Blood seeped from his lips chafed by the wind. Ice crystals had formed from the moisture trickling from his eyes and crusted his lashes together.

"Jesus, Jack!" Craig lunged forward, but Ross and Douglas caught his arms and held him to Sorley land. Jack flinched and tried to shake his head. Sensing their intent to take Jack away, the harp changed the melody. It wove a hypnotic net and flung it at them like a shining web. They covered their ears, but Ross swayed as though he'd been hit in the face. Craig ground his teeth and glared at the harp as if he was going to smash it with his bare hands. *Do it.* Jack sent the wordless plea with a weak nod.

Craig dove at him. His hand reached for the metal pillar.

A feral noise rippled from Jack's throat. Craig recoiled, his mouth agape. Then with a scowl of determination, he snatched the harp and ripped it away. Jack moaned as layers of his skin went with it.

Craig's head flung back with a roar of pain. The smell of burning flesh invaded the glen. He flung it down and lifted his boot to stomp it. Jack's throat clogged. *Do it!*

"Stop!" The cry came from his mouth, but it was as if someone else spoke. He certainly didn't want Craig to stop. He wanted the harp gone.

His bloody hands reached out for it, and Ross and Douglas grabbed his arms to hold him back. Craig raised his foot again, but froze when Jack let out an inhuman scream. He fought his brothers' grasp. They struggled to hold him as he twisted and kicked to get free.

Craig looked to the others for an answer. Exchanging a grim look, they hung their heads and let Jack go. He scrambled on all fours to snatch the harp from under Craig's boot and hug it to his chest. His mind recoiled even as his body wrapped around it.

"What have you done?" Ross murmured. His face was gray.

"You need to get rid of it," said Douglas. Jack nodded even as he cradled the harp like a child.

Chapter 14

Keith was repotting the lavender when they helped Jack inside. The new pot fell out of his hand when he caught sight of Jack. Black soil and clay shards showered the floor. He took one look at Jack's bloody fingertips clutched around the harp and knew exactly what had happened.

"You were right," choked Jack. "I didn't see what it was doing until it was too late."

"And what did it do?" Keith held up his hands as if he suspected the harp would latch onto them from across the room. Jack hung his head.

"I tried to get rid of it, but...it took control."

"It took control?" Keith took another step back.

"I couldn't stop...." Jack raised his bleeding fingers.

"Explain later," said Ross unexpectedly. He shoved Jack in the small of his back. "If you don't thaw those fingers you'll lose them." They ushered him upstairs to the bathroom. Craig grabbed a set of oven mitts and gingerly took the harp and set it in the sink where Jack could still see it. As soon as it left contact with his skin, Jack felt the shackles inside him draw taught.

They stripped him down to his boxers while Keith drew a bath. Ross ran downstairs to heat some hot chocolate. The smell floated up the stairs. Jack's stomach rumbled, but he thought he was going to be sick. He had been marked by faery magic. Their family's protection hadn't saved him.

"Drink," Craig ordered, when Ross returned with the steaming mug. They set Jack in the tub. Though the water was lukewarm it felt like they doused him in flames.

"Look at his hands. Someone feed him," snapped Ross. He rubbed his hands against his leg. "Sorry it's not as good as when Glen makes it. He's working the dinner shift tonight."

"What's going on?" Eira asked from the doorway. Jack hunkered down in the bath, sloshing chocolate into the water. She gasped when saw him shivering in the tub. His brothers crowded the tub so she couldn't get close. She stood on tiptoe for a better look.

"Jack! What did you do?"

"He did what he always does," Keith bit out between clenched teeth. "He ignored me when I warned him to get rid of that damned harp. Now it's sunk its teeth in him and there's nothing we can do about it."

Jack shook his head.

"I can fix this," he mumbled to his chest. The words were barely understandable through his chattering teeth.

"How?" asked Ross with a sneer.

"I'll take it back."

They others exchanged incredulous looks, all except Eira, whose large eyes fixed on his face with something close to hope. Keith exploded.

"Like hell am I letting you waltz off to Faerie so you can hand that stupid thing off to whatever godforsaken demon you think is going to take it back!"

"It could be the only way," said Eira. Jack looked around, surprised. She smiled with solemn understanding. "If it's powerful enough to make him do that to himself then it can't stay in our world where someone else might get their hands on it."

"This is insane." Keith threw his hands in the air and swung to pace but there was no space in the crowded bathroom. Eira leaned against the doorframe. Conviction shadowed her face like a bruise.

"I want to go with you."

Denial ruptured the tenuous hold Jack had on his self-control.

"No! No one's coming with me. I got myself into this mess. I'm not risking you or anyone else to get out of it."

"Oh, get over yourself. I'm a changeling, remember? If that's true then it's past time I went back."

"Speaking of which," said Ross his eyes slits of suspicion, "how is it you've stayed hidden so long? If the Sheriff's been looking for faeries he should have stumbled across you long before now." Blue flames leapt in her eyes.

"How should I know? My life was normal until Grandma died. Since August my world's been coming apart at the seams, no thanks to you guys." She tossed back her hair and charged toward him where he was sandwiched between the tub and the toilet with her finger raised. "And you know what? I'm tired of you acting like any of this is my fault. I didn't ask to be brought into your precious ring of magic secrets, but you all dragged me out here and force-fed me a four-leaf clover without even giving me a choice! So, you can take your paranoia and shove it out your—" She broke off when she saw understanding dart between them.

"What?" she snapped. Ross, with his hands up to protect his face, edged around her and slunk to the door. Douglas stepped between them.

"She was hiding you. Your grandmother knew what you were." He tilted his head to one side with a frown. "But why would she hide you if it meant her real granddaughter stayed trapped in Faerie? I think we need to drive over to your house. Maybe we'll find some answers."

"But I thought it was too dangerous for me to leave," she said in a mocking voice. Keith whipped around so fast he made her flinch.

"You think this is funny? Do you see what they did to Jack? We're vulnerable any time we step outside this house, and you want to complain because we asked you to stay where it's safe?" The color drained from her face. Chastened, she folded her lips and looked at the floor.

"I didn't mean—"

"There's no point arguing," said Jack with a grimace as he flexed feeling back into his fingers. "The fae and Doyle know she's here. The only way any of us can be safe is to figure out what it'll take to make them go away. Turning on her won't change what's happening to me."

"Right, because you're the expert on staying out of danger," said Ross from the safety of the hallway "Tell me, how're those fingers feeling?"

"It makes no sense that the fae would leave a changeling behind and then wait almost twenty years to try and kill her. Clearly, we're missing something. If we can convince Doyle that she's not what he thinks she is then at least that gets him off our backs, but the only place we're going to find any answers is at her house."

Jack's eyes jumped to the harp leaning against the rim of the sink. Would it let him go now that it had him under its spell?

Go, it whispered. *We can play later.*

THE LITTLE HOUSE WAS shabbier than Jack remembered. The aluminum siding had dents in places, and icicles the size of swords hung from the gutters. A foot and a half of snow slathered the steep-pitched roof like coconut cream. As he unbuckled his seatbelt with his taped-up fingers, Jack scanned the front step for signs of the red wolf.

Keith brushed a layer of snow from the shrubs that grew on either side of the stoop.

"Rosemary," he murmured. After doing the same to several more plants in the front garden he discovered primroses, marigolds, and St. John's Wort, all known for their ability to repel the fae.

"What used to hang there?" asked Douglas, pointing to a wrought iron hook above the door. Eira's mouth formed a small 'o' before the corners turned down.

"She and I used to hang holly wreaths this time of year. We collected them ourselves. She made such a big deal about it." Keith and Douglas exchanged a knowing look. At least one part of the mystery had been solved. Her grandmother knew the old lore.

"She was a hearthwitch." Keith wound his scarf around his neck up to his ears.

"A what? Grandma? No way! You didn't know her. She was the most no-nonsense person you've ever met. There's no way she'd have bought into any of this faery stuff."

"Then how do you explain this garden? Whoever planted it knew what to put in to keep fae away."

"First off, according to you I'm a faerie and I lived here quite comfortably for eighteen years." She ticked off on her fingers. "Secondly, she hired a gardener to take care of the yard." Keith frowned, clearly about to ask for the name of her gardener when Ross knocked past him to get to the door. The snow was piled nearly up to his knees. He waited for Eira to unlock the door, but she reached around him and gave it a light tug. It screeched open displacing snow. His brows snapped together in disbelief, but she put her hands on her hips and met his stare.

"How was I supposed to know I wouldn't be back for over a month?"

Deciding to end the argument before it began, Jack ushered everyone into the house. It smelled of dust and medicine buried beneath a pungent layer of vanilla scented candles. Brown shag carpet stretched across the floor, coordinated with the olive and orange-colored wallpaper patterned with watering cans and ivy leaves.

Ross stomped into the bedroom to the right of the door. The crocheted blanket and black and white wedding portrait above the bed suggested it was her grandmother's room. He put his foot against the side of the brass Queen-sized bed and scooted it against the far wall to reveal storage bins filled with loose papers and leather-bound notebooks.

"She kept a diary," Eira explained from the doorway, frowning as Ross rifled through her grandmother's things. Keith and Douglas slid past her to join him. Keith pulled out the drawers of the antique dresser while Douglas stomped on the floor, listening for hollow spaces.

Eira clicked her teeth and turned away. Jack followed her through the living room and down a short hallway. Her room was a breath of fresh air in the time warp of a house. Lavender carpet covered the floor, and a thin strip of wallpaper bisected the walls with a little purple and silver spiral pattern. His breath rose up in front of him the moment he crossed the threshold. Instinctively, he reached to pull her back, but then he spied the open window. Eira groaned.

"My heating bill must be through the roof." Beneath the window ledge the paint chipped and dimpled. "I don't even want to know how much that'll cost to fix."

"So, this is your room, huh?" Jack leaned a shoulder against the doorframe to take it in. It didn't suit her. The pastel palette belonged to a girl half her age. She shook back her hair and surveyed the room with a critical eye.

"I wanted to change it, but Grandma said that was a waste of money. Apparently, Mom used to change up her room all the time when she was my age. My great grandma taught her how to sew, and she would make new curtains and blankets whenever she had money for material. Grandma Winnie didn't like it when I reminded her of Mom." She crossed to a cherrywood jewelry box on the dresser and pulled out a long pendant necklace with a small silver cross.

"I'm sure it wasn't easy dealing with her daughter's death," Jack offered. He found a picture in an oval frame of a tall girl who was all long, stalky legs, slouching in front of a brick wall. Blunt brown bangs covered her eyebrows, and thick kohl rimmed her dark eyes like a domino mask. She bore no similarities to Eira whatsoever, but he knew it had to be her mom.

Eira fastened the necklace behind her head with practiced ease.

"She never said it, but I don't think she liked my mother very much. She loved her—obviously—but she thought Mom had her priorities in the wrong order. That's why she was always on my case, I suppose. She didn't want me flunking out and getting knocked up at sixteen too. Seriously, she barely let me pick out my own clothes. Does this look like something a teenager would wear?" She held up a white blouse with billowy sleeves and a thick lace ruffle that dribbled down the front.

"Maybe if you were a pirate." Eira rolled her eyes and threw the blouse on the bed.

"After I started working at the shop and earning my own money we got into some pretty major fights. I may or may not have bought some things because I knew it would send her head through the roof." She held up a clingy, one-shoulder burgundy dress designed to hug her like a second skin. Jack took one look at the outfit and knew exactly why her conservative, hearth-witch grandma had objected. If her goal had been to keep attention away from her granddaughter, then Eira in that dress destroyed any chance she had at succeeding.

"Where did you plan on wearing that?" he asked with feigned indifference, studying the collection of glass figurines littering the top of her dresser. She laughed.

"I don't know. A date, maybe. Not that she ever let me go out with anyone." She smiled ruefully and tossed the dress onto the bed. Jack studied her through sideways glances.

He wasn't sure what drew him to her. It wasn't her looks. If anything, her fae eyes and complexion warned him to stay away. Her bullheaded determination to get back to what she thought was a normal life amused him even as he admired her for it. She was a product of Faerie, and now because of the harp he was too. Knowing now that the harp had been working to possess him since the moment he touched it, he suspected their mutual ties to Faerie accounted for the strange link between them that gave her a corner of his mind not even the harp could corrupt. The overwhelming protective urge that gripped him any time she was threatened was almost enough to make him think.... He shook his head.

It was dangerous to believe caring about her enough could save him.

The doorbell rang. The rustling noises from her grandmother's room stopped, and Jack and Eira exchanged a look of surprise.

"It's your house," he said, moving aside to let her pass. He hung back, looking at the picture of her mother. The kohl-rimmed eyes stared back as if to remind him that nothing but trouble came from getting involved with the fae, and whether she liked it or not, Eira was fae. He had enough problems without piling on any more. With that thought he pushed his jumbled feelings to the back of his mind and rounded the corner after her. He stepped into the main room just as Eira pulled open the door.

"Daisy?"

"Eira, thank goodness! Where have you been? Mom and I've been so worried about you. You haven't been home in weeks!" His brothers retreated from the door when they caught sight of Logan's ex. However, Jack walked up behind Eira in a show of solidarity against the intrusion.

Daisy's long, ash-blond hair was pulled back in a tight braid that swung to her hips. Her eyes flared momentarily before she relaxed with a grin.

"Jack! It's you. I thought you were him for a minute. You look so much alike." Her voice was light, but disappointment colored her tone like a bruise.

"Genetics are funny that way," he said, taking no pity on her. Eira leaned into him to dig her elbow into his ribs. Daisy watched the exchange closely. She cleared her throat and flashed a toothy, see-through smile.

"Listen, Eira, I'm glad I caught you. Mom's been dying to have you over. She says there's something she's been meaning to tell you but could never find the right time. I think it's about your grandma. You know how close they were." Eira frowned, but tried to hide it. If Jack had to guess he'd say they were about as close as Alaska and Antarctica.

"Uh, okay, but we can't stay long," Eira said after a pause. She reached back and wound her fingers through Jack's. He worked hard not to show his surprise at the gesture. Daisy's mouth opened and closed on a protest, but when Jack looked at her closely she forced another smile and shrugged.

"Great, I'm sure it won't take too long." She led the way across the street to a two-story yellow Victorian with white gingerbread trim. An old tire swing hung from the oak in the front yard.

"Mom, she's here!" Daisy announced as she bounded onto the porch. Jack and Eira exchanged a glance. She tightened her hold on his hand. While he wasn't complaining, he wondered why she was suddenly all over him.

A short woman with close-cropped, frosted, blonde hair opened the door with a bright smile. She wore a green apron around her waist. A cloud of baked cookie and cinnamon apple scent made them close their eyes and inhale in unison.

"Eirawen! I'm so glad Daisy was able to track you down. We were starting to get worried. Come in, come in!" She reached out to pull Eira inside. Jerked off-balance, Eira tripped. Jack leaned in to steady her. Looking down he saw a thin line of white powder sprinkled in front of the door.

Jack dug in his heels, but before he could stop her Eira crossed the threshold. Mrs. Rowe turned back to him. Her eyes dropped to the strap of the backpack hanging off his arm. She wet her lips and held open the door.

"Coming, Mr. Sorley?"

Jack hesitated. She was human. The faded freckles and crows' feet told him so. Why then did her peppermint-green stare give him the creeps?

The moment his foot stepped over the threshold an invisible barrier slid shut behind him. He rocked back, but an impenetrable force held him inside. Uh oh.

Daisy helped Eira out of her coat, but her mother moved up behind Jack.

"You are quite the troublemaker, Jack Sorley." He spun to face her, but before he could say anything she swept past him to guide Eira by the shoulders into the kitchen. Dried arrangements of primroses hung over the doors and windows. Wrought-iron wall art decorated each wall, but it was more than the protective wards. Magic was woven into every thread and floorboard. The walls practically vibrated with it. It was so strong he wondered if he hadn't stepped through another portal into Faerie.

Mrs. Rowe ushered Eira onto one of the white wooden chairs around her painted farmhouse table. Everything in the yellow and green kitchen was bright, neat, and eerily pristine. Jack stood in the doorway, watching Daisy and her mother. Daisy took the chair opposite Eira. Wariness sharpened her features whenever Eira wasn't looking. Mrs. Rowe brought a plate of cookies to the table. Eira reached for one, but Jack cleared his throat and shook his head. Her fingers changed course and swept up through her hair away from the food. Daisy pursed her lips, telling Jack everything he needed to know.

"I think we should head back. My brothers will start wondering where we are." Daisy glanced at her mother, who sat very still, but Eira leaned across the table.

"Daisy said you wanted to tell me something about Grandma Winnie." She kept her tone polite, but her eyes narrowed with determination. Mrs. Rowe heaved a sigh with a hand over her heart.

"Yes, poor Winifred. Such a kind old dear—misguided of course—but you'd never find a woman with a bigger heart."

"Misguided?" Eira repeated, brow arched in quiet warning.

"Yes. She thought she could protect you by keeping you from your father. I warned her that the truth would eventually come out and any precautions she took would only be temporary, but.... She meant well." Eira took a deep breath before staring down at her hands splayed on the tabletop.

"Why should I care about him? If he wanted to be a part of my life he would have stuck around."

"Oh, but he did, sweetie. Your mother was a girl with...let's just say, 'unfortunate' taste in men. I suppose compared to her usual type he must have seemed like a prince. But they never are, are they?" She sent a pointed look Jack's way, and he gritted is teeth. Eira didn't notice.

"What are you talking about?"

"When Gwen realized she'd won the favor of faery lord—shared a bond with him even—she let it go to her head." Jack inhaled sharply, and Eira went still. Mrs. Rowe nodded with exaggerated sympathy. "She thought once you were born you might give her more influence over him, but she didn't realize the price for her audacity would be her life."

"You mean I'm not a changeling?"

Mrs. Rowe looked from Eira to Jack and laughed.

"Is that what they told you? You should be insulted. Changelings are horrible, hideous creatures even fae mothers don't love. Anyone with the eyes to see should know you're of royal stock." When Eira sagged in her seat, Mrs. Rowe pushed the plate of cookies toward her again.

"Winifred did her best to protect you," she continued. Her voice took on a hypnotic rhythm that set Jack's teeth on edge. "But when she died those protection charms began to weaken. You're a midwinter child and Winterthorn's power is at its peak. Surely you've felt his presence?"

"What are you?" Jack asked, unable to hold it in any longer. She spoke of the fae as though she knew them personally. Her nostrils thinned at his interruption, and she sent him a scathing look tinged with envy.

"Honestly, did you think your family was the only one that's learned a trick or two over the years?"

Eira sat back, studying Daisy and her mother. She glanced toward the windows, as if she suddenly sensed the net drawing them in. Magic crackled in the air. It made Jack's skin itch. Eira rubbed her arms.

"I think I've heard enough." She started to rise.

"I don't think so." Mrs. Rowe inspected her fingernails. "I expect they'll be here soon."

"They?" Jack took a step into the room.

"Winterthorn wants his daughter safe. Catching you was just a happy accident. You've made some powerful enemies, Jack Sorley. You shouldn't play with things best left alone." She fixed Eira with a sympathetic smile. "Forgive me, Sweetie. I wish there was an easier way to get his attention. Unfortunately, he only heeds the call of the dead and dying." Before Eira could move, Mrs. Rowe's hand whipped from beneath the table and stabbed a long, silver hair pin into the flesh between her thumb and forefinger. She screamed and clawed at the woman's hand. Jack tackled Mrs. Rowe out of her chair, and Daisy jumped up to protect her mother.

"Stop it! She knows what she's doing!" She braced her hands against his chest, throwing her weight against him.

Dishes rattled in the cupboards, the only warning they received.

The kitchen windows exploded. Howling gray bodies ran circles around the house. Their blurring speed formed a cyclone of single-minded ferocity. One way or another they would break in or tear the house down. Every mirror and glass pane shattered. Furniture scraped across the floorboards, and something heavy toppled upstairs with enough force to make the whole house shudder.

Heads bowed against the gale, Jack and Eira crawled to one another. The doors tore off the cabinets, and plates and dishes flew like missiles. With a great sucking sound, the storm winds gathered to their full concussive force, and the Wild Hunt blasted a hole through the back kitchen wall. The farmhouse table flew across the room. Chips of wood, plaster, and glass sprayed them with machine gun fire.

Jack covered Eira with his body, but a fist of wind knocked him away from her. Out of the madness the wolf pack appeared.

They were on her in an instant. A mass of gray, ghostly shapes formed a whirlwind around her, dragging her outside away from the house. Jack struggled to reach her, but he was no match for a force of nature. One of the creatures broke away, and he found himself staring at a red wolf with embers for eyes.

"You have what you came for, now leave!" Daisy shouted from her place on the floor. Her words were all but lost in the gale. Mrs. Rowe lay unconscious beside her. Blood trickled from the corner of her mouth and a lump swelled just over her eye.

Through the gaping hole in the wall Winterthorn stepped into the house. Orange flames leapt in his eyes as he gazed at the two women on the ground. A wreath of holly circled the base of his enormous antlers that were so large they scraped the ten-foot ceiling. He was bare-chested with a green velvet cloak pinned at his shoulders with silver brooches fashioned into wolf heads with rubies for eyes. His tan buckskin pants contrasted sharply against his chestnut, fae skin. A deep growl rumbled in his chest.

"There she is. Take her!" Daisy flapped her hand toward Eira. "You have what you came for. Now leave us alone."

Raw power exploded out of him, casing the walls in thick slabs of ice. He blazed, outlined in white-blue fire.

"Never presume you know anything about me." He glared down his broad nose at her. When she cowered, he jerked his head up to pin Eira next without so much as a glance at Jack. "Come. There is much I need to explain." At his command, the Wild Hunt herded her toward the hole in the wall.

Jack lunged after her, but the red wolf broke away to face him with a flash of white teeth. He slid to a stop.

"Bite me then!" He darted past it, braced for pain. The snapping jaws passed through his legs like smoke. Eira clung to a chunk of broken drywall as the Hunt tugged and tore at her. Welts, cuts, and wind burns touched every inch of her exposed skin. Jack dove for her, but the red wolf appeared out of midair between them. He veered away even though he knew it couldn't touch him. Eira tossed back her head with a growl of frustration.

Suddenly, the Wild Hunt let out a collective yelp. The smoky bodies melted into the mass of churning gray. Winterthorn's head whipped around before his form dissolved too. The wild winds receded until not a leaf stirred.

Eira twisted to see where they'd all gone. One hand reached for her throat where her silver cross hung. Jack pulled her to her feet, and they ran around the side of the house. But the Red Wolf wasn't giving up the chase. She surged up from the ground to cut off their exit. Jack skidded to a halt. Eira slammed into his back.

Abruptly, the wolf swung its heads toward the street. She let out a thin, frustrated whine.

"Get away from them!" Keith ran at them, swinging his foot as though it was an ordinary stray dogs. Ross was right behind him, better prepared with a baseball bat from his truck. There was a soft crack as the metal bat struck her hind leg.

Howling with rage, the Red Wolf sent one last longing look at Eira before she took to the air and streaked away. Jack swayed, lightheaded with the adrenaline pumping through him. Eira moaned and pressed her forehead between his shoulders. He spun around.

"Are you all right?" He ran his fingers through her hair to shake loose a shard of blue painted china. She stared at the fleck of her blood along its edge and shuddered. Then her eyes rolled back into her head. Her knees gave out and she collapsed into his chest. Jack wrapped his arms around her and looked over her head at his brothers' ashen faces.

Eira clawed at him urgently. When he stepped back she doubled over to clutch her belly. Her face contorted in pain.

"Ja—!"

The muscles of her throat seized, choking off his name.

"Keith!"

His brothers hadn't noticed yet. They were still looking around to make sure the Wild Hunt weren't coming back. At his cry, they all whirled around. Jack sagged as Eira's dead weight pulled him down. Her muscles knotted beneath his hands, drawing tighter and tighter until her body arched in an unnatural bow.

"She needs a hospital," said Keith at the same moment Jack said, "We need to get her to Glen."

"Jack, look at her, she could die before we get her all the way back to the house."

"She'll die if we just keep standing around doing nothing," Ross spoke up. He fished his keys out of his pocket and ran to bring his truck around. Jack lifted Eira into his arms and swung toward the road.

He froze. Standing not ten feet away was Odhran—or what was left of him. His red, blistered skin glistened in the light reflected off the snow. Hate blazed in his bloodshot yellow eyes. No one else saw him. Keith ran to open the cab door, passing through the mutilated faery. The moment he touched him, Odhran faded away. Shaken, Jack shook his head and focused on the girl in his arms.

Eira made a choking noise as they moved her into the back seat. It was impossible to understand what she was trying to say.

"You're going to be okay," Jack said, swinging up behind her. His voice held conviction because the alternative wasn't an option.

ROSS DROVE LIKE A MADMAN. They took back roads Douglas assured them were far from any patrol routes. Eira gurgled against Jack's chest. The harsh noise told him she wasn't getting enough air.

Douglas called ahead so Glen knew they were coming. He handed Jack the phone as they sped up the final hill to their house. Static crackled across the line as Jack started to explain.

"She's seizing!" Douglas shouted. Jack dropped the phone to catch her as a violent spasm lifted her up and slammed her back down.

Ross skidded into the driveway, and Glen ran down the front steps. Jack barely had his seat belt off before Glen was leaning across him to peer into her face. He swore softly at the sight of the cuts Jack hadn't mentioned over the phone. Eira gritted her teeth as her muscles clenched again.

"What happened?" Glen spotted blood trickling from the puncture wound where Mrs. Rowe had stabbed her. He examined it closely. Silver light engulfed him, passing from his hand into hers. Before he could even begin healing the wound he staggered sideways and clutched his head. Eira gasped as the cramp released her with a vicious snap.

"She's been poisoned," said Glen, who looked more tired than Jack had ever seen him. Moving quickly, he instructed them to carry her inside.

"What do you need?" Jack hovered at the foot of his bed where they laid her down. Glen brushed his thinning hair out of his eyes.

"Just stay with her. I don't recognize some of these toxins. I think this might be a Faerie blend. I'll...I'll do the best I can." Mentally, Jack thanked him for not voicing his fear that his best might not be enough. Glen ran from the room, taking Keith with him. Jack heard them arguing over which plants produced the strongest antidote for hemlock poisoning.

Alone in the room, Jack laid his hand on top of hers. The cold touch of her skin felt too much like death. Glen's healing magic had eased her contractions, but until he flushed the poison from her body it only bought her a short reprieve. Eira's eyes closed as she struggled to breathe.

"I knew something was off the moment we stepped in that house. I should have pulled you out of there sooner." Jack buried his face in his hands. Her eyelashes flickered as if she was about to argue, but another spasm caught her in its teeth. Jack caught her hand and dashed tears from his eyes. It didn't matter that he had no control over where she did or didn't go. He'd sensed the danger and let her follow it anyway.

Her eyes flew wide and she sucked in a ragged gasp of air. Cursing with desperation, Jack fastened his lips over hers and breathed air into her lungs. Shakily, she released the air he gave her. That much she could manage on her own. Their eyes met. Already the luster was fading from hers.

Why do you waste time you don't have on a cure that won't be enough? The insidious voice sank like a needle into his mind.

"Go away!" Jack spat the words, uncaring if Eira heard.

You know I can save her. We can save her. The song you need is already here.

"Why would you help her?" Jack screwed his eyes shut against the golden notes beckoning him to play. Piccolo laughter trickled through his mind.

She poses no threat to me. Just because you believe it doesn't make it so.

That rocked him. But then it shouldn't have. The harp was in his mind, sharing his thoughts. Of course it knew what his last hope clung on. And as it knew him, Jack knew it would say anything to convince him he had no way out.

We are bound by music, Jack. What ties you to this girl is nothing more than dreams and delusions. Over time those change and fade, but music breathes inside you. It is my magic that awakened hers to you. Without her you are still you. Without me and my music, you are nothing.

Jack refused to believe anything the harp told him could be true, but it knew where to aim its jabs. Already the melody that would catch hold of her spirit and tempt her back from the darkness danced in his ears. He clenched his fists.

He pushed away from the bed and slung his backpack off his back. He ripped open the zipper where the gleaming instrument waited. The moment his fingers touched the pillar the torn pads on his fingers thickened into sturdy callouses. He stared, stunned by the raw power funneling into his hands.

Well, what are you waiting for? His jaw hardened.

"First, I'm going to save her, and then I'm going to destroy you."

He didn't think. He didn't wait. He just started to play.

Chapter 15

The moment Jack began to play, the harp's power flexed its strength. It seized command of his hands again, though this time Jack relinquished control without a fight. The overhead light flickered and went out, but the room brightened as silver light billowed out from his hands. The heat evaporated, leaving the room feeling like a walk-in freezer. Eira shivered. Before his eyes, her pale skin turned blue.

"What's happening?" Jack stared in horror as a thin layer of frost grew over her skin.

This song was written for the Winter King's coronation. It will freeze her as she is until your brothers return. With her heart frozen the tainted blood cannot spread. But it wasn't just Eira the song was affecting. Outside thick snowflakes poured from the sky. Over the music the house groaned as wind slammed it from all sides.

Jack didn't pay the weather any attention.

"Jack, what are you doing?" Glen ran into the room and nearly slid on the carpet that was soaking wet with the condensation spreading out from the harp.

"Do you have the antidote?" Jack asked through gritted teeth. Even though he was working with the harp, he wasn't immune to the blistering cold. Glen looked down at the mug of dark liquid he carried.

"I can't promise it'll work. Poisons are tricky, and this one's laced with magic. I had to speed up the process and without knowing exactly what—"

"Just give it to her!" Despite the harp's assurance that it could save her Jack knew there was only so long he could stand the cold. Glen grimaced but went to the bedside.

"She's a block of ice, Jack. Stop. You're killing her!"

To Jack's surprise, the harp released its grip on his mind. The unfinished melody hung in the air. The overhead light hummed and came back on. Im-

mediately heat crept back into the room. Glen set the mug against Eira's parted lips to carefully trickle the potion inside. He clutched her wrist and added
his healing energy to hasten her to return back to life.

Before their eyes, her blue pallor faded. Her eyelids flickered, and she
drew her first breath. Though he kept funneling power to her, Glen's face
sagged with relief.

"Just so you guys know, there is a limit to what I can do. You cut it any
closer and I'll have to bring her back from the dead." He was trying to cut
the tension, but Jack's nerves were still too raw. There couldn't be a next time.
These attacks had to stop.

Though Glen assured them she should be fine, she complained that she
still felt cold deep in her bones. Jack ransacked the closet for more blankets,
and when she still lay shivering Glen cleared his throat and looked pointedly
at the bed before he gathered up the coffee mug and headed for the door.
Right. Body heat.

He stood awkwardly beside the bed trying to figure out the best way to
suggest it. Finally, Eira simply pulled back the blankets and raised herself up
to a sitting position so that her back rested against the headboard.

"Hurry up, Jack. I'm cold."

Blushing, Jack slid in beside her, drawing the blankets up around her
shoulders. She rested her temple against his collarbone and wrapped her arms
around his waist. Hesitantly, Jack snaked his arm around her and let his hand
rest above her hip.

A particularly hard gust of wind rattled the glass in the panes. Eira
flinched, and Jack tightened his hold.

"Are you sure you're alright?"

"You know you're not responsible for what happens to me, don't you?"
She eased the sting of the words by burrowing her nose against his ribs. Jack's
arm tightened around her. His eyes darted to the harp. The harp stood on the
edge of the dresser taunting him with its silence.

"I can't help feeling that I brought this craziness back from Faerie with
me."

"Well you didn't. From the sounds of things, I had a target on my back
long before you came along." Bitterness crept into her voice. She rested her

hand over his heart and ran her nose along the hollow of his neck. Jack closed his eyes. His breath stuttered from his chest. What was she doing?

Her hand slid up his neck to turn his face down to hers. She leaned against him, her gentle strength guiding him down.

It didn't matter that she'd nearly died an hour ago. They were caught in the web of another world that was closing in on them fast. Their only escape depended on the other, and their mouths fused together as if that would save them in the end.

"Eira...." Jack's mouth moved across her jaw. His arm locked her to him so she couldn't get away.

Out of nowhere, the memory of her flirting with Logan floated up through the desire washing his better judgment away. *She uses her beauty to get what she wants. Right now, she wants to forget....* The harp's voice was a jet of cold water.

"Wait...!"

Her hands slid under his shirt, raking the skin along his back. A shudder rippled through him. Sensations pounded him like the head of a drum stretched so tight any more might tear him apart. Cruelly, the image of her standing by the register, luring Aiden with her fae eyes and siren smile came back to him. Jack pulled back. The harp's cruel laughter flitted through his head. He stood up and pressed the heels of his palms to his eyes. What was he doing?

"Jack?"

Trying to get his wayward thoughts under control, he dropped his hands to face her. He took one look at her tousled, dark hair and pearlescent skin and wasn't sure whether he wanted to laugh or die. He'd never find another girl like her in a million years, but she could have her pick of a thousand other guys like him.

Jack ran his hand through his hair, wishing he knew what words could navigate him safely through the turbulent emotions rising in her eyes. He saw himself as he had seen Aiden, pathetically reaching for something he was never meant to have.

"Look, I like you," he blurted out without meaning to. Her mouth twisted in a smirk.

"I kinda guessed that."

"Yeah well it's stupid!" The anger was directed at himself, but not surprisingly her face went white with anger. "No, I don't mean it like that! The truth is I like you a lot, and with everything going on I'm trying not to believe that that means anything." She looked confused—and still insulted. The heat in her eyes went cold. After a long moment of tensely held silence while he scrambled to think of a way to explain, she pinched her lips and gave a clipped nod.

"You're right. We've both got a lot on our plates right now. Neither of us can afford any distractions." He winced as her cool dismissal confirmed what he feared. But the flush that rose to her face told him he'd hurt her feelings. In fact, she curled in on herself as if she was crushed. Jack cringed. Her pride was a formidable obstacle. If he'd misread her he'd have more luck moving a mountain than winning her back.

Red and blue flashing lights lit up the room. Eira craned her neck to look out the window. Jack pulled aside the curtain to see Sheriff Doyle climb out of his car and stare up at the house. Leaning against a gust of driving snow he started for the house. A moment later the doorbell rang.

Footsteps pounded the stairs and Logan skidded through the door.

"Hide her!"

Jack and Eira exchanged grim looks. If Doyle came looking, under the bed or in the closet wouldn't keep her hidden for long. She folded her arms, refusing to hide. Logan signaled unnecessarily for quiet as they heard Douglas open the front door.

"Sheriff, what brings you here?"

"I need to speak with your brother Jack," Doyle said in brisk tones. There was a note of triumph in his voice. To his credit, Douglas kept his cool.

"What's this about?"

"It's freezing out here," Doyle complained. "Your wards let me through, which means I have a right to be here."

There was the stomp of boots and the weighty thud of the door. Jack moved to the end of the bed. Logan backed up until they stood shoulder to shoulder, forming a shield.

"My dad used to tell stories of winters like this, where one storm ran into another, but it's been almost twenty years since the last time the weather's turned this bad." Doyle forced a laugh.

"My brother?" clipped Douglas. "What do you need him for?" Doyle's irritation radiated throughout the house.

"I need to know what he was doing at the Rowe's house this afternoon. The back half of her kitchen was blown off by what looks like a bomb, and Jack was spotted by several neighbors fleeing the scene."

Jack's fist clenched. He didn't know who to be angrier at, Doyle for repeating the load of crap, or Mrs. Rowe for trying to feed it to him. Were they working together?

"Why do you insist on treating me like the enemy?" Doyle complained when Douglas didn't say anything. "You're letting them turn us against one another. Sorley, I took an oath to protect this town, and I intend to keep it. Right now, I've got a woman in the hospital and a traumatized teenager, and the only name anyone will mention is your damn brother!"

"Jack!"

Jack and Logan exchanged a look. There was really no use pretending he wasn't home.

"Do you want me to go with you?" Logan asked. Jack shook his head and glanced over his shoulder.

"Stay with her." He meant Eira, but the moment he stepped into the hallway the harp tried to tug him back again. This time when he fought the compulsion, he won.

He took his time on the stairs, trying to look as though he had nothing to hide. Douglas faced Doyle in the entryway. They were the same height, but standing in his light brown Sheriff uniform and thick bomber jacket, Doyle appeared more intimidating. Or maybe that was just Jack's uncertainty over what the man intended to do.

"What?" said Jack. Douglas tilted his head, silently questioning his belligerent tone. Jack ignored him and stared Doyle straight in the face.

"What are you doing here?"

"I have some questions for you. Is there a place we can talk in private?"

Jack shrugged and passed through the French doors into his music room. A keyboard piano stood to the immediate right of the door, and there were several display cases housing his trumpet, saxophone, flute, violin, and cello.

"Does your family have a band?" Doyle asked with a weak stab at humor.

"These are mine," Jack answered shortly. For the first time it occurred to him just how many instruments he owned.

"All of them?"

"I haven't come across an instrument that I couldn't figure out. Now, why are you here?"

"I don't appreciate the attitude, young man." Doyle passed his fingers through his hair, clearly searching for patience.

"I don't appreciate you accusing me of blowing up people's houses," Jack countered coolly.

"Why don't you explain to me why several of the neighbors saw you running away from the crater that used to be the Rowes' kitchen. I assume you're not going to deny you were there?" He folded his arms and drew himself up to his full height. Jack shrugged.

"She asked me to come in, said she had something to tell me. We were standing in the kitchen when the back half of the house blew up. Like any sane person I got out of there as fast as I could."

"You didn't think you should stick around to make sure she was alright?"

Jack clenched his jaw. Nothing he could say now would make it sound any better.

Doyle cleared his throat, looking around at the mahogany paneling.

"Were you and Mrs. Rowe alone in the house?"

"Daisy was there." They both knew he was leaving out one other person.

"Daisy is the one who called in the attack. Are you aware that Mrs. Rowe is currently being treated at Wildwood Hospital for the injuries she sustained when the bomb went off? Since you didn't stick around to find out, aren't you curious to know how badly she was hurt?" Jack saw no reason to pretend that he cared. Indifference didn't make him guilty.

"I'm surprised you're not here to talk about the rise in our local wolf population."

There it was, the subtle tightening around the eyes that told him Doyle knew exactly what he was talking about.

"Wolves, Mr. Sorley? Are you trying to tell me that wolves blew up the Rowes' house?"

Jack raised a shoulder. They had a silent stare down. Doyle desperately wanted to know what Jack knew, and Jack was equally curious to find out what the man was really up to. In an abrupt change of tactics, Doyle smoothed his fingers over an invisible goatee and moved to the nearest window that overlooked the porch and the forest beyond the yard.

"Funny you should mention wolves, Mr. Sorley," he said finally. "Do you pay attention to the local news?"

"Sometimes."

"Then I guess you know that there's been a recent hash of animal attacks in the area. Actually, I'm surprised you and your brothers haven't run into trouble living all the way out here. Three men are dead—had their throats ripped wide open. Coroner thought it looked like the work of wolves, but you're the only person I've talked to that's mentioned seeing wolves in the area."

"Is there something you want to ask me?" Jack put it plainly. They were getting nowhere dancing in circles.

"You've seen her, haven't you?" Doyle's voice changed, became so soft Jack almost couldn't hear him. He thought he meant Eira, and words of denial crowded his tongue. Doyle squinted at the trees. "You've seen the Red Wolf."

Caught off-guard, Jack did a small double-take, and though the Sheriff had his eyes on the forest, the edge of his mouth creased with satisfaction as his trap snapped shut.

"She leads the Hunt," he said in a hollow voice. "I've been after her a long time. She killed my brother."

Jack reared back in surprise. Doyle pinned him with a thin-lipped smile.

"She's dangerous, Mr. Sorley. She looks small and timid, but she'll go for the jugular faster than you can say, 'full moon.' We're on the same team, you and I. It's our job to protect those who don't know what goes bump in the night. So, I'm going to ask you again, what happened at the Rowe's house?"

"It sounds like you already know, Sheriff," Jack said, measuring each word carefully. Doyle's teeth clicked together.

"And where is Ms. Rothchild? Mrs. Rowe's been calling the station nearly every day claiming the girl's been kidnapped, but my son told me he ran into her at the little shop uptown. He says you were with her. I've tried calling her house and I even drove by, but the girl's vanished like smoke."

"I don't know." Jack lied straight-faced and without remorse. Doyle's lips froze somewhere between a smile and a grimace. He reached into the front of his coat, and Jack staggered back, half-expecting him to pull out a gun. Doyle paused with his hand in his jacket.

"If I produce the search warrant that I'm holding in this pocket, do you think you'd have something different to say?"

Jack didn't respond. Not for one second did he believe Doyle had a warrant to search the house. After a moment, Doyle dropped the pretense.

"For the life of me I can't understand why you think I'm the bad guy." Jack pictured a platinum-haired faery held against her will inside a camper whose metal walls poisoned every breath she took. Doyle went on, "Let me do something to earn your trust." In spite of himself, Jack's interest piqued.

"When you're ready, come by the house. I have a case file there that I'm sure you'll find very interesting. It concerns a mutual friend of ours." Just when Jack had been about to give him a chance, the mention of Eira flung his guards back in place. Doyle headed for the door.

"Why don't you just tell me whatever you have to say now? Why do I have to read it from some file?" Jack resented the petulance in his voice. Doyle turned back and Jack was startled by the raw grief he didn't trouble to hide.

"I could tell you a story about forest gods, wild wolves, and ill-fated lovers that would make you see the danger that comes from letting them into our lives. But I see you're committed to believing I'm the dragon instead of St. George. If you want proof, I'll show it to you. Maybe then we can trust each other."

Keith and Douglas hovered in the entryway. They fixed Doyle with cool, appraising stares when he emerged.

"Well, are you going to arrest him?" Keith demanded.

"From the sounds of it your brother's only crime was being in the wrong place at the wrong time. It seems he's been running with a bad crowd lately. I'd get him on the right track if you want to avoid any more of these unpleasant visits in the future." It was a threat, plain and simple, and Keith bristled.

"You should go, Sir," said Douglas softly. "Wouldn't want you to get caught in this weather." Doyle met his eyes for a long moment before flicking his head back to look at Jack.

"Remember my offer." With that, he turned up his collar and let himself out.

"Well?" Keith rounded on Jack. Jack frowned at the door as though he could see through the carved wood to watch the Sheriff stumble down the lawn to his car.

"The Hunt killed his brother. That's what his whole vendetta is about." He told them about the invitation.

"You know that's some kind of trap," said Douglas at once.

"At this point he's offering to share information, which is something we could use. Besides, if he knows more about Eira's past then...." Jack recalled the angular dark-haired girl from the photo in Eira's room. How had that gawky girl convinced such a powerful fae to give her a child, and why had he allowed Eira's mother to die?

"You're going to go, aren't you?" Douglas groaned, watching his face. Jack glanced toward the stairs. He would go.

—If the harp let him.

Chapter 16

Though he had every reason not to go, two days later Jack found himself staring at Doyle's imposing lodge strung now with icicle lights and evergreen garlands. Magic floated over him like settling dust. Logan came around the front of the car to join him.

"I still can't believe you're doing this." Logan eyed the house with distaste. Jack laid his hand on the satchel that rested against his hip. The harp's presence was reassuring—not that he had any choice about bringing it or not. He'd tried leaving it behind, but before he set one foot outside, a crushing panic forced him to his knees. *Where you go I go, Jack.*

As soon as they passed through the gates, a dull ache gathered behind his eyes. It built with every passing second. Logan felt it too, though not as strongly. Faint lines crinkled at the corners of his eyes.

When they rang the doorbell the heavy tread of boots announced Sheriff Doyle's approach. He looked surprised to see Logan, but he took one look at Jack's pinched face and ushered them into them his office through a door to their right.

"What's he doing here?" Aiden stepped out of a den at end of the hall. He made to follow them, but Doyle threw an arm across the doorway.

"It's okay, Aiden. I've got this. Go back to whatever you were doing." He shut the door in his son's startled face.

"You okay, son?"

"No," Jack groaned, rubbing his temples. Though Logan's face was a shade paler than normal, he didn't appear to be suffering as badly. Shooting Jack a concerned look, he stepped forward.

"Look, you told him you had information to share. If you're just jerking us around then you can—" But Doyle held up a hand to stop him before he got started. He crossed to an oak filing cabinet and pulled out a thick paper binder. He undid the elastic clasp and removed a large stack of papers. Without ceremony, he tossed it onto the desk between them. A photograph fell out and slid to rest near Jack's foot. He picked it up and turned it over.

A man lay flat on his back with a red gaping hole where his throat should have been. His blue eyes were frozen open in terror, and there were deep scratches across his face and down his chest. Jack flipped the photo back over and handed it quickly to Logan, who looked at it, paled, and quickly slid it back in with the rest. Doyle's jaw could have been carved from a granite slab.

"What you see there is everything I have regarding Gwen Rothchild's death." Jack hesitated. His heart rate picked up speed. These were the answers they had been searching for, but he knew he wasn't going to like what he found.

There were more photographs. An old woman lay on the floor with a red waterfall pouring down her chest from the jagged chasm across her throat. Doyle's brother hadn't just had his throat ripped out, the animal that attacked him had torn open his belly too. Intestines spilled like sausage links between the shredded flaps in his green, plaid shirt. Jack was relieved he couldn't find Gwen's face amid all the carnage.

Logan quickly gathered the photos and shoved them back in the folder.

Jack picked up the packet of crime notes. Doyle watched him, his eyes two black tunnels leading into the past.

"The neighbors heard the screams, but by the time officers arrived, there was nothing but blood and body parts everywhere. The autopsy concluded that my brother was mauled, but no hair or saliva were found at the scene. It's hard to say whether it was before or during, but Ms. Rothchild went into premature labor. Most of the blood there is hers. It's assumed she bled out, but no body was ever found. For years I believed they took the child with them. If you want proof that the fae can't be trusted, there you have it."

When neither of them showed any signs of understanding he stabbed his fingers through his hair in a split-second of frustration. Then his features smoothed into a mask of control, and he cleared his throat.

"Gwen Rothchild was not a popular girl. She was a desperate, clingy thing who'd let you spit in her face if you said you'd be her friend." Jack and Logan exchanged a look. "My brother was infatuated with the idea of saving her from herself even though she didn't want to be saved."

Jack felt nauseous, though he couldn't tell if it was from the grinding pain in his head or the disgusting way Doyle talked about Eira's mom.

"One night at a party some friends of mine took a prank too far. They'd recorded a phone message she left one of them about a date that was never going to happen. They played it over the stereo for everyone to hear. That night she wrapped her car around a tree. She told everyone she'd swerved to miss a deer. It's a miracle she survived, or at least it seemed like it at the time. One man's miracle is another man's curse I suppose."

Jack's rising anger was doing nothing to ease the pressure in his temples.

"Next thing we know word gets around that she's pregnant. There was no telling who the father was—she refused to say, but my idiot brother decided to step in and make things right. He asked her to marry him—she turned him down. By then I'd gone back to college or else I'd have put a stop to his nonsense." Gravel entered his voice. "Naturally things went bad between them. Well, you see for yourself how it ended." He waved at the folder. "All this time I believed the Hunter came for his child and my brother got in the way out of some misguided need to protect her. I couldn't believe it when I saw the girl on Halloween and realized she'd been sitting right under my nose this whole time."

"I don't understand how you found out about the fae," said Jack with genuine puzzlement. "The official story has holes in it, but no one makes a logical leap to faeries without help." The clouds cleared from Doyle's eyes. Some of the tension ran out of him and he nodded. His jaw relaxed, heartened that Jack was hearing him out.

"There were signs if you knew where to look for them, faery rings in unlikely places, abnormal gaps in people's memories.... You could practically taste the magic hanging over that house. And perhaps I had a little guidance. What the Hunter did was a crime in his world and ours. No one with that much power can wield it without making enemies. From the little I have gleaned, a war's brewing in Faerie and the Hunter has become the hunted. There are more than a few faeries who'd be more than happy to see the girl die."

"And what did the Hunter do that was so terrible? The fae wouldn't care if Gwen lived or died."

"They consider any child created between humans and fae an abomination. They have untold power, but they're restrained by certain rules. We have the gift of free will. When you mix the two together you never know what combination of power and restraint you're going to get."

Dismay slid down the back of Jack's throat. How could he go back and tell any of this to Eira? Even Logan looked green, but then he shook his head.

"If the fae don't consort with humans as a general rule, why would the leader of the dead get a lonely girl pregnant and leave her behind instead of whisking her away to the Otherworld?"

"I don't know why it happened," Doyle admitted gruffly. "Only the Hunter could tell you that. And maybe things weren't so bad when the girl's grandmother was alive and shielding her from the truth. But without the grandmother to hide her, that girl is a walking magnet for trouble. The longer she stays in hiding the more fae will come here searching for her and punishing anyone who gets in their way. The Hunter won't hesitate to bury this town. That's why I need to know where she is. We can use her to stop him. After that we can determine what threats she poses to the rest of us."

This one meddles with forces he can't hope to control. When Death comes for him he will beg for release. If the harp had teeth they would have snapped. The fury channeling through him from the instrument made Jack queasy. Doyle misunderstood the uneasy look in his eye. He opened his arms.

"I understand why you're afraid, Jack. I can't imagine the things you must have seen in their world. I know your family believes that it's safer to keep out of their way, that we can ever be safe. But you have insights I desperately need. Use the gifts the faery gave you, and help me protect our world."

Jack flinched. He tried to hide it, but Doyle was watching him, waiting for his reaction, and the sudden light in his eyes meant that he'd seen.

"Yes, I've been well-informed about your family's history with the faery lady. Perhaps you would like to meet her?"

"You're holding her prisoner?" Logan's voice could have cut steel. Doyle struck the wall with his fist.

"I'm an officer of the law, not a barbarian! She's committed no crimes that I'm aware of, therefore she's simply in custody. I've made her accommodations comfortable enough. We have an understanding. As it turns out her goals are quite similar to mine. It's only her pride that's tweaked at the moment because I've taken the necessary precautions to hold her powers in check."

Logan's hands balled into fists, but Jack caught his elbow. The movement jangled the harp which let out a low hum. Doyle stepped back, eyes alert and wary.

"What was that?"

"Jack's on his way to a music lesson," Logan lied before Jack could flounder. Without thinking, he used a push of compulsion to make Doyle believe it. The silver fog issuing from his mouth had the effect of liquid nitrogen on every moving thing in the room. A devastating silence stretched between them as both parties had their worst suspicions confirmed.

"We should go or you'll be late for that lesson," said Logan, his cheeks flaming.

"Well, since you're such a musician, Jack, perhaps you'll be interested in performing at a party I'm throwing a week from tonight? Consider it an olive branch. We don't have to be allies if you and your brothers aren't willing to stand on the front lines, but I would hate to think we have to be enemies. We've both lost people we cared about. No one else should have to lose family and friends."

"I really ought to get to that lesson," Jack said, not quite meeting Doyle's eyes. He turned to go.

"Don't make the mistake of thinking you can save her, Jack. There's no point trying to hang on to something that was never meant to be."

Logan put a hand on Jack's shoulder, urging him toward the door, but Jack had to say something, had to wipe away the man's cool certainty that he knew what he was talking about. When he turned back, Doyle held out the case file.

"Take them. Take a good look. Not everyone has safeguards to hide behind like you and I do. Before you decide where you stand ask yourself if you want to be responsible for more scenes like these."

BACK AT THE HOUSE, Jack and Logan told the others everything. The contents of the case folder spread across the coffee table. Eira positioned herself as far away as possible, and not once since the pictures slipped out had she come near enough to see.

"Winterthorn didn't kill her mother—he saved her!" Ross shot up from the couch. His eyes bulged, and he looked around wildly to see if anyone shared his epiphany. Nonplussed stares looked back at him.

"Does that look like a rescue to you?" Logan snapped up one of the gorier photos and waved it in Ross' face. Ross brushed him aside and began to pace back and forth as he worked through his theory.

"The wolves attacked Doyle's brother, but they didn't leave any of her mom behind. That's because they took her with them. I think...I think the Red Wolf is her mother."

"What?" Logan snorted.

"Let me see those photos." Ross got up from the couch and rifled through the stack of pictures. He separated out three and laid them out on the coffee table. Eira averted her face, but the others crowded closer. They all showed various angles of a thick pool of blood with smeared paw prints.

"Look, there's none coming from his body where the wolf clearly was. Maybe her mother was dying and turning her was the only way to save her. Maybe she made a pact with Winterthorn, and he came to collect—I don't know! But I saw the Red Wolf. I communicated with it, and it wasn't like the other wolves. She views Eira as pack. I thought maybe it was because they were both from Faerie, but I get it now."

Something like pain flashed across Eira's features. She shook her head, but Jack sensed the horror rising up inside her as she reexamined every encounter she'd had with the Hunt. Not once had the Red Wolf shown aggression toward her. Only when Jack or his brothers got involved did the animal snap and snarl.

"Doyle said she crashed her car into a tree after a party when she swerved to miss a deer," said Jack in a hollow voice. "That must've been when they met."

Abruptly Eira's head came up.

"Does this mean my mother is alive?" There was such blank hope on her face that Jack felt a fist squeeze around his heart. Ross ducked his head.

"I wouldn't put it that way," he said gruffly. "She's part of the Hunt now."

She hid her disappointment as best she could. Her lips folded, and she gave a curt nod.

"So," she said, packing the single syllable with grim resignation. "What does Doyle expect you to do with this?"

"She's right." Craig lifted his head. "I mean, sure, faeries are dangerous, but what makes him think any of this is going to make us rise up against them? All things considered they've left us alone unless we messed with them first." Though no one said anything, Jack imagined every head turning in his direction at that last part.

"I can ask him when I go to his party next week." Eira stretched her arm across her body as if she was limbering up for a fight.

"Are you out of your mind?" Ross exploded. "You want to go to that nut job's house—after everything they just told you?"

"What's he going to do? If he's throwing a party then he can't try anything crazy in front of his guests."

Keith groaned and pinched the bridge of his nose. He wasn't even going to try talking her out of it.

Chapter 17

Jack was uneasy. Sheriff Doyle's party smelled like a trap, but Eira wouldn't hear any of the arguments against going. The knowledge of who her father was had hardened her, though whether it was from pride or shame he couldn't tell.

She sent Logan with specific instructions to go back to her house to pick out her outfit for the party. For once she was in perfect agreement with Keith that she wasn't leaving their property. Jack should have known it would be the burgundy, one-shoulder dress. When she descended the stairs in sculpted, knee-high boots that flashed an inch or two of pale skin between black leather and pressed velvet his mind went back to that moment in his bedroom and he wanted to kick himself.

Jack wasn't the only one impressed. Craig let out a low whistle. Logan gulped audibly and smoothed his fingers through his hair. Even Glen stood a little straighter.

"You look nice, Jack," said Eira, coming to stand beside him. Her eyes never quite met his as she flicked a wave of black hair away from her cheek. All week she'd kept a cool distance between them, shooting him impatient sidelong glances. It left him feeling uncertain and confused.

The strap of a tan, one-shoulder satchel crossed his chest. He laid a protective hand over the bag, and it gave a telltale hum.

Since saving Eira, the harp had been relatively quiet. It sensed the forces gathering against them. Jack spent his evenings losing himself in playing. It was no use trying to keep his hands off it when it sang and whispered in his head. He hadn't tried to get rid of it again. Not yet. He had the feeling he would need it before long.

Eira's gaze hardened as she stared at the satchel. After a moment, she pursed her lips and her large eyes searched his with a fierceness that was terrifying. Not sure what she was looking for, Jack turned away.

It took three cars to transport everyone. They formed a caravan. Douglas led the way with Glen in the Cruiser. Keith, Ross, and Craig took Keith's faded brown truck. The Mustang took up the rear.

Logan drove with one hand resting casually on the console so his forearm 'accidentally' brushed Eira's whenever they took a sharp turn.

"Oh!" Eira gasped and clutched her belly when they passed through Doyle's iron gates.

"What is it?" Jack sat forward to grip her shoulder. She braced one hand on the dashboard and covered her mouth with the other. Logan leaned away, horrified she was going to be sick all over his front seat.

"It's the same feeling I got the first time I came onto your property. There's something that doesn't want me to come through."

"His land has faery safeguards too." Logan muttered mostly to himself. It wasn't something they didn't already know—Doyle couldn't exactly torture and kill out in the open where any faery could call for help or seek revenge. Still, it was disconcerting to see that Eira, who was immune to most spells and wards felt the effects so strongly.

"Stop the car!" Jack said. Logan hit the brake so hard all three of them jerked against their seat belts. The car behind them honked.

"Look." Jack pointed beyond the iron fence to a figure half-hidden by the large apple tree. Those sweeping antlers couldn't possibly belong to an ordinary deer. Eira's hand fell limply into her lap.

Seeing that he had their attention, the stag stomped and tossed his head in obvious irritation. For the moment at least, the weather remained clear. Logan leaned over the steering wheel to study the stag. The red SUV behind them honked again. Swearing under his breath, Logan started moving again, but he craned his neck to keep Winterthorn in sight. Eira pressed her nose to the window until the procession of cars forced them to turn into Doyle's circle drive.

"We'll figure out what he wants." Jack whispered. Her eyes were round, but she nodded.

Logan dropped them off at the foot of the porch before going to find a place to park. Guests milled around the covered porch with drinks in their hands. Aiden hovered near the front door, and when he saw Eira slide out of the passenger seat, he bounded down the steps, nearly knocking Mrs. Summers over the railing into a holly bush.

"Eira, hey! Glad you could make it." He ignored Jack to pull her into a hug. Jack counted each second before Eira politely pushed him to arms' length.

"Your dad invited us," he said loudly, forcing Aiden to acknowledge his presence. Aiden flicked him the briefest glance out of the corner of his eye.

"Yeah, that's right. He says you're supposed to perform tonight or something. With all the money he spent on the spread I guess he had to cut corners somewhere." Jack nearly snorted at the cheap jab, but he managed to keep a straight face. Eira cleared her throat.

"Your house is nice," she said with forced brightness. Aiden blinked and turned to look at the impressive lodge as if he'd never seen it before.

"Thanks. D'you want a tour?"

Before she could answer, a figure filled the open doorway. Sheriff Doyle regarded them with a beer in his hand. When his eyes met Jack's, he lifted the brown bottle in a sarcastic toast.

"Stay here," Jack whispered in Eira's ear before he climbed the steps to meet him. Doyle's eyes fixed on the satchel that bounced off his left thigh before snapping back to Jack's face with squinty-eyed malice.

"Sheriff," said Jack coldly when he reached him. The smell of beer mingled with his wintergreen aftershave to form a cologne that made Jack's head swim. Doyle's hands were steady, but his eyes blazed like a furnace. Instinctively, Jack knew he'd be an angry drunk.

"Mr. Sorley." Doyle tipped back his bottle without breaking eye contact. "You found the girl I see." His dark eyes fixed on Eira like black, polished marbles. He curled his lip and spat off the edge of the porch. Jack, aware of the people watching, took a steadying breath.

"Not what, Sheriff. Who."

Doyle stiffened. Then he burst into a deep rumbling laugh that caused several nearby guests to turn with vague, curious smiles.

"She's done her job on you, hasn't she? Shame. I figger'd you were made of stronger stuff." His words slurred.

"I didn't realize my brother was so amusing," Douglas said softly from behind Jack's left shoulder. Jack sensed the arrival of the other five as they fanned out in a semi-circle around the door. Doyle's smile turned brittle.

"You're going to take her side." His hand clenched around his bottle. "After everything I showed you, you're going to side with that little —"

"Dad," Aiden came toward them looking embarrassed.

"Careful," warned Craig, cracking his knuckles suggestively. Rudolph's nose blinked on his flamboyant holiday sweater. Doyle sent him a bland look and indicated the twenty or so guests arranged around them on the porch with a sweep of his drink. Some stared openly at the unmistakable standoff.

"You'd turn against your own race for one of them?" Somehow, Doyle managed to pack a well of contempt into his low voice. "You've see them. You know what they've done, what they're capable of doing if we don't stand up and fight back. And rather than bring others into the light you'd shelter one of their spawn?" This was not the urbane sheriff Jack was used to. He didn't know what to think of the drunk making a spectacle on his front porch.

"What do you mean, 'bring others into the light'?" Keith pushed past Douglas. Unlike Doyle he couldn't keep his voice down, and more heads turned in their direction. Frowning, Aiden put a hand on his father's arm, stopping him from taking another swig.

"Maybe you should check on the music, huh? You know how that last track always skips when it gets to the end."

Doyle's eyebrow twitched. He focused on Aiden's pleading face and as Jack watched, the glazed look in his eyes hardened to cold purpose. He rested his hand on his son's shoulder and squeezed with rigid affection. His mouth pulled into a smile dripping with charm.

"You're right, son. I think it's time we all headed in." He raised his voice. "Everyone, if you'd be so kind, I'd like to move into the living room. It's time for a holiday toast!"

The Sorleys stood their ground as people jostled past them into the house. Jack glanced around for Eira. At first, he didn't see her and a surge of adrenaline shot through him at the thought that she had gone in alone, but then he spotted her sitting on the wooden porch swing tucked into the shadows. Aiden sat next to her, hunched forward with his face buried in his hands. Her hand lightly stroked his arm.

Blistering jealousy struck hot and fast before he could hold it back. It roused the monster. *You see? You would value a girl like that above all the power I can give you?*

As he stared, Eira leaned in close to whisper in Aiden's ear. The only word Jack could read was 'camper,' and his blood went cold. Aiden nodded, lifting his eyes to meet hers. She touched his shoulder and smiled. Jack's fingers curled.

Sensing his gaze, Eira looked up. Her mouth quirked in reproach.

Noticing that her attention had wandered, Aiden lifted his head too. Seeing Jack watching them, he stood abruptly and pulled her from the swing into the darker shadows around the porch. Jack took a step after them, reluctant to leave her alone with him even when she was clearly willing to go. His circle of brothers blocked his way.

"She'll be fine for a few minutes," Douglas muttered dryly. "She can handle him." He grabbed Jack by the scruff of the neck and steered him into the house.

During his previous visits Jack hadn't seen beyond the entryway and therefore didn't realize just how big the house was. Thick oak beams stretched over the heads of more than fifty guests in the living room. Among them were Mayor Heidrich and his wife, an anchor and weatherman from the local news station, and several officers from the police department. Across the room Jack spotted Daisy. There were stitches on her cheek. The moment their eyes met she darted away like a minnow into the sea of bodies.

The crowd arranged themselves in a semicircle around Doyle, who stood with his back to a cast iron mantelpiece. Somewhere he had traded his beer bottle for a paper cup of punch. He scanned the faces before him with cold calculation despite his welcoming smile. Servers, or rather a couple of guys off the football team dressed in black slacks and white collared shirts, moved throughout the room with trays of punch for everyone.

Jack raised a warning brow when one of the boys approached him with an outstretched glass. Glen reached around him to accept the drink, but as soon as the boy moved away he swirled the contents and gave it a sniff.

Doyle lifted his free hand.

"Thank you all for coming. I know how miserable this weather has been, and I'm glad so many of you made the effort to be here." Scattered applause and raised glasses answered him. Someone quipped about never turning down free food. Doyle waited for the laughter to subside before he continued. "As Sheriff it's my job to see that our district is safe. Since I took office I've worked tirelessly toward that end, and the town has made great strides—but we're still not safe."

Here and there people stirred. Candle flame smiles flickered. Doyle stared into his punch. He grimaced.

"This winter alone three of our finest were savaged in the night. Just last week my officers responded to the scene of a home with the back half blown off. No one was apprehended, and there was no evidence left at the scenes. But this isn't the first time a mystery has gone unsolved in our town, is it?" His hand shook, but his jaw tightened. Christmas carols chirped in the background from an old CD player, at odds with the tension condensing the guests into an uneasy knot.

"Never again!" Doyle raised his drink and pink liquid sloshed over his arm. "No more will we hide from enemies who escape into the night. Tonight, I want you all to raise your glasses and join me in a solemn pledge to rid our city of the vermin that lurk in the shadows." He drank deeply. Reluctantly, his audience followed suit—everyone except for the Sorleys.

"He's put clover in it," hissed Glen as the color drained from his face. "My god, he's given them all Faery Sight!" And just that quickly Doyle's plan laid itself bare. He had gathered the most influential people in Straifield together to open their eyes to the fae.

"We've got to get Eira out of here!" Jack spun for the door.

"I want you all to welcome my special guest. She's condescended to grace us mere mortals with her presence. Believe me, it took plenty of convincing to bring her here." Doyle's slur became more pronounced with his derision. He opened the door to a room off the living room.

Jack felt her presence at his back like a bonfire. Gasps scuttled here and there. He almost couldn't drum up the courage to look.

Her eyes were suns blazing between the strands of starlight that coiled from her head. Despite the snow outside she wore a billowing sky-blue gown pinned at her shoulders with living lilacs. Thick iron bracers lined in silver sheathed her forearms connected by thin chain links as deceptively delicate as the force of nature they contained. The sick-sweet, charred-apricot smell of her burning flesh made everyone's eyes water. Her face was sculpted marble, crumbling under the strain of pain and fury.

"My god, what is that?" Mayor Heidrich drew his wife under the shelter of his arm. Jack frowned. What did they see? Credeilia was spring personified, the closest any of them would probably ever come to an actual deity. Why were they not flinging themselves at her feet in awe?

Doyle moved to stand beside her. He prodded her in the back so that she stumbled toward the crowd. More metal jangled from beneath her diaphanous skirts.

"Take a good look. She and her kind are the ones responsible for the disappearances and deaths no one can explain. They're scavengers and parasites feeding off us because we haven't had the resources to send them back to where they belong."

He took up the end of the chain that draped between her wrists and jerked her upright so that she had to stretch onto her toes. She stifled a cry. Power rolled off her in waves. The temperature in the packed room went up five degrees. The Sorleys backed away. If Doyle's control slipped for even a moment she would obliterate every living thing in the room.

"What is it?" asked an officer Jack didn't know without his name badge. The man's hand crept to his belt as if he'd forgotten he wasn't armed. Doyle lowered the chain so Credeilia could stand flat-footed again. His mouth curled.

"She is a daughter of Finvarra—a faery king from the Otherworld."

There was general puzzlement as his guests tried to assimilate the creature before them with their preconceived notions of 'fairies' and magic. Credeilia bared her teeth and hissed like a cat when a curious town hall official moved closer for a better look. Doyle yanked on her chain. She staggered, and her hands caught the front of his shirt.

Her eyes swooped up to snare his for an instant before he shoved her away, white-faced. When she lifted her head, satisfaction simmered in her gaze. He had nearly fallen under her sway. One second was all it would take to sink into those bottomless pupils and never come back up again.

Doyle raked his fingers through his hair, unnerved by the near-catastrophe.

"You see? If it weren't for these metal restraints she would kill us all where we stand. Iron is the only weakness that all of them share. Anything less will only provoke them."

"If she's as dangerous as you say then why haven't you done something about it?" called the officer, shoving his way to the front. Jack backed toward the door. With each passing second it became more apparent that Eira could not be anywhere near this. Doyle was orchestrating a witch hunt, and he wouldn't hesitate to direct it after her. Where was she? Why hadn't she come in yet? Aiden was still missing too.

His brothers stood frozen, transfixed by what was happening. Keith hovered against the wall looking torn. Logan gazed at Credeilia in open adoration. He gripped Glen's sleeve, stretching the fabric around his fist.

"She's not a dancing bear!" he shouted. Ross covered his eyes with a low groan and slunk back into the shadows as every head turned in their direction. Keith grimaced. Glen tried to grab Logan's arm to hold him back, but he shook him off and moved through the crowd.

"People, you're standing in the presence of a living, breathing goddess and you're acting like you can just get rid of her without any consequences? What do you think the fae will do if they find out he's been holding her hostage? For all we know the reason we've been buried under all this snow is because he's trying to contain forces he has no chance of controlling." Logan jabbed his finger in Doyle's direction. Doyle's brows snapped together.

"He's under her spell! She's given him a silver tongue and he's trying to use it to save her." Even though he spoke the truth, it sounded like a desperate accusation. Logan's mouth curled with a grim smile. The crowd clustered together, looking between them, uncertain who to believe.

Jack slipped out into the hallway. Credeilia's fury was a coiled dragon. The moment it had space to breathe it would incinerate everything in its path. He dashed for the front door and open air.

The chill night was welcome after the stifling heat of too many bodies. He shivered as the cold kissed the sweat clinging to his skin. He scanned the porch.

Eira and Aiden were nowhere in sight. He ran the length of the wrap-around porch then jumped over the railing onto a packed snowdrift. The yellow glow from the icicle lights hanging off the porch cast a dim halo around the house, but an unsettling darkness cloaked the rest of the yard.

"Eira!" Jack cupped his hands around his mouth.

"Help! She's not breathing!"

Jack whipped around. The shout came from the road. His feet devoured the distance to the fence. The awkward weight of the harp slapped his thigh as he ran. Straining his eyes, he could barely make out the two figures. Aiden knelt over Eira, whose black hair fanned around her like spilled ink on the snow.

"Eira!" Jack dropped to his knees and reached for her hand. He held it against his cheek, but it was ice-cold. Here eyelids didn't so much as flutter. He whirled on Aiden.

"What did you do?"

"Nothing! She just fainted." Aiden held up his hands and shuffled back. Panic made him forget that he was taller and stronger than Jack.

"Did she touch anything? Anything!" Jack turned her hands palm-up to make certain they were empty. Aiden edged nearer, wide-eyed and stammering.

"No. She said she wanted to see Dad's camper. I took her in and she said it gave her the creeps so we came out here, and then this giant deer came out of nowhere. It reared up in front of us and I thought maybe it kicked her because she just dropped like a stone."

"The stag got past the fence?"

"No, we were over there by the old apple tree." He pointed to the large tree Logan had parked beneath on their failed reconnaissance mission. "When she wouldn't wake up I tried to carry her back, but this was as far as I got before I heard you yelling."

"Where did the stag go?" Jack slashed his head left and right, certain Winterthorn couldn't be far away. Aiden frowned.

"Who cares? Listen, one of us needs to get help. She's—"

"Where did it go?" Jack's entire body clenched with the effort not to strangle the information out of him. For once, Aiden wasn't baiting him on purpose.

"I don't know, man. After she went down, he took off." Jack gathered her into his lap. From her serene expression he could almost believe she was sleeping. His heart was pumping so fast that he wouldn't have been able to separate her pulse from his even if he could find it.

"Go inside and get my brother, Glen. He's a doctor. Hurry!"

Eager for something to do, Aiden nodded. His sneakers kicked up snow as he dashed for the house. When he was gone, Jack raised Eira's face.

"Come on Eira, please. Open your eyes!" He patted her cheek—light, rapid taps to get any kind of reaction. He looked over his shoulder, but Aiden had only just reached the front steps.

"What did you do?" He hurled his frustration at the night.

A sorrow-filled whine answered him, only ten feet away. Jack's blood iced. He hugged Eira tighter before lifting his head to face Winterthorn.

He wasn't disguised as an animal anymore. He wore his true faery shape—nearly foot tall with hot coals for eyes and a long, arrow-tipped nose.

"What did you do?" Jack growled against her hair. To his surprise, Winterthorn bowed his head in unmistakable relief.

"It was the only way." He lifted his chin to indicate the lodge. "This man bears an old grudge, a cyst that has festered and infected his mind. He seeks to strike at me through those I hold most dear." His rage pulsated. Hoarfrost grew over the iron fence, only to hiss and melt away. Winterthorn towered over Jack, flexing his fingers in impotent rage.

"One byproduct of the protection your father wrought from me with his lies meant I could not communicate with you unless you spoke to me first. When I would have reached out through her, you kept her from me. This was the surest way to establish an audience with you." Jack felt as though he'd stumbled into oncoming traffic. He shook his head.

"You're lying!"

Winterthorn's laugh was an avalanche, cold and merciless, a deep rumble of strength. Jack clenched his jaw, realizing how stupid the accusation was.

"But she's your daughter!" He lifted her up so Winterthorn could admire his handiwork.

"To atone for damage she sustained at our first meeting, I gave her the thing that she wanted most—to know unconditional love. She should have died that night on the road, and I could only prolong her death for so long. So, I gave her an untarnished soul to bring into the world, so that for a moment she could experience true love. Tonight, I took it back. What was done once can be done again."

"How?"

"I offer an exchange—your father was fond of them."

Jack's hand crept protectively to the strap of his bag. The faery's eyes missed nothing, but he snorted his disdain.

"I have no need for your treasure. There are others who seek that prize. No, you will help free my lady, and then I will tell you how you may save yours." Winterthorn stepped back and scrutinized the fence. The metal twined in a pattern of intricate knots across the horizontal bars.

"I cannot cross the boundary this one has set with his iron and incantations. I need only for you to grant me a way in."

"What am I supposed to do? Doyle's inciting a witch hunt in there right now. At the rate he was going I'd be surprised if they haven't crucified her by now." It was probably not the smartest thing to say.

Winterthorn went stone still. The temperature plunged. He lunged to within an inch of the iron. His face contorted—half-beast and half-man. Jack scrambled back.

"Bring down the barriers! This mortal will pay for his crimes with his blood!"

He melted into a shower of flurries just as Aiden returned with Glen. Jack's fingers curled around Eira's hand, willing it to squeeze back.

"No!" Glen leaned over her to go through the same inspection Jack had already completed. "She's dead!"

Aiden flinched.

"We've got to go," said Jack, grabbing Glen's sleeve. "Aiden, stay with Eira. We'll be back." He hardly recognized his own voice. Glen stumbled after him, fighting to return to Eira's prone form.

"What are you doing?"

"Winterthorn killed her so he could blackmail us with her soul. If we save Credeilia he'll tell us how to save Eira." He ground out the words, seething with hatred for the fae and their games. Glen froze, just as horrified by the proposition as Jack had been. Jack grimaced.

"We can still save her. If we don't do this, she'll have died for nothing."

"What are we supposed to do?"

His brothers stood at the edge of the crowd, watching as Doyle guided Credeilia to stand on a chair so everyone could see her. Blue flames danced in her eyes, but Doyle took no notice. His confidence was making him cocky. Jack waited in the doorway as Glen caught the others' attention. He studied Credeilia.

How could she have allowed herself to be captured? Her powers were as great as Winterthorn's. What power did Doyle possess that he could hold a faery hostage? Doyle beckoned Mrs. Heidrich forward to touch the ends of Credeilia's long, blonde hair. She stepped forward with child-like delight, petting one waist-length braid while the faery endured it in stubborn silence.

"Did you find Eira?" Logan asked, leading the others over to the doorway.

In an urgent whisper Glen recounted Winterthorn's ultimatum.

Shock rocked them all back on their heels, but Glen made a quick slashing movement to remind them not to draw attention. As one they looked at Credeilia, who turned to face the window with sudden alertness.

"You say he just needs to be able to get on the grounds?" Keith clarified in a hushed voice. Jack nodded, eyes burning. Keith walked to the nearest window. He scanned the frozen landscape through narrowed eyes. Jack thought tears clouded his vision when Keith's body began to blur, but a few seconds more, and his brother projected a thin halo of power. Suddenly, his hands jumped to his temples and he hunched forward. The silver aura winked out.

"Apparently his safeguards don't just suppress faeries' magic," he muttered.

Despite everything that was going on in the living room, Credeilia's head snapped around. Her gaze speared them, unfathomable and intense. Careful not to look directly into her eyes, Jack gave a short nod. Yes. Help was coming.

"Ross, buy me some time," Keith groaned, putting his fingers to his temples. Silver waves poured out of him to seep through the floorboards. Ross frowned but opened the nearest window. He sent out a call and an answer came almost immediately.

Jack threw himself to the ground as dozens of blackbirds streamed into the house. People screamed as the little black bodies pelted them like darts, raking, pecking, flapping. Lamps broke, people stampeded, and Doyle roared out over the noise.

"What's she doing?" cried the Mrs. Heidrich. "I thought you said her magic was contained!" Her words ended on a shriek as a fat bird got tangled in her downy, gray hair. She and her husband were the last to evacuate the room.

Doyle rounded on Credeilia, who fell off the chair. Her skirts splashed up from her ankles, revealing ugly black manacles connecting her feet. Logan, Douglas, and Jack ran to intercept Doyle while Craig reached for the chains. His hand closed around her wrists and power spiraled up through his arms.

"Don't!" Doyle gasped. Douglas had him in a chokehold, his fists pulled tight under Doyle's right ear. Craig funneled his magic out through his hands. The iron glowed red-hot. Credeilia screamed, and Craig muttered an apology as sweat dripped from his brow. He released the metal that had transformed into pure silver. Doyle doubled his efforts to get free.

"Stop! You don't know what you're doing!"

His words were drowned by the hurricane roar that exploded from Credeilia. Invisible limbs of high-powered wind flung them all to the four corners of the room. Jack slammed into the fifteen-foot pine tree. Glass ornaments shattered and slashed him as he crashed through the branches.

"You think you can hold me prisoner?" Credeilia's voice thrummed deep, and low. Lifting one hand to her temple, she pointed the five fingers of the other at Keith. A jet of lightning shot from her fingertips and struck him square in the chest. He lit up like a Christmas tree.

"No!" Jack shouted hoarsely. But instead of hurt him she added her power to his.

The house shuddered and groaned. Thin twisting vines curled up through the floorboards. Jack scrambled over the smashed baubles and lights, stepping over the grasping green creepers that wound around chair legs and scaled the walls with impossible speed. Within seconds, a moving green carpet covered the floor.

Jack ran to Logan sprawled face-down by the fireplace. The thick garland from the mantle tangled around his legs. He hadn't moved since the wind knocked him into the wall. When Jack turned him over a lump the size of a goose egg stood out above his left eye. Logan groaned and put a hand to his head.

"Ugh, I think the hall just decked me with a bough of holly."

Jack rolled his eyes and hefted him over his shoulder. They were built along the same lines, and Jack staggered to one knee. Ivy wrapped around his ankle. Jack surged up, kicking free. The only safe space was a narrow circle around Keith. He was on his knees as Credeilia continued to pump her power into him. Jack set Logan down and peered through the shattered window. The attack wasn't isolated to the house.

The forest was encroaching onto the lawn. Saplings speared up from the ground. Thick roots shredded the clean sheet of snow, anchoring cars and latching around ankles and feet as Doyle's guests tried to escape. More vines stretched down from the trees, uprooting shingles to peel back the roof.

"No!" Doyle pulled out a pocket knife. Before anyone could stop him, he jumped on Credeilia and stabbed her leg.

An explosion of thunder tore open the sky. A fork of lightning struck the copse of trees by the road. The large apple tree fell over, tearing down part of the fence.

Craig and Douglas dragged Doyle back from Credeilia. Glen crawled forward to inspect the wound in her calf, but the heat of iron had cauterized the skin. She bared sharp, cat's teeth, and drew back her leg. Doyle laughed.

"See? Even when you try to help them they'll still turn on you."

The room iced over. It happened so quickly that the house and all the vines were coated in thin, platinum frost before Jack realized he couldn't feel his fingertips. There was a crash as something massive plowed through the front door. Then the great stag stood in the living room. Doyle flung off Craig and Douglas as if they weighed no more than paper.

The stag leapt for him, transforming in midair. Winterthorn lifted Doyle by the front of his shirt with one hand. He formed a long, jagged icicle in the other and plunged it deep into Doyle's chest.

His body convulsed. Ice shards ricocheted through his veins, severing vessels, freezing him from the inside out. A thick crust of frost caked over his skin and hardened until he became a solid block of ice.

Winterthorn let him fall. He shattered when he hit the ground with a splintering crash.

With blurring speed Winterthorn went to Credeilia and gathered her in his arms. Gentle as a deer, he brushed her face with his, soft feathering touches against cheeks and brows. Neither said a word that Jack could hear, but emotion swirled around them like a gathering storm.

"Hey! We rescued your girlfriend, now bring Eira back." Jack intruded deliberately. The tender touches and unmistakable love between them ignited bitterness inside him. How dare Winterthorn look so happy after what he'd done. Credeilia tensed. Winterthorn looked up. There was a challenge in his dark, predatory eyes, an alpha sizing up a potential rival.

A shower of flurries whirled, blurring the two faeries from view.

"Wait!" Jack jumped forward, intending to pull them back. But as his hand connected with ice-cold flesh, his feet lifted off the ground. He heard his brothers shout his name, and then he was spinning and weaving, helpless as a snowflake tumbled on the wind.

Chapter 18

"Get your hands off me! How dare you! Let me go!"

Shouts dragged Jack from the swirling fog. He winced and put a hand to his temple. When he looked up, he was kneeling on the rocky bank of a lake. Silver mist danced over its black, satin surface. The shouting came from behind him.

Cringing against a whirl of vertigo, Jack turned to see Winterthorn catch Credeilia shoulders. Her forearms were an angry red where the bracers had been, but he avoided the fresh burns while holding her at arm's length. Dewdrops glittered in the thicket of her lashes as she fought. He held her easily, but intense lines of sorrow etched themselves across his ancient face.

"I gave up my kingdom for you!" She raked her nails along his cheek. He didn't make a sound but pulled her against his chest, imprisoning her so she couldn't do more harm. She thrust out her chin.

"How many more of your foul creations have you loosed upon the earth?"

"None." It was the first word he had uttered, and it was a ragged shred. Even Jack, who wished the immortal nothing but pain, couldn't help the flare of pity that single sound sparked. Credeilia wasn't so easily swayed. She raised her burned wrists.

"He bound me in iron. He stripped me of my powers. I needed you, but you left me in darkness to protect her instead."

"It was my duty to protect her," he said in a voice that carried the weight of mountains. Lightning struck a rotted tree. The hollow trunk exploded.

"Ah yes, your protection." The scorn in her voice made Winterthorn raise an arm as if to ward off a physical blow. "As I recall, your protection left me trapped in the roots of a tree and cast out of my own world, not jealously guarded like some precious jewel!"

"Once my battle with Darragh was over I scoured that forest for you. In calling for you I drew her mother instead." The emeralds on his stag brooch flashed as his broad shoulders sagged. "The injuries she sustained attempting to avoid me should have claimed her life. I thought I could atone by granting her heart's desire."

Thunder rumbled in the distance. Jack flinched.

"It is against our laws, or have you become so drunk on your own power you no longer feel they apply to you?"

"She is merely a fae soul bonded to a dream. She poses no threat to our world or theirs."

Jack frowned, trying to make sense of Winterthorn's explanation. If he understood correctly then Winterthorn's power was even greater than he'd ever believed. He could create new life from lost souls?

"You should have left the girl to die as you left me to rot in that tree!"

The cloak of shame draped heavily upon his shoulders. Her anger was a palpable heat. But he was not the leader of the Wild Hunt for nothing. Despite his immense sorrow he looked straight into her eyes.

"And you, My Lady? When the woodcarver freed you, why did you not return to me? For a thousand Faerie years I could not detect your light, and then for one moment I sensed you in the mortal realm, but by the time I arrived that light extinguished as if it had never been. To make matters worse the human you called to awaken you was a liar and a cheat. He sent me on a wild goose after I gave a vow of protection in good faith. Even in mortal time that was decades ago."

"When I first awakened even the secret doorways to Faerie were barred against me thanks to your banishing spell. My powers were weak with disuse and Darragh was very close. I dared not reveal myself for fear that he would find me first. And then I discovered your betrayal." Her nose wrinkled in a snarl.

"I could not allow that insult to stand. After my first attempt to destroy her failed, I thought a mortal tool would have truer aim. However, I underestimated the hatred you inspire in others. Once that fool realized he could use me against you not even my word was enough to convince him we could remain allies."

Jack gaped. She was the one behind the attacks on Eira? If it shocked him, it rocked Winterthorn to his core.

"Credeilia..." The sound of her name was pain in its most piercing form. Power rippled around the glade and slammed into Jack's chest. He doubled over with a small moan, and for the first time the two faeries took note of him.

Despite what she'd just revealed, Winterthorn leapt between Jack and his lady. Antlers erupted from his hair, massive and threatening and unnerving to see when the rest of him remained a man. Jack held up his hands, but it was Credeilia who diffused the situation.

"I know you. You are his son—the one who freed me. I see his light in you. What are you doing here?" She stepped out from behind Winterthorn and approached Jack with a gentle smile of welcome. Moments ago, he'd thought her beautiful, but now he saw nothing but bitterness and hate. Her hand cupped his chin and tilted his face up for inspection. Jack thrust his finger at Winterthorn.

"He swore that if my brothers and I freed you he would save Eira." He knew it was not the smartest thing to say, but the longer he waited the further Eira slipped away. At the mention of her name, Credeilia's fingernails scored his face.

"My blessing lays upon you. I gave you a gift that would see you a king among men, and even you betray me for her?"

"He promised her life for yours." Blood trickled down his neck.

"And if I take her life, what will you do?" Her delicate features hardened. Jack gulped. It was as if she'd reached inside him and tore out his heart.

"Before he can do anything he must stand trial for crimes laid against him in the Ash Queen's court," said Winterthorn in a deep rumble. The empty place in Jack's chest became a black hole. He jerked his chin free and clenched his fingers around the strap across his chest.

"This was a trap."

"I am the Hunter. You stole one of the great relics of Faerie. I am duty-bound to retrieve it—and you." White teeth flashed in his dark face. "I cannot recall the last time I was led on such a merry chase. Your father chose his rewards wisely."

Credeilia looked at him with renewed interest.

"Uaithne chose you? I have never heard of her choosing a mortal. Your talent must be exceptional indeed." Winterthorn flicked his cape over one shoulder.

"That remains to be seen. If you wish to save my daughter's soul you must journey to the Ash Queen's court and await judgment for what you have done. It is a grave offense to take one of our sacred treasures beyond the borders of Faerie. The Hunt will lead you to the boundary of the Ash Queen's realm."

No sooner were the words out of his mouth than gleaming red eyes appeared in the surrounding shadows. A familiar red wolf loped forward. Her mouth dropped open in a silent smile before she turned and headed back into the trees. Jack glanced back at the faeries, but they were gone. There was only the black lake and its creeping mist.

He had to run to catch up to Gwen. Though she moved at a steady pace her dark coat blended easily with the shadows. The knowledge of who she was left Jack feeling awkward as he trailed behind her.

"You were protecting her, weren't you?" he said finally. Her ears twitched and she paused to swing her head back.

"That first day on her porch, you were guarding her in case the fae came back. And then at our house, you were trying to make her turn back, not take her away."

Her pink tongue lolled.

"I'm sorry. I thought you were hunting her."

She kept walking. His apology meant nothing to her. She took two more paces and froze. Her hackles rose and a growl rippled from her chest before she melted back into the trees. Jack raised his head.

His only warning was a soft whistle before a coarse whip coiled around his neck. The cord pulled tight, choking off his cry of surprise. He clawed at the whip, but its owner gave a savage yank that spun him around and lifted him off his feet. Jack landed hard.

"Not so proud now, are we?" hissed a voice from the shadows of a large hole carved into the side of a hill. Jack's jaw clenched as he recognized the lisping sound. Cruel fingers seized a fistful of his hair and yanked without mercy.

Slick, blistered flesh brushed Jack's cheek, and he jerked away, earning a deep stab of thorns into his throat.

"Now you shall suffer as I have suffered, thief." Odhran spat in his face.

"I'm not a thief," said Jack through gritted teeth. "It chose me."

"Liar! Uaithne would never choose gutter scum like you. She belongs with me."

"You can have her! I don't want it. I'm here for Eira. I'll stand trial but her soul goes free." It was comforting to pretend he had any control over the situation. Odhran's lip curled.

He turned on his heel, dragging Jack by the cord of thorns around his neck. Jack had to scramble to his feet before the whip tightened and gouged holes into his skin. Odhran walked straight -backed into the mouth of the cave. The passage opened abruptly into the ghastly hall Jack remembered. As the crowd parted to let Odhran pass, they caught sight of Jack stumbling in his wake and hissed. A hulking figure approached. Only one eye peered out from beneath his fleshy forehead. Jack shrank back.

"Human?" it grunted. The cyclops stretched out a three-fingered hand to touch Jack's hair, but snatched it back again when Jack jerked his head.

"Out of the way, oaf!" Odhran snapped. He shoved the cyclops aside even though he only reached the monster's waist. More fae crowded close, nearly all of them grotesque. The few females Jack could make out were hunch-backed crones with yellow, broken teeth and warped bodies bowed until they touched the floor. The males gestured crudely, and Jack averted his eyes. He was relieved that none of the musicians from his previous trip were playing their macabre instruments this time.

"Now." Odhran snatched Jack's hair again and spun him around. "Now, we will see who the true bard is."

A loud commotion erupted from the back of the hall. Squawks, shrieks, and howls rose to the cave roof. The ground rumbled and shook. If not for the faery's hold on his hair, Jack would have fallen. Up from the ground an enormous crystal emerged like a pillar of ice. Trapped deep within the prism was a large, blinding ball of light.

Jack tore free of Odhran, sacrificing several strands of hair, and ran toward it. Odhran yanked on his lead rope with a cackle. Jack's spine arched against the agony of a dozen needle-sharp spikes gouging his throat. He sank his teeth into his lower lip to bite back a cry, but as he coughed and choked, a film of blood flowed over his tongue.

Odhran waited for Jack's look of defiance, and the moment their eyes locked, Jack's muscles froze. He circled Jack slowly.

"That I have suffered so on your account is beyond bearing," he muttered mostly to himself. "Even by mortal standards you are frail." He stepped forward and tore the bag from Jack's side. The leather strap snapped, nearly dislocating Jack's shoulder. Odhran held the harp between his two hands, inhaling the carved gold blossoms as if they were real fragrant blooms. "At last.!" Reverently, he tucked it in the crook of his arm and laid his fingers against the strings.

One golden string snapped.

"This cannot be!" he said, astonished. "What have you done? She is broken!"

"She wasn't the last time I played her."

Habit made him say it, made him respond to the faery's overinflated sense of authority with the same disregard he'd always shown Keith. But Keith was his brother who restrained himself out of love. Odhran backhanded Jack with enough force to lift him from the ground and fling him several feet away.

His head struck stone. Stars flashed before his eyes. The volume of blood in his mouth doubled, and agony popped in his jaw like a berry. Pleased, Odhran raised his arm to swat him again. Jack shut his eyes, but the blow never came.

"Let the Queen pass judgement on you for your crimes."

Odhran snapped his fingers and the giant crystal cracked in two. A figure fashioned from starlight staggered out. Her feet hovered a foot above the ground, but if he squinted he could make out Eira in the center of the light.

She—it, he wasn't sure which—flew to where Jack lay on the ground. With another wince, he rolled onto his side. Experimentally he feathered his fingers over the lump swelling under his cheekbone. Eira's fire-bright hands unwound the vines that circled his throat.

Jack shivered, unnerved that he was staring at a ghost. No, he corrected himself. Not a ghost—a soul. Eira's soul. And it was shining. It belonged with her body back in their world, not trapped deep in the belly of this hollow hill.

He shifted his jaw from side to side with another grimace. The willowisp gave a hiccup of warning that Odhran was approaching. Jack tried to thrust her behind him, but his hand passed right through her arm. Odhran, on the other hand, snatched her out of the air.

"Only a mortal would wager a prize like Uaithne for you." He squeezed her arm, and she hissed and dropped to one knee.

Jack froze, paralyzed with rage. Eira's spirit tossed back the shadow of her hair. Her blazing eyes promised revenge. Odhran's lip curled.

"You should never have allied yourself with him. He is already condemned, and now your fates are tied. When he dies, so will you."

Fire spewed up from the ground, enclosing the three of them in a tight circle. Jack scrambled back as flames licked his sneakers. The willowisp flickered in surprise.

"You will control yourself, Odhran, if you wish me to pay any heed to your petty complaint." Smoke and shadow poured itself into the enormous throne situated beneath a swag of calcified drapery that glittered in the firelight.

Jack grunted as Odhran materialized behind him and forced him to the ground with a boot to the back of his knees.

"My Queen, I bring you the vagrant who stole Uaithne from our hall. Let him stand and be punished. Restore her to me so that I might bring pleasure to your court once again."

Lounging on the throne with one leg curled over an armrest was the Ash Queen. She wore a gown of black leather armor. Dozens of throwing blades crisscrossed her bodice and long ropes of chainmail looped down from her waist. Jack shrank back. Danger coiled around her like a snake.

The Queen stroked a small, glowing, glass vial dangling from a silver chain around her neck. One by one she took in the willowisp, Odhran, and Jack. Her blackberry-stained lips peeled back from her teeth.

"The Harp of Seasons cannot be taken or given, Odhran. She chooses. You know this." Her eyes cut him like a razor blade.

Jack tried to swallow the fear pinching his vocal chords. The Queen's voice was raw power, throaty and deep. His body leaned toward her even as his mind rebelled.

Odhran hissed a denial.

"This mortal took her to his world where our powers could not follow. He has corrupted her against me." He kicked Jack's outer thigh to show his contempt. The Ash Queen traced a silver-tipped fingernail up the base of her throat to the outer corner of her lips and tapped her cheek. Boredom left her eyes heavy-lidded.

"What punishment would you suggest for such a crime?" She spoke with disinterest, but her amber eyes were alight. She knew what Odhran wanted. His intentions weren't exactly subtle. Odhran puffed out his chest.

"His death must be an example—" He meant to say more, but she waved her hand for silence.

"An example to whom?" she asked with sultry amusement. "Are there a bevy of young mortals capable of breaching our borders with designs on our most sacred relics?"

A chaotic jumble of emotions flapped leathery wings in Jack's chest. Chief among them was satisfaction that the former harper's plans were falling apart. Odhran drew himself up, affronted.

"Your Majesty, I seek justice for—"

"What you seek is salve for your pride. The Harp of Seasons has chosen a mortal, yet you persist in thinking yourself his superior. Though it is unwise of you to persist, a trial by song will be enough to settle this dispute."

If this was what Odhran wanted, he wasn't happy to get it. His fleshless lips pulled back from his teeth.

"Uaithne is broken. The boy damaged her—" His throat constricted around the lie, and warm laughter rippled over them as the Queen tipped back her head. She set her booted feet on the ground and approached Eira, whose image flickered again. The Ash Queen reached down to slide her fingers beneath Eira's ghostly chin, but when she saw the face looking up at her the monster she concealed leapt to the surface. Her eyes flashed like sunlight across polished steel.

"Pass me the harp." Eira didn't move, but the Ash Queen gave her no chance to resist. She locked her eyes on Eira's and it was as though invisible hands took hold of her limbs, unbent her spine and controlled her fingers to first grasp the harp and then hand it over. The Queen took the instrument, and at once the threads binding Eira to her will snapped. Eira fell to all fours while the Queen lazily inspected the harp.

"An unworthy hand attempted to play music on these strings. As Odhran says, this offense is punishable by death." Her tongue drew a slow line along the arch of her lip. "I myself have heard Odhran's talent bring her harmonies to life. But, if her favor no longer shines on him then the transgression is his. The Harp of Seasons can hardly be expected to remain impartial."

She waved her hand and two wooden harps appeared. Eira gaped at the open display of magic, but Jack's spirit recoiled. The harps floated toward him and Odhran, who accepted his with distaste. The faery bard shot the gold harp a petulant look.

Jack gathered his courage. His hands shook. He couldn't let the combative atmosphere cloud his purpose. Already he felt the harp flex its control over his mind. He gulped.

"Eira isn't part of this. Let her go."

Eira glared at him. The Ash Queen looked between them and smiled.

"I see Winterthorn's skills as a hunter have not diminished since he withdrew from the world. He baited this trap well." She glided toward him, long liquid movements he couldn't help but drink in. Fear raked low in his belly like a trapped animal clawing to get out. She tickled her fingernails along the underside of his chin. He shuddered.

"If you wish to save the girl's soul you must save yourself first. Should you prove unworthy of the harp's power, your life is forfeit and she will share your fate." Eira darted forward.

"Jack's not responsible for what happens to me." No one paid any attention to her. This was about possessing the harp's ancient power, and if Jack wouldn't use his talent to harness that power for himself, the fae would use anything at their disposal they knew he'd fight for.

"How are we to be judged?" Odhran asked sourly. This contest did nothing to assuage his pride. He couldn't hide his bitterness even in front of his Queen. The Ash Queen's eyes swept over Eira. A tremor passed over her again, sending her light flickering again. The need to protect her was a pounding drum in Jack's chest.

"You will pit your skill against one another for the soul of this young woman. It is nothing for music to move one to dance or weep, but to live or die—that is a feat worthy of the Harp of Seasons."

Odhran gave a wet laugh. Jack felt like he was drowning. An impossible task. Why had he expected anything else? Like an idiot he'd charged headfirst into an ambush, and now he and Eira were going to die.

I care nothing for the girl, but you *are mine.*

"I accept, My Queen." Odhran bowed until the stump of his nose brushed the floor. The Ash Queen turned to Jack. He dropped his head.

"I accept," he whispered.

Odhran struck first with the opening chords of a funeral dirge. Eira moaned. The color of her aura faded to gray. Jack fumbled to settle the strange harp into place. His hands shook trying to find the notes for an upbeat pop song. The effect was instantaneous. Eira's form grew more solid, and her light intensified.

Use me.

Jack screwed his eyes shut and frantically switched to a song he'd composed in the basement. The cave rang with the dueling music. There was no harmony, just noise. It threw off his timing. His hands slipped on the strings. Eira's face grew gaunt. Deep hollows appeared beneath her cheekbones that sliced through her skin sharp as razor blades.

Let me help you. Uaithne was a breath against his ear. Jack glanced at the Ash Queen who looked unimpressed as she inspected her silver nails. *I will not allow you to lose, but without me there is no way the girl will last long enough for you to win.*

Jack knew what it wanted. If he tapped into the music it imparted to him then he would find the power he needed to hold Eira to the light. Credeilia's blessing had given him talent but no magic of his own. Even without the harp's influence Odhran was fae. He had every advantage, but Jack was afraid. There was no such thing as a faery gift without strings.

Odhran's tune changed keys. Eira's form wavered. She would have collapsed if the Queen's magic didn't hold her upright. Her light changed from gray to blue.

Jack poured his heart into his song. Instead of competing with Odhran he decided to complement him, siphoning his magic to use against him. The cacophony relaxed into a mournful lament. The fae looked around, stunned to hear the echoes flung back to layer melody upon countermelody, until it was as if an entire orchestra of strings joined in.

The fullness returned to Eira's face. She smiled, and her image faded into the center of her light. Relief split Jack's face. He felt a tear slide down his cheek. It was working!

The Ash Queen swung her head, eyes gleaming with fascination. Jack pushed his fear to the back of his mind and focused on keeping pace with Odhran. The faery tried to outplay him, executing a series of intricate arpeggios that rippled to life a story of unrequited love playing out in shadowy swirls through the air.

Eira moaned. Almost at once she was opaque again, her light nearly gone. Jack's mouth went dry. He tried to counter the complexity of the faery's song with simplicity.

It wasn't enough.

Although it eased the lines around her mouth, Eira's eyes fluttered closed and her luminescence ebbed.

Jack's fingers stilled his strings.

Without his music to counter Odhran's, Eira's light all but winked out. A cry of denial tore from her mouth.

Help me! He shrieked the words into the echoing chamber in his mind. Silence answered him. For one soul-shattering moment he thought the harp was going to punish him again.

I thought you'd never ask.

For the second time in his life Jack felt his head split open as the harp poured its power into his mind. Eons of compositions lay at his fingertips. *No, none of those. This one is for us....*

Jack began to play again. Invisible fingers settled over his, guiding him through a confession ripped straight from his soul. It was her song, his feelings captured in each blinding note. The cavern rang with his song. He willed it into every crack and corner until Odhran's playing could barely be heard as anything more than a low hum.

Eira's lashes sprang apart. The shadows receded and her light blazed so bright it was blinding. That was nothing compared to the pride glowing in her eyes.

"Enough!" The Ash Queen held up a hand and both harps vanished into mist. She touched a finger to her eye and it came away with a touch of moisture. She stared at the droplet as though she'd ever seen such a thing before.

When she spoke, her voice was soft with awe. "Well done, mortal. You have won the girl her life."

Eira launched herself at Jack. Though he knew she wasn't really there, his arms came around her anyway. Victory and terror clung to him as she engulfed him in her light.

Odhran's scream echoed throughout the cavern. The Ash Queen pointed at him, and he rose into the air. His body bowed, bending backward until his spine snapped with a loud crack. The Queen let him fall with a careless flick of her wrist. She turned away while her court devoured him like a swarm of ants.

"I had grown weary of his preening anyway." She fixed her gaze upon Jack and Eira, who moved to place herself in front of him, acting as a shield. The Ash Queen looked through her to stab Jack with a look laced with promise. The attraction he thought he'd felt earlier shriveled. Though she wore her mask of beauty well a monster lurked underneath, waiting and hoping to be provoked into violence.

"You have but a moment to say your farewells."

Eira's spirit flickered with shock.

"You said if I won we could go free!" Jack shouted. "You said our fates were tied together." The Queen looked over her shoulder, savoring his anguish. Then he understood. His heart was a jackhammer inside his chest. He'd known what accepting the harp would mean, and still he'd held onto the hope that the fae would keep their word.

Eira's furrowed brow told him she didn't understand yet what the true price of her freedom was. The Ash Queen was more than happy to fill her in.

"In winning, he has earned the right to claim the Harp of Seasons as his own. But the harp is a thing of power. It will be...instrumental," she savored the word, "in the coming war between our worlds. Things are in motion now that cannot be reversed. In good conscience, I cannot allow such a weapon to fall into my enemy's hands." Jack swayed as her cage closed with a definitive snap.

"Take it back then," he said through gritted teeth. "I don't want it." The Queen touched the vial around her throat again.

"Uaithne chose you. You will find it...unpleasant if you try to leave without her." Jack knew only too well how unpleasant it would be. His head fell forward onto his chest. It was as though someone had torn out his heart and stitched up a stone in its place.

"But Eira—" The Queen cut him off before he could erect another false hope to cower behind.

"Winterthorn's child has been spared. You waste time arguing that would be better suited returning her to her corporal form. There is a limit to how long a soul can exist outside its body."

Jack wanted to argue. He wanted to fling the harp into the fire and never set eyes on it again, but already he felt its power creeping back into his mind. Soft notes like laughter dripped into his ear. *You will learn to love me.*

He had just beaten the best bard that Faerie had to offer. There was no way it would let him go now. Like the man who ate beneath the faery hill, Jack was bound forever. Despair settled over him like dirt over a grave.

He turned to Eira, or the part of her that was still there. Already she had begun to fade away. The fae never gave anything without taking something in return. His eyes burned.

Eira took one look at his face and shook her head. Wildly, she looked around for a platter of food or goblet of wine, but slowly her form dissolve. From across the distance of time and space her body called her back. She reached for fistfuls of his sweater as if she might anchor herself to him, but her hands passed through him, as substantial as smoke.

"Jack...!"

He tried to clasp both sides of her face, but it was like trying to catch a rainbow in his hand. He'd thought she could save him, that caring enough could break the harp's grip. At least he'd managed to save one of them.

The pearl of a tear slid down her cheek. She covered his hands with her own transparent ones.

"I'll find a way to get you out of here. Whatever happens, however long, please don't give up! I will come back!"

She was nearly gone. Jack bent forward to kiss her cheek in farewell, but as their lips touched, she became less than air, sailing back to a world that would go on without him. Jack blinked at the space where she had last stood. He willed some trace of her to remain. There was only a cold ache that settled in and made itself a home.

A hand landed on his shoulder. He flinched, but didn't turn.

"You are destined for greatness, Jack Sorley. You'll forget her in time." The Ash Queen spun him around and regarded him with the same fascination as before. He recoiled. He might be her prisoner, but he would never become her tool. Even as he thought it, the reality of his situation mocked him. She had forever to wear down his resistance. Though she clearly wished to strip his mind bare to plumb the depths of his talent, she could afford to wait.

You are mine now, Jack Sorley, and now all of Faerie knows it. And because he dropped his eyes to the ground he was not sure whether it was the Queen or the harp that claimed him his fate.

Chapter 19

"**S**how him to his quarters, Sindriel." Jack recognized the faery Scatha summoned the moment he saw the braided flame of red-gold curls. The twisted and distorted members of the Ash Court drew back to let her pass. She wore a different dress this time, a knee-length sheath of spider silk that made him think of an insect trapped in a web.

The Ash Queen leaned toward Jack, inspecting him with an unblinking stare that made him feel like a new blade she was studying for imperfections. She withdrew one of the knives from her bodice and tucked the point between her teeth.

"A Solitary Queen has never sat on a Faerie throne, and the Harp of Seasons has never bound herself to a human. We are destined to change this world of ours, you and I."

Not on your life, Jack wanted to say, but dejection locked his jaw.

Executing a deep curtsy, the faery maid led him from the hall. Jack barely saw anything as he shuffled one foot in front of the other through the long twisting tunnels. Not once did Sindriel look over her shoulder to see if he followed. Jack glanced down a dark corridor to his right, wondering if she would stop him if he tried to escape. After all, she'd let him go the last time. But he didn't have the heart to try.

They came to a round wooden door inlaid with a pattern of gold filigree vines. The door swung open and Sindriel stepped back to let him through.

Not knowing what to expect, Jack was surprised to see an ornate four-poster bed with green velvet covers against the opposite wall. A gold music stand stood in the center of the room with sheet music already waiting for him. Gold ornaments and statues decorated the shelves carved from the walls.

To the left of the door facing the bed hung a large tapestry depicting a woman with flowing black hair. She stood on a snowy meadow wearing a scarlet gown blown back by the wind. The details were so lifelike he swore he saw her breathe.

"I told you it was impossible to escape," murmured Sindriel from the corridor. Jack flinched.

"Go away." He moved further into the room. Forest-green robes lay folded for him at the end of his bed. For the moment, Jack ignored them. The sheet music piqued his curiosity though.

"There is one thing I should show you before I go." Sindriel glided over to the tapestry. Jack gritted his teeth, planning to tear it off the wall as soon as she was gone. She pulled it aside to reveal a large oval mirror. The solid gold border echoed the apple tree motif of the harp.

"I assume you're familiar with the use of a scrying glass?" She arched a brow as if it was a skill even a child should know. He had no idea how to use one, but he knew what they were. Hope ballooned in his chest, but he stabbed it with suspicion. He refused to give her a weapon to torture him with. She watched him, her expression unfathomable.

"You will be able to watch your family through this glass. It should provide comfort...for a while at least." She trailed off, and Jack's blood went cold. What she didn't say was that he could watch them until they grew old and died. In Faerie, he would remain exactly the way he was while his brothers found wives, married, and had families of their own. His hands closed into fists.

"Does the Queen treat all her prisoners like this?" He indicated the gold furnishings with a sarcastic wave of his hand.

"In spite of what you believe, you hold a revered position in this world. Uaithne is one of Faerie's oldest treasures, nearly as respected as the Four Relics themselves. As her keeper, your status is equal to that of any prince." She tilted her head to the side, considering him. Jack looked away first.

"I get why the other guy wanted it so badly," he said grudgingly. "But I don't. I don't belong here. I belong with—" The words died on his lips as a familiar face filled the glass. He took a step toward the mirror with his heart in his throat. He saw as clearly as if he stood in the room with them, but there was no sound.

Eira lay on the ground with Aiden's tear-streaked face above her. He and his brothers had carried her inside the vine-covered ruins of Doyle's house.

Though Glen and Logan attempted to pull him back, Aiden shrugged them off to pinch her nose and cover her mouth with his. As soon as he did Eira lit up with silver light. His brothers flung up their arms to shield themselves, and Aiden scrambled back in fright. She gasped and her lashes lifted. Aiden hugged her, crushing her face into his shoulder. Jack flattened his palms on either side of the glass.

Eira pushed at his chest, her movements jerky like a foal learning to use its limbs for the first time. Glen moved in to help her, but as soon as she saw his face her eyes filled with tears. She waved him away. Jack's eyes burned and his throat felt as though he'd gargled with rusty nails.

She shouldn't have to be the one to tell them. His brothers moved in, pestering her with questions, no doubt demanding to know where he was.

Jack let the tapestry fall back to hide the glass. The last thing he saw was Keith's horrified face before Ross started shouting with veins standing out in his throat. He didn't want to watch them turn on her. He didn't want Sindriel to know about the double-edged bond that still tethered him to Eira, that as she gave his brothers the truth he shared every ounce of her guilt. It was just like the fae to make him feel the joys and sorrows of the life he'd given his freedom to save.

A shadow filled the doorway.

"Leave us." Scatha's low voice rippled throughout the room.

Jack held his breath as the door swung shut. Unchecked power rolled off her in waves. Trembling, he kept his back turned. Her sigh rattled from her throat like the warning hiss of a snake.

"I can see you will be useless to me until you receive closure from your previous life." His nerves jolted beneath his skin when her warm breath fanned the back of his neck. He shivered and flinched away.

"What are you talking about?" He didn't look at her. She terrified him.

"Do you know how I came to power, Jack?" Her chainmail rustled as she glided around in front of him. He shook his head.

"I infiltrated the court of the previous Ash Queen. After I gained her trust I orchestrated a coup and assassinated our High King." Jack didn't raise his gaze above her navel, but as she was so tall that was still about eye-level. "It was past time those prancing court pigs learned the power we Solitary Fae wield. You should have seen their faces when Finvarra fell." She tipped her face up like she was tasting the first drop of rain. Jack feigned interest in a solid gold statue shaped like a goose near his foot.

"What does this have to do with me?"

"I am a warrior first. I know that battles can be won and lost based on morale. It occurs to me," she gave another rattlesnake sigh, "that I would be doing myself a disservice by crippling one of my greatest assets before I get the chance to use it in the field."

"So what are you saying?"

"I am willing to offer you a deal."

Jack froze. His spirits were too battered to hope, but he held perfectly still to hear what she had to say.

"Go back to your world. Take the harp. Your family's lands are as well-guarded as any temple here." She swung away to run her hands along the velvet curtains draped from the four-poster bed. "My condition is this: when I am ready I will summon you, and regardless of where you are or what you're doing you will drop everything to answer my call." She turned and pierced him with her soulless eyes. "Are we agreed?"

Jack's fingers flexed. He wanted to take what she was offering, but he knew he would get burned even worse if he did. Scatha glided to the tapestry and unveiled the mirror. Jack closed his eyes, but not before he saw Aiden pull Eira behind him and square off against Keith. His face was a mask of anguish, the horror of the night written in unchecked tears from his eyes. Eira struggled to get between them, trying to comfort Aiden while drawing Keith's rage.

Just the fact that he knew they were there was enough to crumble Jack's resolve. Scatha watched him, enjoying the battle he waged within himself. He gritted his teeth.

"I don't trust you." He wanted to. He wanted to believe everything would be just as she said. She regarded him through slitted dark eyes and moved along the edge of the room with the slow confidence of a predator stalking its prey.

"I don't care if you trust me. You need only obey." She moved to the door. "Your way back is through that mirror. If you would go you have only moments to do it. The portal will close, and I will not open it again." She vanished, and the smell of brimstone filled the air. Jack swung around to look at the mirror. Instead of his brothers he saw his bedroom back home.

He hesitated. What trouble would he bring back from Faerie this time?

The sheet music caught his eye. Notes penned in gold ink skipped back and forth in a dizzying dance. His mind translated the language of lines and dots into Eira's declaration of freedom and his sentence of a fate worse than death.

He gathered the sheets of parchment and held them over the nearest torch. With a soft crackle, the pages caught fire. The flames fed greedily until there was nothing left. Clutching the harp against his side, Jack ran for the mirror.

Whatever came next, he and his brothers could face it. At the very least he was determined to try.

Acknowledgements

I have a lot of people to thank for helping make this book possible. First of all, I owe a huge thank you to Holly Mullis who let me talk her ear off for years about my progress and changes along the way. I need to also thank Chris Rox, Christy Kimmerly, and Marie Collins for reading early drafts and sharing their insights and encouragement. Naturally, I need to thank my family; my parents; my husband, Josh; and my son, Jericho. Your support was, and still is, invaluable to me.

About the Author

Alicia Gaile is the author of YA contemporary fantasy and fairy tale retellings. She wrote her first fairy story at the age of twelve after visiting the Goll Woods Old-Growth forest in Ohio with her aunt. She came across a meadow with a fallen down tree where she could practically see fairies and leprechauns dancing with unicorns in the dappled sunlight. After receiving a Creative Writing degree from Georgia College and State University she began writing early versions of Trial by Song while living abroad in southeast Asia. She currently resides in El Paso, Texas with her family and two dogs.

If You Enjoyed This Book, Check Out These Other Titles from Snowy Wings Publishing!

Phoenix Descending (Book One of Curse of the Phoenix) by Dorothy Dreyer

Who must she become in order to survive?

Since the outbreak of the phoenix fever in Drothidia, Tori Kagari has already lost one family member to the fatal disease. Now, with the fever threatening to wipe out her entire family, she must go against everything she believes in order to save them—even if that means making a deal with the enemy.

When Tori agrees to join forces with the unscrupulous Khadulians, she must take on a false identity in order to infiltrate the queendom of Avarell and fulfill her part of the bargain, all while under the watchful eye of the unforgiving Queen's Guard. But time is running out, and every lie, theft, and abduction she is forced to carry out may not be enough to free her family or herself from death.

CROWN OF ICE (BOOK One of The Mirror of Immortality) by Vicki L. Weavil

Snow Queen Thyra Winther is immortal, but if she can't reassemble a shattered enchanted mirror by her eighteenth birthday she's doomed to spend eternity as a wraith.

Armed with magic granted by a ruthless wizard, Thyra schemes to survive with her mind and body intact. Unencumbered by kindness, she kidnaps local boy Kai Thorsen, whose mathematical skills rival her own. Two logical minds, Thyra calculates, are better than one. With time rapidly melting away she needs all the help she can steal.

A cruel lie ensnares Kai in her plan, but three missing mirror shards and Kai's childhood friend, Gerda, present more formidable obstacles.

Thyra's willing to do anything—venture into uncharted lands, outwit sorcerers, or battle enchanted beasts—to reconstruct the mirror, yet her most dangerous adversary lies within her. Touched by the warmth of a wolf pup's devotion and the fire of a young man's love, the thawing of Thyra's frozen heart could prove her ultimate undoing.

Golden (Book One of the Golden Trilogy) by K.M. Robinson

When the girl with the golden hair betrays everyone, not even she has hope of surviving.

The stories say that Goldilocks was a naïve girl who wandered into a house one day. Those stories were wrong. She was never naïve. It was all a perfectly executed plan to get her into the Baers' group to destroy them.

Trained by her cousin, Lowell, and handler, Shadoe, Auluria's mission is to destroy the Baers by getting close to the youngest brother, Dov, his brother and sister-in-law and the leaders of the Baers' group. When she realizes Dov isn't as evil as her cousin led her to believe, she must figure out how to play both sides or her deception will cause everyone in her world to burn.

If her allegiances are discovered, either side could destroy her...if the Society doesn't get her first.

About the Publisher

Snowy Wings Publishing is an independent, author-driven publisher of Middle Grade, Young Adult and New Adult fiction. From sci-fi and fantasy set in fantastic new worlds to contemporary stories that will warm—or break—your heart, your imagination will take flight in bold new directions on Snowy Wings.